THE POSSIBILITY OF NOW

KIM CULBERTSON

Point

Library of Congress Cataloging-in-Publication Data

Culbertson, Kim A., author.
   The possibility of now / Kim Culbertson. — First edition.
      pages cm
   Summary: After years of overachieving at her elite school, Mara James has a
complete meltdown during her calculus exam and, embarrassed by the incident
and the viral video evidence, goes to live with her ski bum father in Squaw Valley,
where she hopes to find a place to figure out where her life is headed, and maybe
even finally understand her father.
   ISBN 978-0-545-73146-1
   1. Life change events—Juvenile fiction. 2. Fathers and daughters —
Juvenile fiction. 3. Squaw Valley (Calif.) —Juvenile fiction. [1. Self-perception —
Fiction. 2. Perfectionism (Personality trait) — Fiction. 3. Fathers and
daughters — Fiction. 4. Squaw Valley (Calif.) — Fiction.] I. Title.
   PZ7.C8945Po 2016
   813.6 — dc23
   [Fic]
                                                              2015016518

10 9 8 7 6 5 4 3 2 1   16 17 18 19 20

Printed in the U.S.A.   23
First edition, February 2016

Book design by Yaffa Jaskoll

To the Jedi-Fairy-Sage-Dixons,

the best ski team a girl could ask for —

thanks for always reminding me to

stop and smell the alpenglow

And to

Melissa Sarver White and Jody Corbett,

who helped Mara find her way

ONE

make lists to survive. I'm not alone in this. You can't Google anything without getting hit in the face with a list. Once, I searched for "Why do people make lists?" Besides giving me 127 reasons why we love lists, I stumbled onto even more lists: 11 New Uses for a Paper Clip, 15 Regrettable Marriage Proposals, 23 Places to See Before You Die.

When did we start doing that? Maybe on a wall way back in a dark cave, a shaggy-headed caveman scratched: *Kill mammoth, make fire, stand upright.*

As humans, we must just crave them. And after what happened to me, I need my lists now more than ever.

"What are you thinking about?" Mom's eyes flick to me, then back to the road in front of us.

"Nothing." I shift in my seat, staring out the car window at the beige California scenery along the I-5. Every fifty miles or so, Mom finds a new way to ask if I want her to *turn around, go home, forget this whole thing.* Each time, watching the landscape outside slip farther from the bleached earth tones we left behind in San Diego, I tell her a version of *I want to do this, keep driving, I have a plan.*

Scratch that. I have *a list.* And I love lists. It's just not like any list I've made before.

We're heading north, tracing the 5, until eventually we will reach the highways that connect us to a dense stretch of Tahoe National Forest and, soon after, to Squaw Valley.

To Trick McHale, my biological father.

That's how Mom always refers to him. Trick McHale, *your biological father*. I got an A in AP bio freshman year. She doesn't have to remind me of the genetics. Besides, that's not how I think of him. Mostly, I don't think about him at all. To me, Trick McHale is another list: nine birthday cards (three with twenty-dollar bills), five phone calls, and one visit to the San Diego Zoo when I was seven. Which is why, when I blurted out five days ago that I wanted to go live with him for a while, just to take a break, to put my *bad day* (Mom's words) behind me, Mom's surprise was second only to my own. I don't blame her. It was random. Especially for me. It hadn't been on any list of mine anywhere. But here I am. Heading north.

What's more shocking than the asking is that Mom said yes.

That's how bad it is.

Only it's really not that bad. It's Not. That. Bad. The day after my bad day, I made a list and taped it to the back of my bedroom door. My Get a Grip List.

No one has died.

No one has cancer.

No one has dropped me in the middle of a war-torn country.

I have not been sold into child slavery.

I have not joined a cult where I only eat wheatgrass and limes.

I have not lost a limb.

2

Only it feels a little like I have. Lost a limb.

"If I turn around at this exit, we could be back home by dinner." Mom peers into the rearview mirror before changing lanes, passing a dusty white minivan. A little boy in the backseat watches us glide by, pressing his small hand flat against the glass.

"Maybe I'll feel like eating in Squaw Valley." I adjust the red half-inch binder resting on my lap. I like to put my long-term-goal lists into binders, real ones I can hold and not just electronic ones. I'm old school that way. I have a system. Yesterday, I printed out a cover for it, reading THE NOW LIST against the backdrop of a Hawaiian sunset. Nothing says live in the now like a sunset, right? I squint at it, bubbles of doubt forming in my gut.

The semi trucks on the 5 stack up like toy trains, and Mom pushes the Lexus past a line of them. We pick up speed as Mom adds, "Or we could just turn around. I really think it's starting to blow over."

If by "blowing over" she means "still going viral." The YouTube video had 616,487 views the last time I checked it.

I clear my throat and try for a bright voice. "No, I'm good. I think this will be great!" I sound like a Disney princess on her third helium balloon.

Mom notices and frowns sideways at me. "Yeah, you sound great."

I try to dial it down. "Seriously, think of this like my semester abroad, only I'm going for a quarter and it's Tahoe instead of Italy or South America. Like an exchange student. But without having to change money or wonder why they don't put ice in my drink."

Her frown lines deepen, telling me she feels this trip is nothing like an exchange program. She's already told me what she thinks this is.

3

Running away.

I still don't know what happened. Not really. I mean, I *know* what happened; I've seen the video footage. But I still don't know *how* it happened. One minute, my calculus teacher, Mr. Henly, was telling us to use a number two pencil, and the next minute I was shredding the test and sobbing, "It doesn't matter, none of this matters, it doesn't matter," over and over until Mr. Henly called someone from the office to come get me.

"I swear, this is going to be great," I say again, my voice thin, watching the blank middle of California spool away behind me. "I made a list."

Mom purses her lips and stares at the road before us.

A few hours later, as we trade Southern for Northern, replacing palms for pines, Mom asks again, "Are you sure you don't want me to turn around?"

I wish she'd stop asking. "We're basically there." I clench my binder in sweaty hands and try to breathe in the quiet scenery.

She pulls onto Highway 89 toward Squaw Valley, passing campgrounds on our left, dark tops of picnic tables peeking through the snow, the campground sign draped in plastic. It's hard to believe we left San Diego this morning and now we're here. Where Trick lives. We stopped only once, to grab some sandwiches and more coffee, so we made good time. Mom loves to make good time when we're driving, so I don't tell her I have to pee. We're close and I can't stand to watch her check all her clocks any more than she already has. Mom always seems to have backup timepieces. On her wrist. On her phone. The car dashboard. She checks and double-checks their synchronicity. It seems to both calm her down and rev her up.

"I'm not sure what Trick's living situation will be like." Mom peers at the snowy road ahead. "I'm just giving you a heads-up. He, well, lives differently than we do." She says it as if he lives in a tent in the middle of a field. Looking around, this seems suddenly like an actual possibility.

My only memory of Trick McHale in person is the day he took me to the San Diego Zoo. Mom had given us passes and money for lunch and told me she'd wait in the parking lot in case I needed her. Inside the zoo, Trick wandered around with me, sipping at a beer he'd smuggled in by tucking it into his sock. What I remember most about that day is the way he laughed a deep rumble at my horrified reaction to the naked mole rats. "It says they aren't completely naked," he said, studying the sign where it explained that they had over a hundred hairs that helped them find their way around. "But they seem butt naked to me." I lost it then, one of those little-girl belly laughs I still sometimes get with my best friend, Josie, and he looked so surprised and pleased. I didn't stop laughing until we reached the Arctic fox.

Almost a decade has passed and I haven't seen him again, the time between birthday cards and calls elongating. Mom has never told me I couldn't see Trick. It wasn't like that. There was never any animosity — only absence. All those years, she'd rarely mentioned him, and he'd never made an effort, so I hadn't, either. I was busy. I had Mom and my stepdad, Will, and my little twin brothers, Seth and Liam, and a busy school life. Our one trip to the zoo felt like a dream, but once, a few years ago, I found a children's book called *Naked Mole Rat Gets Dressed* and sent it to Trick because it made me think about that laugh and the way it had surprised him.

I don't know if he ever got it.

"You doing okay over there?" Mom glances at me. She's been asking me that a lot lately.

I fiddle with the heating vent, letting warm air wash over me. "Yeah, thanks."

After my bad day, I barricaded myself in the house for the entire holiday break. Mom and Will spoke in overly bright voices. Josie came with pizza and movies and tried to coax me to the mall, but I wouldn't go. A Christmas tree went up and down. I stared at the sea of wrapping paper and plastic toy packages Seth and Liam had left in their wake. Mostly, I tried not to think about the numbers of views my excruciatingly public meltdown was now racking up online.

Miss Perfect's Epic Meltdown.

When I watched it, just once, I barely recognized the girl with the ash-blond ponytail, wearing the pale blue O'Neill hoodie Will had bought me on a windy day in Hawaii last April. But it was my face, pinched like a peach pit, ripping my test and all those other tests into paper rain. All those bits of test confetti filtering through the shocked air of the classroom while, outside the tall windows, the palm trees bent against the blue Windex sky of San Diego. I never want to watch it again.

But I told myself it was Not. That. Bad.

Each day, I added things to my Get a Grip List.

I have not spiraled into drug addiction.

I have not been kidnapped.

I have not lost the love of my life to a terrible disease.

Only I kind of had. If the love of my life was being valedictorian and the disease had hashtags like #checkoutthisfreak and #whatadramaqueen and #ihatethisgirl.

6

Still, I thought I could go back to Ranfield Academy. After all, my parents and Ranfield and countless movies and bumper stickers had raised me to rebound. All those years in tennis and soccer and the early years of swim team, the mottoes had been clear: Shake it off. Get up. Get back out there. It's a mental game.

It definitely is.

Because in the grocery store five days ago, my first trip out of the house, the small hairs prickled on the back of my neck as people whispered behind their hands in the milk aisle and the produce section and near the bakery.

"The girl who freaked out."

"That valedictorian girl from the video."

"What a psycho."

Finally, I told Mom I'd just wait in the car. When she'd deposited the groceries in the back and slipped in beside me, I blurted, "I want to go live with Trick in Tahoe for a while."

Mom told me that you can't care what other people think.

Josie told me people are jerks; don't worry about them.

Will told me humans have the attention span of gnats; let it go.

Great advice. I'm just not sure how to actually *do* any of that. Not care. Not worry. Let it go. Am I missing a certain gene?

Through the window, I see the Truckee River tumble into view on our left side, glittery in the pale sunlight. Everything in this landscape is sharp — white, blue, gray, silver. Even the green is deep and charcoaled. It *will* be like studying abroad — a foreign country where the only whispering sounds will be the snow falling through the pines.

Mom slows at a light and turns right at a large sign reading SQUAW VALLEY USA, INTERNATIONAL MOUNTAIN RESORT. "Squaw Valley

7

hosted the 1960 Winter Olympics," she tells me, gliding along Squaw Valley Road. We wind back into the valley, passing a turn-off for the Resort at Squaw Creek. As we curve to the left, a snow meadow comes into view, and beyond it, a wall of winter mountains.

"Wow," I breathe, taking in the snowy peaks.

"Yeah, I know. It's gorgeous." Mom pulls the car into a parking lot near a massive cluster of brown alpine-style buildings. "The Village," she tells me, her voice holding a trace of the distaste that appears the few times I've asked her about why she left Squaw Valley when I was barely three. "We're here." She shuts off the engine, hesitating, her fingers plucking the keys swiftly from the ignition. As she studies the resort in front of her, I can almost see the flashes of memories move across her features. She goes quiet, whatever it was that took her away from here crawling back out from under all the snow.

"Mom?" She must be freaking out. Mom also makes lists, keeps color-coded files of necessary forms, and has a master Google calendar for me and for the twins with different-colored fonts for each of us. Purple. Blue. Green.

My bad day in the middle of junior year wasn't anywhere on her lists.

"Right, sorry." She jingles her keys slightly and then, without warning, reaches across and grabs my hand. "You can say hello, just stay for a night and clear your head, and get in this car with me tomorrow and drive home. You know that, right?"

A vulture of doubt circles me. "I know."

I also know she doesn't want me to do this. She's thinking now is not the time to change directions and she's probably right. I realize that if I get out of this car and walk to meet Trick, I will take myself off the path we've planned, the one that would have me show up at school today with my head held high, not worried about everyone's whispering, the one where I do shake it off and get back on track and win a scholarship to the right sort of college. One of the schools on Mom's ever-evolving list.

On this right path, I pity the person who posted that video of me because they are mean and petty and small. I write a college essay about how I hit a rough patch but righted myself and stayed steady and faced my fears and it made me stronger. Maybe I start a support group for kids like me, victims of cyber shaming. Those future admissions committees would nod understandingly and applaud me for getting back up, dusting myself off, and making the best of a bad situation.

Mara James. Accepted. Future secured. Take that, high school.

That sounds a lot like what old Mara would do.

Problem is, I can't seem to bring myself to hold up my chin, start that support group, write that essay. I don't feel pity or strength or resolve. I feel broken and small and confused.

"I'm ready," I lie.

Mom slips on a periwinkle knit beanie, the purplish-blue darkening her eyes. Or maybe it's disappointment that darkens them. "Okay, then." She sighs. "Let's go see how Neverland's holding up."

THE NOW LIST

1. Learn to ski: green runs, blue runs, black runs??
2. Internet cleanse (no social media, no news, Skype okay!)
3. Meditation — at least 10 minutes a day!!
4. Sleep until 8 on a school day
5. Essential oils to relax — lavender, chamomile, orange
6. Simplify & downsize!!
7. Kiss a cute snowboarder!! (Josie's suggestion)
8. Breathe! (obviously)
9. Be brave (from Will)
10. Read for fun? (see attached suggested book lists)

TWO

Stepping out of the car, the first thing I discover is that it's freaking cold in Tahoe. I mean, I've been cold before, but this is a bite-you-in-your-face-and-shake-you-around-like-a-chew-toy sort of cold. Mom said to dress in layers. She just hadn't mentioned one of the layers should be an electric blanket. But at least I'm out of the car. I hurry in search of a bathroom, grateful to find it heated.

My phone buzzes just as I'm drying my hands. I check it — Josie.

are you there yet?

I call her and she picks up immediately. "Have you frozen to death yet?" Our connection sounds a little crackly.

"Yes. This is frozen me calling you from beyond the grave." On her end, I can make out the faint sounds of tennis balls hitting racquets. "Coach Jeffers is not going to like you calling me from practice."

"He thinks I'm getting some Advil for my lady issues." With our coach, you basically just have to say *lady issues*, and he's done. He wants no further information. It comes in handy.

"I can't really talk. I'm in a bathroom." My voice echoes off the walls. "We're about to go meet Trick."

"Wait, you're meeting him in a bathroom?" Josie asks loudly.

11

"No, we're heading to meet him!" I lower my voice. "Josie, are people, you know, talking about it?"

She doesn't answer. Instead, I hear Coach Jeffers bellow, "Martinez, you better not be on your phone!"

"Gotta go," Josie says quickly, and then she's gone.

I stuff my phone into the pocket of the ice-blue down parka Mom bought me at REI and head out to find her.

After Mom finishes a quick coffee (double espresso, no milk), we walk through the Village, past ski shops and restaurants. It's not even five but the light fades, the walkways filling with shadows, the sky an emerging bruise. Combined with the knife of cold, the beauty of it all makes it suddenly difficult to breathe in an ordinary way.

It's a Tuesday, and the Village isn't crowded. Around me, a scattering of people lounge around fire pits, sipping coffees and beers, exchanging stories about their day, their sentences peppered with words like *shred* and *zipper line*, their boots propped on the edges of the stone pits, skis or snowboards leaning against empty chairs. They remind me of the packs of surfers in Oceanside, their terminology its own barrier between them and the rest of the world.

It's quite possible my jeans have now frozen to my legs. Apparently, I will be wearing the long underwear Mom bought me all the time and not just for skiing.

After walking the length of the Village, we find ourselves standing in front of a ski shop. A sign out front reads NEVERLAND in large white letters made to look like they'd been written in snow. The store seems to sell clothing and gear but also advertises ski and snowboard rentals. One of the bumper stickers featured in the window declares TAHOE LOCAL: MY LIFE IS BETTER THAN YOUR

VACATION. Mom notices it, rolls her eyes, and pushes through the main door, sending an unseen jingle bell shivering.

It's warm inside and melting patches of snow puddle on the worn carpets where people have tracked it in on their boots. The store is packed with racks of ski pants, jackets, helmets, goggles, socks, and boots, but it's empty of people. I scan the warm wooden walls behind the register. In the center of pictures of skiers and snowboarders, a glossy sign reads NEVERLAND again, and beneath it, a quote from J. M. Barrie's *Peter Pan*:

WHICH OF THESE ADVENTURES SHALL WE CHOOSE?

Before I can point it out to Mom, a man pushes through a swinging door that reads SHOP in the back of the store. He wears faded jeans, a beat-up Santa Cruz sweatshirt that might have once been black, and a trucker hat with an orange bill.

Trick McHale.

I can't stop my mind from adding, *your biological father.*

My body buzzes with nerves. He hasn't seen us yet, and it gives me a moment to openly study him in his natural habitat. He holds something in his hand, something that looks like it should be attached to a ski. A binding, maybe? He chews at his lip, his eyes locked to the binding. I do that. When I work on a particularly difficult chemistry equation.

"Hello, Trick." Mom speaks first, her voice the tone she uses with clients.

His head jerks up, startled. "Oh, Lauren — whoa, didn't see you there." His voice holds the deep rumble of the laugh I remember from our zoo day, all surfer-dude soft edges. He takes me in, his green eyes surprised. "Awww, Mara, no way. Look at you."

I don't know what to do with my body. Should I give him a hug?

13

Would that be the normal thing to do? Nothing about this feels normal. The acceptable time window for a hug passes, and I just stand here, eyes straying back to the *Peter Pan* quote. "Hi, um, Trick."

He nods, his eyes slipping from my face, maybe noticing I said *Trick*, not *Dad*. He clears his throat. Then clears it again. Should I have called him Dad? No, that would be too weird. I've talked to our mailman more times than I've talked to Trick McHale.

The silence around us condenses.

Finally, Trick says to Mom, "You look good, Lauren." His voice falters.

Mom pulls off her beanie and shakes out her highlighted hair. "Oh, well, thanks." She doesn't return the compliment. Instead, she opens her purse and digs around for something. She does this sometimes, to look productive, even when there is nothing really to find. She's doing it now. I can tell. To avoid talking, to put some action into the middle of all the thick silence.

Trick watches her, his expression growing slightly amused. Does he know she creates distractions to look busy when she's uncomfortable? He must, because he asks, "You looking for something in there?"

Mom flushes. "Oh, wait — found it!" She hurriedly applies the victorious tube of lipstick as if to say, *See — this, I was looking for this, thank you very much.* I gape at her. Mom never acts like a spaz; she's always cool, organized. What's going on?

Trick grins. "Good thing. We almost had a lipstick crisis on our hands."

Mom's expression shifts, her eyes narrowing. Uh-oh. The look. When she gives us that look, my brothers and I are usually inspired to suddenly go clean our rooms. "Well, some of us care about how

14

we appear to other people." She tries to keep her voice light but doesn't really pull it off. The look muscles must be connected to the voice muscles.

Trick's smile dies. We could medal in the Awkward Olympics right now and it might be a three-way tie for gold.

Luckily, the front door jingles and a pack of boys bursts into the store. There is something territorial about the way they bang through the door, laughing, their voices raised. At first they seem to move as a single unit, but eventually, I make out individual boys. Five of them. All but one wear odd, tight suits, like a quartet of teenage superheroes without their capes. They must be ski suits, because their boots look like they should be attached to skis. The tallest, his slim, athletic body clad in midnight blue with spiderwebs all over the chest, heads straight toward the counter. He moves behind it, checking shelves.

Trick joins Midnight Spider-Man behind the counter. "Here, Logan," he says, pulling a pair of skis from a rack. "They're all set."

"Thanks, Trick." Logan grabs the skis and throws them over his shoulder, and the boys clomp back toward the door. The non-superhero boy hangs back. He wears a shiny black parka and jeans, slips of auburn hair curling out from under a red beanie. He crumples his empty bag of chips and leaves it on the counter. He's good-looking in an overly confident way, which usually annoys me, but when he winks at me as he follows the others out the door, I feel my face flame. Trick's gaze follows the boy's exit before he tosses the chip bag into an unseen trash can beneath the counter.

My mom has been watching them, too, her mouth slightly open. "Was that Logan Never?" she asks when the door has closed, leaving us alone again.

Trick nods. Something passes between them, a version of the look Mom had in the car when we pulled up, that memory ghost.

"Who's Logan Never?" I ask.

"The tall boy with the skis," Mom mumbles, staring at the empty door for a moment. "His parents own this store. Matt and Jessica."

"That other kid was Beck Davis," Trick tells her, and I know he means the one who left his chip bag on the counter.

Mom's face noticeably alters, like she's eaten something sour.

"Who?" I ask. The shared history that floods the room makes me feel like I missed a memo or something.

"Boys I used to know," she says.

"Yep," Trick says from behind the counter. "We're all still here."

THREE

"I'm seeing a *shrink?*" I blink at Mom as we drive the darkening highway back into Truckee, the mountain town we'd seen signs for on our way to meet Trick in Squaw Valley. This announcement is perhaps the most shocking part of our trip so far. Never in a million years would I have thought Mom would sign me up for therapy. Not that Mom has anything against therapy. Therapy's fine. For *other* people. That guy who talks to himself in front of Trader Joe's, for example, or people who decide to shave their heads and start painting their skin neon green.

"He comes highly recommended," she insists, chattering at me about Dr. Elliot's credentials. Blah-blah-blah UCLA. Blah-blah-blah specializes in teens. I can't get a word in over the staccato of her Manic Mom Talk. Will always jokes that Mom's brain is like one of those news tickers scrolling across the bottom of CNN. She continually makes lists, finalizes plans, and sets goals while simultaneously checking off each completed task as more multiply and take their place. That slim blue leather notebook in her purse is embossed with a gold clock for a reason. It's the hard copy of her Productivity System. It's full of the things she accomplishes, crossed through with a single inked line when she finishes them, and she

17

simultaneously cross-checks it with the Google calendar on her smartphone and laptop.

"I don't need a therapist," I say when she finally breaks to take in some air.

"I gave you an option to come home. If you want to stay in Squaw Valley, you will meet with Dr. Elliot," Mom tells me. There is no room for argument.

Several minutes later, we pull into a parking spot in downtown Truckee, its warmly lit lamps a stark contrast to the shock of cold when we open the car doors. I clutch my binder to my chest as if it could add some warmth.

We walk the icy cobblestone sidewalk past several brick storefronts until finding the small sign for Dr. Jonathan Elliot, where we push through the door and climb a flight of steps. Mom explained to me in the car that tonight won't be a full session, just a chance for us to meet each other and talk about how these sessions will work.

I hesitate on the last step, feeling a wash of nausea. I'm not really the kind of girl who talks about her feelings. I've always tried a more head-down-eyes-on-the-prize approach to life, burying my head in a pile of textbooks until I graduate from college. I saw a psychiatrist at the hospital immediately following my bad day and it didn't go so well. After ten awkward minutes, he basically told me I'd had a panic attack. Meanwhile, I lost five pounds in sweat weight from his mile-long list of questions.

A door at the end of the hall opens and a man appears in the hallway. Sweet-faced and slim, he wears a pair of thick-rimmed tortoiseshell glasses and his brown hair recedes just slightly. He's dressed in khakis and a wool vest with a long-sleeved tech-fabric shirt under it. So far, everyone in Tahoe looks like they just got back from hiking the Pacific Crest Trail.

"Mara and Lauren?"

"Dr. Elliot." Mom moves in front of me, offering her hand. "We spoke on the phone. Thanks for meeting us so late in the evening."

"My pleasure. How was the drive up?" As Mom answers him, he moves to hold open the door to his office so we can go inside. The room, long and narrow, faces the street, a wide window running the length of it boasting a rooftop view of the building across the main street and out to the distant pines beyond. I take in the cream walls of the office, settling on a trickling fountain of smooth rocks in the corner, the Truckee River in miniature. Everything about this office whispers, *You're in Tahoe, relax.*

I immediately feel defensive.

"Have a seat," Dr. Elliot says, sitting down in a velvety armchair speckled with grays, whites, and blacks as if the chair had been carved from spongy granite. There is no desk. No clipboard. The San Diego guy had a clipboard. Mom and I settle into matching burgundy armchairs across a glass coffee table.

"Help yourself to water or tea," Dr. Elliot offers, motioning with his hand toward a small kitchenette where the counter holds a hot water pot, a basket of assorted teas, a pitcher of water with lemon slices, and some cookies on a white plate. "Whenever you want it."

I glance at Mom. Therapy has cookies? This might be okay. She nods, so I stand and help myself to a snickerdoodle and a cup of chamomile tea. Chamomile's on the Now List — good for relaxation. "Thanks."

Dr. Elliot rubs his hands together. "Mara, I talked to your mom and she told me you've been pretty stressed out lately, that you had a rough calculus exam." I nod, the cookie turning to paste in my mouth. *A rough calculus exam.* Like describing a cyclone as a bit breezy. Is understatement part of therapy? "Can you talk about what happened that day?" His voice murmurs just above the sound of the fountain.

I tell him about my bad day — the hum in the room, the way I felt the test shift in front of me, how sweaty my hands got, how I mostly can't remember ripping up other people's tests. He listens, nodding slightly, and waits until I'm completely finished before he says, "Sounds like you had a panic attack."

Maybe Dr. Clipboard and this guy went to school together at the University of Stating the Obvious.

Mom leans forward in her chair. "She saw a doctor in San Diego who said the same thing."

"But I'm fine now," I tell him, smoothing my hand over my binder.

"She's only left the house twice since it happened and one time was to get in the car to drive up here," Mom says, her voice catching. "That doesn't seem fine." She fiddles with the strap of her purse. "At back-to-school night, they said junior year is challenging, the hardest one."

I look down. "I'm just overwhelmed."

She glances at Dr. Elliot, doing that grown-up telepathy look they think we can't see, the one that says, *See what I've been dealing with?* But I'm not sure Mom could understand if she wanted to. Probably because she has never seemed overwhelmed. All her lists and forms and rules keep overwhelmed on its right side of the fence, too scared to even peek over. In Lauren James's world, there is a right way (hers) and a wrong way (anyone else's). Doubt is scared to death of my mother.

"Maybe she should drop an AP class? Or a club, maybe? She's in a lot of clubs."

Dr. Elliot doesn't respond, which seems weird. Isn't he supposed to referee the conversation or something? "I'm not sure dropping a class will help, Mom — it's not just one thing." Was it one thing? I scroll through the morning of the test and the days leading up to it. Normal studying. Normal five hours of sleep at night. That morning, Ranfield had posted the class rankings in our online portal. Still number one then. Not anymore.

"Do you think it would help to drop a class, Mara?" Dr. Elliot asks.

Um, isn't *he* supposed to be able to tell me that? "It's not about dropping a class. It's more than that." I make a sweeping motion in the air with my arms, as if overwhelmed might be best portrayed as a puppet show. "It's the bigger stuff. The world is so terrible right now. War, poverty, global warming . . . the Internet . . . *all* of it." My chest tightens. "It's too much. And then I was sitting there and . . . school seemed so small and —" I mime ripping up tests. "I'm sorry. I don't know what you want me to say."

My mom throws another pained look at Dr. Elliot. "She takes too much on. She needs to block it out."

"Me blocking things out isn't going to make them go away, Mom. It's not like I drop Eco Club and — bam! — the world is suddenly rainbows and puppies."

"But would it help *right now*?" she asks, clicking her manicure against the wooden arms of the chair. "Right now you have to worry

21

about *your* future, and then you can worry about the rest of the world." We've had this discussion before, too.

Dr. Elliot finally decides to join the conversation. "I looked at your school's web page. Very prestigious and highly competitive. Could that culture be contributing to feeling overwhelmed?"

I bite my lip, but Mom is quick to say, "That's not the problem."

"Maybe it is," I interrupt. But it's been a gradual build, like rainwater after weeks of drizzle. "Sometimes, Ranfield feels too extreme. All the rankings and intense scrutiny. It just feels indulgent when the rest of the world is, I don't know, barely hanging on to clean water? When you stop and think about it, like really think about it, the values are screwed up." I take a breath, trying to organize the thoughts in my head. "At Ranfield, they're always telling us to be global leaders, global contributors, but I feel like the real goal is to be constantly better than everyone else. All the time. With everything. Even if you're not the best, you should be *trying* to be." I imitate a PA voice, holding a fake microphone to my mouth. "Good morning, Ravens. The rest of the world is falling apart around you, but make sure you're wearing the right jeans! Collecting the right awards! Getting the right test scores! There may or may not be a world left once you graduate because everything is going to go up in flames and earthquakes and hurricanes, but make sure you get Student of the Month!"

A smile catches the edges of Mom's mouth. "Flames *and* earthquakes *and* hurricanes? All at once?" She shrugs apologetically at Dr. Elliot. "That's a bit dramatic."

I drop my fake microphone bit. "It's not," I insist. "Also torna-does. And homeless people."

Mom can't help herself — she laughs. "Tornadoes of home-less people?!"

"It's not funny!" Okay, it's a little funny. My brothers and Will would totally go see a movie with all of that. Well, not the homeless-people part. That's too awful. But the tornado-hurricane-earthquake part. Sold.

Mom tucks her hair behind her ears and gives me a look usually reserved for a person poised on the edge of a bridge. "Sweetie, you can't fix what's wrong with the whole world."

I drop my eyes. "I know." Right now, I can't even fix my own life. World, you might be on your own.

Dr. Elliot clears his throat. "You mentioned the Internet. I know there was a YouTube posting that got quite a few views. Do you want to talk about that?"

My gaze slips to the pines outside the window, dark against a deep purple sky. "I don't care about that."

"Did it contribute to your not wanting to go back to school?"

I tap my binder. "I have a better plan."

"Tell me about it," he prompts.

I study the sunset cover. "Well, obviously, in the big picture of all that is wrong in the world, my problems are pretty stupid." Mom wants to say something — I feel it radiate off her — but she restrains herself.

Dr. Elliot pushes at the bridge of his glasses. "You alluded to that before. Why do you think your problems are stupid?"

I shrug. "You know, I keep reading about 'first-world problems,' like being upset about a cell phone contract or being mad that your latte wasn't hot enough, and, well, being stressed out about school feels like that."

His eyes flit to Mom, then back to me. "You feel like caring about your schoolwork is the same as needing your latte to be a certain temperature?"

I hurry to explain. "That's not exactly what I mean. It's just that everywhere, people are dying in wars and kids are starving to death and I sat there staring at that test and I was so tired and it felt so small of me, to worry about tests, to worry about grades so much. I've always cared so much about each grade, award, test score, because I've set this huge goal for my future. To be valedictorian, to get into the best college I can. Everything I do is for the future and I don't even know what that is, what I want. Not really. It's just sitting out there. This huge unknown. And suddenly, all of the work, all the stress, seemed so . . . I just need a break. People are always saying live in the now and I've never done that." I hold up the binder. "So I made some notes."

"About living in the now?" He leans back and the lamplight flashes across his glasses, turning them opaque.

"Yes."

"What type of notes?"

"Some research." I flip open the cover. "Okay, so I like to make lists and this is a list of things I can do while I'm in Tahoe to learn how to live in the now and not be so stressed out all the time."

"List making can be very helpful." He leans in, his eyes warm. Is he laughing at me? No, maybe just the light again catching his glasses. Therapists aren't allowed to laugh at you, right? At least

24

not to your face. "So you think living in Tahoe can help you feel less stressed?"

"Well, sure. I mean, it's Tahoe." I glance at Mom, who nods in agreement. If Mom's version of Tahoe is even close to accurate, everyone here hangs out and skis and goes to parties and relaxes all day by the light of a roaring fire pit while contributing approximately *nothing* to the greater good of society. Now that I think of it, Mom's version looks a lot like a beer commercial.

Dr. Elliot cuts into my thoughts. "What does Tahoe mean to you?"

I shrug. "People here are just more relaxed, right? I'm hoping it's contagious." Frowning, I realize I might have just insulted him. I mean, *he's* working all day up here in this nice office. Not hanging out with a Heineken at one in the afternoon next to a chairlift. A spidery crack appears in Mom's version of this place. Which I decide to ignore.

But he doesn't look offended. "Would you share an item from your list?"

"Sure." I scan the list. "Some of these I stole from Google searches, but a few of them I came up with on my own. And my stepdad, Will, and my friend Josie helped me." I flush at #7, where Josie wrote, *Kiss a cute snowboarder!!* Won't be sharing that one. #2 is Internet cleanse. I'm staying off the Internet and all social media while I'm here unless I need to research something for school. That one is from Dr. Clipboard in San Diego, but it seems boring, so I start at the beginning. "Okay, number one: Learn to ski."

Mom sits up suddenly. "Wait, no — that's not part of the deal."

Dr. Elliot and I both stare at her sudden stricken look. "Mom, I'm in *Tahoe*. The first thing that came up when I Googled 'things to do in Tahoe' was skiing or snowboarding. Of course I should learn to ski. What else do people even do here?"

This makes Dr. Elliot laugh out loud. Apparently, therapists *do* laugh at their clients. "Well, amazingly, there are people in Tahoe who don't ski or snowboard," he insists, but motions to my binder. "Okay, what else?"

I scan the list. "Um, number four: Sleep until eight on a school day." I look up at him. "I never get to do that. Unless I'm sick." Uncapping my pen, I add *when I'm not sick* to #4.

"Sounds good." Dr. Elliot picks up his tea and takes a sip.

Mom fiddles with her purse strap again. "I think, though, it's important she keep a schedule while she's here. Ranfield has enrolled her in their Home Hospital program, which lets her keep her scholarship, but she can't slack off. She still has to do the work." She looks seriously at me. "You aren't here to ski all day."

"I need PE credits," I argue feebly.

Dr. Elliot chimes in before Mom can respond. "I think she can finish her schoolwork and manage to take a ski lesson and sleep in until eight." He steeples his fingers in front of his face. "I'm curious, though, because you haven't brought up your father. You'll be staying with him while you're here, right?"

"With Trick, yes. My biological father." My face flames. Why did I just say that as if Dr. Elliot needed a science lesson? He's a *doctor*.

"Where does he fit on that list?"

He's not on the list.

"I don't really know him at all." The words hang heavy in the air.

He glances at Mom. "And why is that?"

We both freeze.

Even with all the lists I'd written and research articles I'd printed out and organized in my binder about skiing and resting and Zen teachings and essential oils that help with relaxation, in each of my pages in the binder of ideas for living in the now, how did I not consider the fact that I don't know *anything* about Trick McHale? Nothing. Except that he thinks naked mole rats are hilarious and he can smuggle a beer in his sock. Not the strongest basis for a room-mate arrangement.

"I, um, don't know," I finally say, my throat tight.

Mom adds quietly, "He's never really been a part of her life."

The fountain burbles, suddenly intrusive, and Dr. Elliot seems to use it as his cue to stand. "Well, Mara, we'll have plenty of time to get into all of that when you come back."

We thank him and hurry from the room.

Outside, Truckee has faded into night. A chilly blast of air hits us as we push open the door to the street. It feels cold and remote but in a peaceful, yielding way. No billboards, no honking traffic, no newsfeed on the horrible state of the world. As Mom and I move carefully down the icy street toward the car, I hold my binder close to my chest, noticing my heartbeat steady, going quiet like the sky just beginning to blink with stars.

We slip into the car, and Mom gets the heater going. "I think that went well," she says, pulling out of the parking spot. As we drive down the street, the snow warm with lamplight, I flip open my binder and add #11 to the Now List: *Get to know Trick McHale.*

FOUR

Annoyed, Mom checks the door of Ethan's Grill again for Trick. I think she mutters, "Typical," under her breath, but when I ask her what she said, she says brightly, "Nothing!" She spins her watch around her wrist. I sip my Diet Coke and watch the hostess seat a couple of snowboarders my age near the window. #7: Kiss a cute snowboarder!! I look quickly away, scanning the menu again. Mom will want me to have something with veggies as my green intake has been slim today.

"I'm sorry I can't stay longer to help you settle in." Mom pretends to read the menu for the tenth time, her eyes straying again to the door. "Will really can't afford to take any time off from work right now, and the twins need me there."

"I know." The mention of Liam and Seth sends a ripple of homesickness through me even though they can be super annoying sometimes (most of the time). People think it's adorable that I have nine-year-old twin brothers. And it's true. They *are* adorable. When they aren't leaving their disgusting socks on the kitchen counter or making gross noises with their armpits or creating a mine field with their LEGO pieces in the hallway that makes every venture to the bathroom a firewalk. But they were sad about me leaving. They drew me a picture of a girl wearing a snow hat (me) with a big goofy smile. Of course, this smiling me is also being attacked by mutant robots. Cute. Mom and Will told them I was going away to a special camp, which was probably a mistake. Now they both also want to go to snow camp when they get to high school. Mom told them this particular snow camp was only for girls. Girls named Mara. I'm not sure they're buying it.

Mom takes a drink of her white wine, watching me over the glass. Sighing, she sets it down. "Mara, the important thing is you use this time to settle down and get your work done. You'll see. It's slow here. You'll be bored in a week." As she takes another sip of her wine, I sense a *but* coming. "But," she continues (there it is), "I want you to be careful, stay aware. This place has a way of just creeping in."

Like Tahoe is a horror movie.

Before I can respond, a photo text comes through from my stepdad: a group of seashells and smooth rocks spelling out BRAVE. Ever since I can remember, Will and I have collected seashells and cool-looking rocks and we leave our collection on a shelf in the living room. For the last couple of years, he arranges them each week into a word or phrase like DREAM or AIM HIGH. His Shells of Wisdom, he calls them. Once, he spelled out PERSPIRE, and I laughed for days. My stepdad works ridiculously long hours as a medical malpractice attorney, but he's never failed to change the shells each week.

He texts again: Btw: What's a six-letter word for "ability to make good judgments, quick decisions, in a specific area"? Ends in "N."

Will and his crossword. Grinning, I text back: acumen.

Will: Thx. That SAT prep class just paid for itself!

I text back: yeah, and who knew SAT words could be so ironic?

29

He resends the BRAVE shell picture.

My chest tightens.

Maybe Tahoe is a mistake.

"Mom?" I start, but I'm stopped by the arrival of Trick pushing through the heavy wood door of the restaurant. He smiles at the hostess, who clearly knows him. She gives him a kiss on the cheek and laughs at something he says. Is my father funny? When he spots us, his smile falters, and motioning toward us, he crosses the room with the barest trace of a limp. He limps? I don't remember a limp from the zoo trip.

He slides into the seat across from me and next to Mom. "Hey," he exhales, fumbling with the menu. "Can I get a Sierra Nevada, Maggie?" he says to the hostess, who nods and heads off toward the bar. He looks at Mom's almost empty glass of Chardonnay. "You want another one?"

Her eyebrows lift slightly. "No, thanks. I'm driving."

"And what about you?" He motions to my almost empty Diet Coke, grinning. "Shall we get you another round? A hearty IPA maybe?" Mom narrows her eyes and his smile wavers, a shadow of annoyance passing over his rough features. "Oh, relax, Lauren. I'm not going to actually get our kid a beer."

Our kid.

"I should hope not," she says, her voice clipped.

Awkward Olympics. Round two.

When Maggie returns with Trick's beer, we order our pizzas. Then, Mom asks Trick generic questions that he answers like he's at a job interview. Yes, he still likes working in the shop at Neverland. No, he's not too worried about how terrible the snow's been on and off the last few years; that's just life in a ski town — bad years and good years. He seems surprised when she tells him she loves being a real estate agent.

"You *love* it?" he echoes, his voice laced with doubt. He tries to hide it by taking a gulp of beer.

"I do," she responds coolly, sipping the last of her wine. "I don't really expect you to understand."

He glances at me, clears his throat. "So I don't know if she mentioned it, but your mom used to shred this mountain."

"You skied?" I'm shocked. Mom has never once mentioned skiing, and we almost never travel anywhere that doesn't have palm trees, sand, and an endless stretch of blue water.

"We should probably talk about Mara's schedule." She sidesteps my question and flips open her clock-faced notebook.

I take a bite of the pizza Mom ordered, some pine-nut-spinach-goat-cheese concoction that seems more like a salad than a pizza, and Mom walks Trick through my schedule. Trick chews his own sausage-and-mushroom pizza as he listens. He needs to drive me to my therapy sessions with Dr. Elliot. He needs to know that I'm staying off all social media (Now List #2: done). And he should make sure I'm completing my Home Hospital assignments and submitting them properly to Ms. Raff, my supervising teacher, through Ranfield Academy's online portal.

"Sounds like military school. Sir, yes, sir!" He fake salutes me. I giggle but only until I catch the dark look on Mom's face.

She pauses over a page of my schedule. "Ranfield is a very prestigious private school. Mara won an academic scholarship that she has maintained since sixth grade that covers a huge part of her tuition."

"Sweet." He nods at me. "Good job."

Blushing, I say, "Thanks."

"So tuition, huh? What's that running you?" He signals Maggie for another beer as he downs the last of his.

"We only pay fourteen thousand a year," I tell him proudly, then shrink beneath Mom's glower.

Trick spits beer onto the table. "Fourteen grand *a year?*" He chokes, wiping his mouth and then mopping up the table with a napkin. "Are you serious?"

Mom says evenly, "I would prefer to not discuss finances with you."

"Okay," Trick mumbles into his pizza before adding, "but that's practically what I live on each year." The air crackles between them and we eat in silence for a minute. Finally, Trick wipes his hand on a paper napkin and plucks the schedule from the pile of paper. "So, okay, this is all online? She just logs in and submits all her work?"

Mom looks relieved. "Yes, they have a portal, see." She shows him on her phone. "Her subject teachers assign all the work she would normally be doing in their classes and she sends it all in to Alice Raff, who coordinates it."

Trick looks impressed. "Man, where was all this when I was in school?" He takes a long swallow of beer. "You're a lucky kid."

Mom blinks at him. "Mara would rather be at school, Trick. She'd rather not be dealing with this whole thing at all. They've given her this quarter to recover from what happened to her, but then she has to come home or she loses her scholarship. It's serious."

He flashes me an apologetic look. "Right, sure — sorry."

I pluck a stray bit of cheese from my plate, chewing it as Mom signals Maggie for the check. Mom's right. It's serious.

Always so serious.

．　．　．

After dinner, we follow Trick's beat-up truck back through the shadowy valley, turning left on a road that winds up a hill. I take a minute to text Josie: getting settled — check out the snow! and send her a picture I took earlier in Truckee, the frosted pines, the purpling sky. She doesn't text me back. They have a chem quiz already tomorrow, so she's probably studying. Which is what I should be doing since I have to take it online. My stomach starts to knot.

I stare out the window at the dark houses. Every so often, we pass the lit windows of houses with chimneys releasing a curl of smoke, but most of the houses we pass sit in shadow. "Why do so many of these houses seem empty?"

"Many are second homes," Mom explains, turning into a long driveway, Trick's taillights glowing up ahead. His truck crawls past an enormous glass-and-wood alpine house and around the back of it until we reach a tiny bungalow tucked against a dense grove of trees. A single porch light glows next to its front door. During our drive up this morning, Mom told me that Trick works as a caretaker for a vacation home, helps maintain the house in exchange for living rent-free in their backyard cottage. The squat rectangular box in front of me isn't what I'd imagined when she said cottage. This looks more like a storage container.

Trick unlocks the door and waits for us to follow him inside. He snaps on a light, revealing a narrow space much like the inside of a motor home. To the left, a kitchenette runs the length of the wall — a counter with a hot plate, a sink, and a mini-fridge. The rest of the room seems divided into an eating area — a small black card table and two folding chairs with ratty seat cushions — and a living room, a threadbare overstuffed chair that might be trying to be a love seat and an old TV perched on a board resting on cinder blocks. When Mom told me about Trick's cottage, I'd imagined a cozy storybook type of place — a roaring fire, a warm kitchen. Not furniture that looks like someone left it by the side of the road. My brain immediately starts listing improvements:

new couch
new kitchen table with real chairs
some curtains on the bare windows

"So, have you, uh, lived here a while?" I lick my lips, hoping that he actually moved in yesterday and is planning to replace the décor because the last resident was a nearsighted frat boy.

"Eight years," he says, looking around. "The Stones — that's the family I caretake for — are only here, like, three or four times a year. It's free and it's warm. Can't beat that." He nods affectionately at the woodstove nestled in the corner behind the card table, the source of the soft warmth in the room. "And here" — he motions to a door — "the bedroom. I thought you could have it."

I peek through the open door. The room holds a full-size bed heaped with blankets, and another woodstove gives off an orange glow in the corner. There's no room for much else. I glance at Trick. "Where will you sleep?"

"The couch pulls out into a twin bed." It's generous of him to call it a couch.

Mom's face constricts. "I thought you said you had room for her."

Trick frowns. "I do."

"So you're just going to sleep *there*" — she motions to the chair-couch, her voice pinched and tight — "for the next two months?"

He shrugs, scratching his head through his beanie. "When have I ever minded sleeping on a couch?" He winks at me, partly settling the tremor of nerves bubbling in my stomach. "Feel free to decorate."

Later, I sit cross-legged on the bed, watching Mom brush her hair in the cracked and spotted mirror that hangs over the empty bookcase where Trick told me I could stack my clothes. Probably to give us a little privacy in the minuscule bathroom, Trick went out to fetch some more wood. I hear him rustling around outside. Mom catches my eye in the mirror. "You still liking your plan?"

I tug the sleeves of my pajamas over my hands. "If you were selling this place, you could call it cozy ski-bum chic in the ad." I nod at the posters of skiers all over the walls. LEGENDS OF SQUAW VALLEY, they say. JONNY MOSELEY. TAMARA MCKINNEY. MARCO SULLIVAN. The names don't mean much to me.

She glances around. "*Warm* and cozy ski-bum chic," she agrees. She sets the brush down on top of the bookshelf and pulls back the covers of the bed. "Scooch over." I make room for her as I crawl under the blankets. She wrinkles her nose, mumbling, "Ugh, does he ever wash these sheets?" and leans to click off the switch for the overhead light. I can still make out her face in the pale glow of the woodstove.

The room smells musty but also warm and woodsy. I like it. "Don't worry about me, okay? Number six on my Now List is to simplify and downsize. I'd say I can cross number six off my list just by living here." We both giggle into the dark.

She huddles close to me in bed, both of us willing the cold sheets to soak in the heat of our bodies. After a moment, she whispers, "Honey, I know you keep saying not to worry, but I can't help it. After everything that happened . . . why would you choose to come *here*?"

I stare up at the dark ceiling, her words knocking around my mind, triggering a secret place there I'd never noticed before. I ask, "Why don't you ever talk about what happened with you and Trick and Tahoe?"

Her body stills. I hear the front door open and close and then Trick stacking wood in the other room. Mom exhales next to me. I can feel her hesitating, but then she shifts onto her side, facing me under the blankets, and squeezes my hand. "Sometimes people can grow miles apart, Mara. Even in the smallest of houses."

FIVE

Mom kisses me good-bye in the blue light of dawn. "I'm going to get on the road," she whispers, and I see the outline of her through sleepy eyes. "Don't get up." I roll over as she tiptoes out of the room and pulls the front door shut behind her. Distantly, already dozing, I hear her car start and drive away. When I wake again, sun streams through the window. I sit up, the room cold against my face. I can actually see the breath leaving my body in small clouds. Shivering, I yank on some long underwear, jeans, and black Uggs and pull on a Patagonia fleece. Still freezing, I add my parka.

I find Trick sitting at the card table, eating a bowl of off-brand fruity loops. "My room . . . is freezing," I chatter, migrating toward the glowing woodstove and holding out my hands.

Trick's spoon hovers over his bowl. "Yeah, you're going to want to leave your door open at night. Or else keep stocking your stove." At my confused look, he laughs. "Here, let me show you."

We head back into my room where, crouching down, he shows me how to get the fire going again, how to angle the wood and stuff paper in between. "Here, now you try it." I settle on my heels next to him and it's strange to be so close to him, our shoulders touching. When the fire catches, he wipes his ashy hands on the rag sticking out of the woodbin. "Make sense?"

37

I feel dizzy. "Yeah, thanks." I need food. I get light-headed when I don't eat enough.

"No sweat." He stands. "I've got to get to work."

"What time is it?"

"About eight-thirty."

Now List #4. Done. That was easy.

He moves into the other room, asking, "You want a lift to the Village?"

"Great." I'm sure there's a café where I can get some food and start my schoolwork. Grabbing my bag, I follow him into the cold morning. It snowed a bit in the night, just a dusting that disappears beneath our boots, but it still stops me. I turn a slow circle, taking in the quiet, the sugar-sifted trees, the enormous house, dormant and angular from across the wide stretch of yard. Trick watches me take it all in, this snow-globe world, from where he sits behind the wheel. Scrambling in next to him, I say, "Sorry. You're used to it, I know, but it's just so beautiful."

He starts the truck. "You never get used to how beautiful it is."

•　•　•

I follow Trick into Neverland mostly because I don't really know what else to do. He didn't say anything the whole ride into the Village and hasn't offered any suggestions for where I should do my schoolwork. By now, Mom would have given me three different detailed options with a clear front-runner. Probably color-coded on index cards. She's always talking to me about being independent while inadvertently tipping my decisions toward her preference with a frown or a just-visible narrowing of her eyes.

Where are those stupid index cards when you need them?

Instead, I stand marooned in a ski shop in Squaw Valley, holding on to the straps of my backpack for dear life. A man stands behind the counter. Tall and broad-shouldered, he wears a pair of reading glasses as he sorts through a stack of papers. He glances up when he hears us come in, but before he can say anything, a golden retriever appears from nowhere, all fur and slobber and energy, and jams her muzzle into my crotch.

"Oh! Hi there, nosy," I gasp, trying to push her away, which she mistakes for petting.

"Piper!" the man behind the counter shouts, and the dog makes a U-turn back to him, her tail wagging. "Sorry about that," he says, coming out from behind the counter. "She's a little overzealous. You must be Mara." He offers his hand.

"Uh, yeah. Hi," I say, shaking his hand even though mine is covered in slobber.

"Matt Never."

Trick elaborates. "He and his wife, Jessica, own Neverland." The parents of Midnight Spider-Man.

Mr. Never pushes his reading glasses to the top of his head. "Wow, I haven't seen you since you were tiny." His voice is low and kind. "You sure have grown up." Then he grins. "Of course."

"Nice to see you. Again," I add, feeling strange to have no memory of someone who seems to know me.

The door behind us jingles and Midnight Spider-Man comes into the store. Piper leaps to her feet, tail wagging, and rushes to greet him. Now dressed in street clothes, his dark hair messy, he has a cup of coffee in a stainless steel travel mug in one hand with a laptop tucked under his arm. He bends to pet Piper. "Morning, Pipe, good girl."

"Oh, Logan!" Mr. Never motions for him to come closer. "Mara, this is my son, Logan. You two probably don't remember, but you were in diapers together."

Logan looks a lot like his dad and gives me his version of their crooked smile. "Hi. Sorry, don't much recall the diaper years."

"Me either, but nice to see you've grown out of them." We both quickly look away, probably because I just said the weird thing about growing out of diapers. That was slick. Almost made valedictorian, but put a cute boy in front of me and I'm a complete idiot.

Trick lets his amused gaze slip from Logan to me. "Logan's a junior in high school, like you."

"Why aren't you in school right now?" I blurt, because, apparently, I'm also training to become a truancy officer.

Logan just grins. "My school has a flexible schedule. We meet two or three times a week for classes and labs and stuff, but otherwise I get all the work done on my own. So I have time to race." He sounds like he's clearly had to explain this before.

"Race?"

"Ski," Logan clarifies.

Before I can stop myself, I morph into my mother. "So you don't go to a real school?"

Instead of getting defensive, though, Logan laughs. "Real enough. I take all the same classes as regular school." I notice he says *regular* with the same inflection someone might use for *prison* or *bacteria*. "It's great, actually."

I want to sound breezy but end up spitting out something that sounds like "Ofcourseitsoundssupercoolandamazing," yet not

40

sounding at all like I think it's super cool or amazing. Logan and Trick exchange glances, their eyes widening at my spew.

"It works for me," Logan says, then adds, "I know that other type of school works for a lot of people. It's just, for me, sitting in a seat all day every day would give me hives. I'd freak out." As soon as he says this, though, he colors and drops his gaze, and I realize he knows exactly why I'm here in Tahoe. Logan hurries on, trying to extract his foot from his mouth. "Whoa, sorry — I didn't mean anything by that . . ."

Mortified, I stare at Trick, who won't meet my eyes. Is he *telling* people? The whole reason I'm here is so people *aren't* talking about me. Aren't whispering about the super-stressed-out girl who went mental on her math class.

"Right, okay," I stammer. "Speaking of school, mine's the opposite of flexible and I have work I need to turn in. Is there a place, I could, you know" — I hold up my laptop — "plug in?" *So I can get out of here*, I manage not to add.

Looking relieved, Logan nods. "You could hang next door at Elevation. Their coffee's sick and you totally have to try the cheese bagel."

"Sick coffee, cheese bagel, got it. Thanks." Without looking again at Trick, I hurry out of the store, welcoming the wash of cold against my burning cheeks.

•   •   •

Next door, I find a table near an outlet and dump my bag and laptop, my stomach churning at the whole exchange with Logan, or, as I now plan on calling the list in my head, How to Repel a Cute Boy in Under Two Minutes.

say something weird about diapers

insult his school

talk really fast

flee the premises

I inhale the coffee-scented air and remind myself to breathe (#8!). Elevation is glass and chrome and glossy black tables. A few people sit in armchairs near a fire, chatting or talking on their phones or writing in journals. Everyone either wears a down jacket like mine or has one over a chair, just in different colors. Tahoe is like attending a down-jacket convention. It's clearly the staple of the uniform. As evidence, I hang my own jacket on the back of a chair and power up my laptop so it can load while I order.

At the counter, I choose a vanilla latte and, after a moment's hesitation, a cheese bagel. "Do you want that toasted?" The barista wears a silver beanie that matches her Elevation apron, the front silk-screened with a shot of a skier jumping across the outline of a moon. Her glossy black hair falls in two perfect braids. Her name tag says NATALIE. And underneath that, SINGAPORE.

"Um, sure." I pull a ten-dollar bill from my wallet and hand it to her. "You're from Singapore?"

She hands me my change. "Yeah, but I've lived in Squaw for six years." Rolling her eyes, she adds, "The company who owns us wants our 'home country' on our name tags. You know, *international* resort and all that." She points at the guy with white-blond hair behind the espresso machine. "That's Finn. Netherlands." Finn gives me a quick wave. Natalie from Singapore pops a bagel in the toaster. "Butter or cream cheese?"

"Butter, please."

"I'll bring them out to you." She nods toward the table where I left my stuff.

Settling into a chair, I log on to my school portal. As it loads, I pull out my English binder, the slim volume of poetry I'm reading for my project, three sharp pencils, and the tight loop of my earbuds. I plug them into my laptop and click on my study playlist, mainly classical with some new "relaxation" music Josie found for me that mostly consists of some form of water noise — rain, stream, ocean. If I listen to it too long, it makes me need to pee.

Natalie sets down my drink and bagel, the smell of butter soaking into me. There's a snowflake in the foam on the top of my latte. "Wow, cool design," I tell her, admiring the intricate pattern.

"Thanks. It's my signature. Whoa, you've got yourself quite a setup here." She nods to the various school supplies I've placed on the table.

I flush as she notices the Now List binder, and I quickly set my poetry book on top of it. "I promise I'm not moving in."

"We have plenty of room." Her eyes stray over my head. "Beck, get your nasty boots off my table."

I turn to see the Chip Bag Boy from yesterday tipped back in his chair, his legs resting on the next table, his auburn hair rumpled with an alarming case of bed head. His smile widening, he swings them off, his heavy boots thumping to the ground. "Sorry, Nats. Won't happen again."

"Right." She disappears through a door to the back of the café.

I get to work, but after twenty minutes of rain music, I need to pee. I yank the earbuds out and find a bathroom. Returning, I pass Beck's table, where he has been joined by two girls my age. A petite girl in a white beanie has her back to me, but as I pass by their table,

43

the other girl briefly catches my eye over her soup bowl–size mug of tea, then shakes her mane of dark red hair at something Beck has been saying, her large brown eyes slipping back to him. "You're one hundred percent full of crap," she tells him. It piques my interest, and sliding back into my chair, I can't help but listen in.

Beck laughs. "I'm not, Isabel. This is the way I see it. We sit around all the time just rehashing other people's opinions. Other people's ideas. That's all school is — one massive recycling program." He puts on a stuffy-sounding voice. "Here, students, let's stuff your head with everything the whole world already knows so you can go out in the world and keep up the status quo." He shifts out of his pseudo-teacher voice. "It's a total waste of time. If I want to be a true independent thinker, I have to be done with school. Out of the system."

Ugh. Listen to this guy. I shake my head and try to concentrate on the assignment on my screen. I can hear the girl who must be Isabel say wryly, "It sounds like a convenient rationalization for not doing your homework." *Exactly*, I want to say, but of course I don't because I'm not supposed to be eavesdropping. I'm supposed to be doing my English essay on Emily Dickinson. I open the book of poetry and try to skim a few lines.

But my ears steal back to the conversation behind me. Beck elaborates on his theory. "Think about it. It's all about fear — people are so scared to step off the treadmill; they don't take any chances with their own minds. They just blindly follow everything that's been done before. I mean, seriously, nothing worth learning can be taught."

They must hear the low snorting sound that comes out of me because their table goes silent. Then, I hear Beck say, "You got something to add to that, San Diego?"

44

My neck prickles. Did Trick make *Have you seen this girl* hand-outs? Send out an email blast? Turning to face them, I clear my throat. "Sorry?"

Tipping in his chair again, Beck eyes me with a mix of confidence and amusement he has clearly cultivated. "It seems like you have something you wanted to add."

I feign innocence, shrugging. "Nope." I start to turn back to my computer, catching sight of my Now binder, and Will's contribution flashes to the front of my mind.

9. Be brave

I turn to Beck's table. "Actually, okay, yeah. It's just something you said struck me as . . . funny."

His eyebrows shoot up and he drops the chair back onto its four legs. "Oh, yeah? Which part?"

"You said something about school just being one . . . how did you put it? One massive recycling program for ideas?"

"Sounds like something I'd say." He grins.

I steady my hands against the back of the chair. "But then you essentially rehashed Oscar Wilde. 'Nothing worth knowing can be taught.' That's Oscar Wilde."

The girl he called Isabel cracks up into her tea. "Oh, wow, Beck — you're so busted. You see that on a meme somewhere?" The other girl giggles and takes a last sip of her espresso before she starts putting on her coat.

I'm surprised when Beck's grin just gets wider, his eyes brightening. "Well, I happen to think Oscar Wilde was a pretty cool guy."

"Clearly enough to plagiarize him," I say, trying to tease him, but something about him makes me nervous and I hope he can't hear the wobble in my voice. There are kids like Beck at Ranfield, always up for an argument. They populate the debate team and student government, and use up most of the air in the AP history discussions. Only that's not why Beck makes me nervous. More likely, it's because he looks like he belongs on the cover of a magazine called *Gorgeous Skier Boys*. The Disarming Smile issue. I don't generally talk to boys who look like Beck. Or, more honestly, they don't usually talk to me.

My phone buzzes. It's Mom's Google calendar, reminding me I should be wrapping up English and moving on to AP history. Great. I've barely started my Emily Dickinson assignment. First morning here and I'm already behind.

Isabel and her friend push back their chairs, stand, and pull on beanies. As Isabel slips into her down jacket, I'm struck by how tall she is. The word that comes to mind is *Amazonian*. She grabs her mug. "Well, kids, while this I'll-show-you-my-brain-if-you-show-me-yours is a hoot for all of us, Joy and I have practice." To me, she says, "By the way, I'm Isabel Hughes and this is Joy Chang." I notice she doesn't introduce Beck.

"Hi." I smile at Joy, who gives a wave before winding a scarf around her neck.

To Beck, Isabel says, "Behave yourself, Oscar." The girls say good-bye to Natalie and Finn before leaving the café.

When they're gone, Beck slides into the other chair at my table. "It's Mara, right?"

"Beck, stop harassing random customers," Natalie calls from behind the counter. She tries to sound tough, but her voice is fringed with affection.

"She's not random. She's Trick McHale's kid." He leans his forearms on the table, tipping it enough that I have to catch my three pencils from rolling off the side of it. "I know about her."

To hide the tremor his words send through me, I log back into my portal, the session having expired during my eavesdropping. "What do you think you know about me?"

He runs his hands through his hair, only adding to the bed head. "I know you're named after Tamara McKinney." At my blank look, he clarifies, "First female skier to win the overall Alpine Cup in 1983. Grew up in Squaw Valley. Only American skier to hold that title until Lindsey Vonn in 2008. Maybe you've heard of *her*?"

I shake my head, thinking of the poster in Trick's bedroom. Tamara McKinney. Mom never told me I was named after a skier. Even though my legal name is Tamara, she's only ever called me Mara.

Why does this boy know things about me I don't?

Annoyed, I try for a polite smile, avoiding his hazel eyes, and stare intently at my screen. "Listen, I don't mean to be rude, but I'm busy. I have a paper due tomorrow." I nod in the direction of the book of poems on the table. "I happen to care very much about my massive recycling program."

He takes it in stride by not moving an inch. "What's your paper on?"

"Emily Dickinson."

He pushes back from the table. "Righto. Then I'll leave you to *dwell in Possibility*. Capital *P*. Oh, that's Miss Dickinson, by the way. Don't want to be accused of plagiarism twice in one day."

SIX

"Why do you look so purple?" I squint into my laptop screen at Josie.

"It's my new side-table light. It changes colors!" She squints back at me, flipping her long, dark ponytail over her shoulder. "See?" She switches it from purple to red to blue, each light changing the hue of the white stripes on her black-and-white sweater tights. Josie is always in shades of black, gray, and blue. In tennis, we call her the Human Bruise. For many reasons. Seeing her sitting on her familiar bed in her familiar room makes me feel farther than six hundred miles away. Aside from the posters of tennis stars John Isner and Rafael Nadal plastered everywhere, her room feels like a beach, all sun-bleached colors and posters of waves. One wall is just a map of Earth's oceans and their currents. Josie wants to be an oceanographer someday like her older brother, Reuben.

She notices my expression but mistakes it for criticism. "You don't like the light. I know, I know, it's dorky. But I love it." She switches the light back to purple.

I shake my head. "That's not it . . . I just, well, I miss you," I tell her, trying not to sound like a sappy idiot.

She perks up. "Come home! What are you even doing there?"

I try to keep defensiveness from leaking into my voice. "I think this is really going to help me, being here. I just need some time to get my head on straight."

Josie narrows her eyes. "Do they have special head-straightening gear in Antarctica? Why can't you get your head on straight in a warmer climate?"

For Josie, anything under sixty degrees is Antarctica.

I glance around my new room. No changing bedside-table lights here. No bedside table, actually. Outside, snow flutters past the window, dusting the green fence of trees behind the cottage. When I told Josie that I wanted to come to Squaw Valley, you would have thought I'd told her I wanted to try living in a snow cave in Alaska without electricity or light. So in my defense, I reminded her that for someone who wants to be an oceanographer, she should remember that many oceans in the world are freezing.

Still, she knows this isn't about geography.

Josie sips her Diet Coke loudly through a straw. "So how are things with the biological father?"

"Okay. He's not very talkative. But he taught me how to build a fire."

She looks skeptical. "Congratulations. He's a caveman." I pretend to shut the laptop cover. "Kidding!" she pleads. When I reopen it, she says, "I'm glad you're getting to know him better." I drop my eyes, and she hurries to ask about school. "Are you bored? What do you do all day?"

I hold up a pile of books and binders. "Impossible to be bored with the bucket-load of assignments Ranfield gave me for this whole Home Hospital thing." Apparently, Ranfield's version of a hospital involves producing large volumes of *I promise I'm actually learning something*. Maybe even more than when I was in real school. "Oh, and Mom's making me see a shrink."

Josie's eyes widen. "She is?" Tons of kids at Ranfield see shrinks, so I know Josie's reaction is about Mom and not the actual shrink part. "That's not like her."

"I know, right? The queen of solving your own problems. I couldn't believe it. I guess she wants to figure out why I decided to become a human paper-shredder."

Josie makes a sympathetic face. "Well . . . why *did* you?"

Shrugging, I push aside images from that terrible day — the numbers shifting on the page in front of me, the sound of paper ripping, my classmates' horrified faces. "I had a panic attack." Before she can reply, I hurry to change the subject again. "Want to help me figure out how to redecorate this place? Because, well, see . . ." I move my laptop around so Josie can view the bed, the woodstove, the bookcase now stacked with my clothes in neat, even rows. "It's a work in progress."

"What's with all the ski posters?" she asks, her voice sounding far away. One of the things I've always loved about Josie is she doesn't press me when she knows I'm done talking about something.

I set the laptop back on the bed in front of me. "These are the legends of Squaw Valley," I say in my best movie trailer voice-over.

"Don't you people have a Target?"

"Mom's sending me bedding."

"Well, I'm sending some better wall décor," Josie insists. "Text me the address."

Before I can respond, she says, "Oh, wait —" and she's suddenly off camera. Seconds later, she's back, holding up a pair of pants. "Our new warm-ups."

Another tug in my chest. "Oh, no way — he let us get the green ones?" Coach Jeffers told us we had to stick to our usual dove gray for warm-ups. Figures right after I leave he caves on the pretty pale green ones we've all been begging him for since August.

She hesitates. "I had him order you some. For when you . . . you know, come home."

"Thanks, Jo." My eyes sting. "How's school for you?" Josie and I both came to Ranfield on scholarship in sixth grade, and she's always been the only one there I can actually talk to.

She rolls her eyes. "School is school. We have a thousand poems to read in American lit, and Mr. Roberts is trying to raise, like, a million dollars for the Eco Club trip to Costa Rica. Same old same old. Oh, and Chris Locke is having a party tomorrow night."

"That should be fun." She knows I don't really think it will be fun. I'm not much of a party girl; it's embarrassing how boring I am. Josie always ends up hanging by someone's pool with me, but listening to her chatter about it, I wonder if she'll be able to have more fun without me there.

"You know, Mar," Josie says. "He was really pissed at whoever posted that video."

"Who?"

"Chris Locke."

I don't respond, my mind flashing to an image of Chris Locke in his baseball uniform. I don't know him very well. He's quiet and hangs out with other sporty guys.

Josie mistakes my silence for disagreement. "He is! *Most* people thought it was a horrible thing to do."

My skin tingles. "I know." But I don't really know. I don't really want to think about any of it, actually. The test. My classmates' wide O mouths. The YouTube video. I shake my head. "*Most* people aren't the problem."

Josie breathes out, clearly trying to choose her words. "Chris says it's the jerks who ruin it for everyone else."

Why are we still talking about Chris Locke? "Right, key word *ruin*."

"We can't let them. I mean, they're only, like, ten percent of the population."

"Do you have actual data to support that? Because it seems like the jerks are winning." But Mom and Will said the same thing. Let haters be haters and all that. Don't give them the energy. Don't let them win by running away, which is what I'm sure everyone thinks I'm doing by coming here.

A voice floats into the background of Josie's world. "Dinner, *mija!*" My mouth waters at the thought of one of Mrs. Martinez's amazing meals.

"Coming!" Josie shouts back. "Gotta go, Mar. Get in a little trouble, will ya? You're in Tahoe."

Looking around the empty room, I pull my Now binder across the bed to me and add:

12. Get in a little trouble

Not that I have any idea how to do that.

•　　•　　•

52

Trick waits for me outside in his truck while I have my appointment with Dr. Elliot the next morning. "How'd it go?" he asks after I get back into the truck. He heads out of Truckee toward Squaw Valley.

"Okay. He's nice or whatever. I made more lists."

He pulls into the McDonald's drive-thru. After ordering, he asks, "What do you mean, 'lists'?" He hands me a bag of food and my Diet Coke.

I tuck my drink between my thighs and open my box of chicken nuggets. "You know — what I'm grateful for, what I can and cannot control, beautiful things in my life — that sort of thing. Can I open this sauce in here?"

He motions at the ratty interior, much of it patched with duct tape. "You worried about messing up the fine upholstery?"

I pop open a barbecue sauce, licking a bit from my finger. Trick digs around in the bag on his lap for some fries as he pulls the truck back onto Highway 89. "So these lists — they help you feel better?"

"I guess." Of course, having me create lists to help me is like asking a dolphin, *Have you thought about living in water?*

I've made these assignment lists before.

Last year my sophomore history teacher, Ms. Diaz, made us keep gratitude lists as part of our current events folder. Maybe she saw it on Facebook or something. She called it the Current State of Me project. I made endless lists for her — the sun on the water, the smell of brunch on Sunday, the way my brothers laugh at funny movies. I got an A+ on it and she'd written, *Such a strong sense of what's good in your life!* in her scrawling purple pen.

What Ms. Diaz and her exclamation point didn't know was that I used to sit and stare at the posters on the walls of her classroom

53

and get these horrible stomachaches. Ms. Diaz's posters had sayings like LIFE IS SHORT; HISTORY IS LONG with pictures of a Roman building, once great, now in ruin. One poster read IN THE GRAND SCHEME OF THINGS, THAT PROBLEM'S PRETTY SMALL! written over a dot showing where our generation lands on the Time Line of Humans. I hated that poster. I wanted to write underneath it: *Shut up, poster!* History, she told us (over and over), teaches us that we are but small parts of a much bigger struggle and so we must make the best of where we land. So I made her list after list after list to show her I could make the best of where I'd landed.

I got an A+ in the class. And dozens of secret stomachaches.

"Well, I'm glad they're helping," Trick says now, turning the truck down Squaw Valley Road. "Sounds like you're a girl who knows what works for her."

"Yeah," I mumble, munching fries and staring out at the strange white world, not adding, *Or at least convincing people I do.*

•   •   •

I officially suck at meditation.

For the past hour, I've been sitting here by this flickering fire, wearing yoga pants, with the snow falling outside, trying to follow an article titled "5 Handy Tips for Meditation."

I'm stuck on step 1: Quiet the mind.

But my mind won't shut up.

Be quiet, mind!

Thing is, I don't have a quiet mind. I've *never* had a quiet mind. My mind is shouty and bossy and makes a weird sort of buzzing sound like a malfunctioning space heater. If I don't distract my mind by reading or studying or exercising or *doing* something, it gets even louder.

Psssssst, growls my mind, my eyes squeezed shut, *you suck at this.*

When Trick walks in with a pizza at a little after six on Thursday evening, I have stopped quieting and started crying. "Oh — hey?" He dumps the pizza on the card table. "What's wrong?" He takes in the pile of books, notes, binders, pencils, and paper I left spread all over the coffee table an hour ago. He also notices the binder I *might* have thrown across the room earlier, which now rests facedown in the dregs of the ripped-up sunset picture.

"I . . . I'm meditating." I look up from my cross-legged position, my face flushed from sitting too close to the fire. And from the binder throwing.

He shakes some snow from his shoulders and starts peeling off layers until he's just wearing his jeans, wool socks, and a long-sleeve shirt that says SQUAW VALLEY across the chest. "Meditating. Okay, well, nice job on the fire." He hunkers down in front of it, warming his hands. He smells cold like outside.

I swallow and wipe some tears from my cheeks. "I suck at meditation."

He looks sideways at me. "I thought maybe you were into some style that encourages crying. You know, lets out all the inner tension. Through your eyes. Or whatever."

Is that a thing? Can I count this? "Nope. Just sitting here in fail mode."

He gives me a funny look. "I'm not sure that's how it works."

"I read three different articles telling me that I need to just accept where I am in my mind and go with it. But I don't know how to do that yet." I crawl to my binder and pull it onto my lap. I flip through the articles I'd printed out about meditation. I'd highlighted the line "Settle into your mind" and written *???* after it. "It says to quiet your mind, but it doesn't really tell me how to do that. It's missing a step." I hold it up. "These are faulty instructions."

Shaking his head, Trick stands and slips into a seat at the card table, flipping open the lid of the pizza box and grabbing a slice. The smell of pepperoni makes my stomach growl. He chews his slice halfway through before saying, "Maybe the point is to just sit and be still and not fight it so much." At my blank look, he says, "Don't try to be *good* at it."

I shut the binder. "What's the point of doing something if you're not trying to get good at it?"

He gives me a funny look. "To just experience it." He nods at the box. "Want a slice?"

I join him at the table. "Should I get a plate?"

"Nah. Then we just have to do dishes." Outside, the sky darkens. Trick doesn't say anything else and we eat our pizza in silence, watching the fire, its warm glow reminding me of at least one thing I managed to get right today.

SEVEN

I spend much of Friday at Elevation finishing my schoolwork for the week. A little after two, I rub my eyes, feeling slightly sick. Note to self: Three lattes and two cheese bagels do not fall under the "healthy choice" category for daily dining. Ready for a change of scenery, I pack up and head next door to Neverland to see if Trick might be able to run me back to the cottage. I should probably start studying for the chemistry test I have on Monday. The bells tinkle on the door as I push through it, and Logan Never comes out of the back dressed in jeans and a sweatshirt that says THE FROST BOYS across the front. "Oh, hey — thought you might be Isabel."

"Nope, just me." To fill the awkward silence, I say, "That's a nice sweatshirt. I've seen other guys wearing them around. Are they for your ski team?"

He looks down at it. "Yeah, the shop partly sponsors our team, so, you know — Lost Boys, Frost Boys. Are you impressed with our cleverness?"

"Oh, sure." I think of Isabel and Joy. "But what do the girls wear?"

"Their sweatshirts have Tinker Bell and say 'Eat my fairy dust.'" His phone beeps and he checks it, his face falling. "Aw, man."

"What?"

He doesn't look up. "Our friend Bodie can't make it today. He forgot he has a dentist appointment. Isabel's going to kill him." Logan texts back, chewing his lip.

"Where are you going?"

"Goggles." He tucks his phone back into his pocket. "It's this program that meets on Friday afternoons at one of the middle schools up here. For at-risk kids. We play games with them and talk about how to stay on the right track."

"Cool." They have stuff like that at Ranfield, too, since we're required to have one hundred hours of community service every year, but I always end up tutoring math or something in our learning center because it fits better into my schedule, instead of having to go off campus.

Isabel comes through the door in a down jacket and jeans. "Where's Bodie? We're going to be late," she announces, as if Logan hasn't been hanging out waiting for her. "Hey," she says, noticing me.

Before I can respond, Logan tells her, "He's not coming."

Her brown eyes widen. "What?! Our entire talk today is about not skipping out on your commitments. And Bodie *flakes*? Great example."

Logan grabs his jacket from a hook on the wall. "He has a dentist appointment."

"We're building a 'triangle of accountability' with our bodies," Isabel fumes, flipping her braid over her shoulder, her eyes flashing. "Can't have much of a triangle with just two of us. Kind of defeats the *triangle* part of it!" She squeezes her hands into fists. "I'm going to crush him into a million tiny pieces until he's just a pile of broken Bodie on the ground."

Whoa. Kind of scared of Isabel right now. "I can go," I say. "I can be an arm of a triangle."

Logan looks relieved. "Great — my dad's waiting for us at the car."

I follow them out, thinking, *Bodie, whoever you are, you owe me your life.*

•   •   •

Turns out, being the third arm of a "triangle of accountability" means having Logan step on your face.

"Does it hurt?" he asks, handing me the ice pack he went in search of minutes earlier, wincing as he looks at me. I sit in a metal folding chair near the stage in the multipurpose room of the middle school. After the face stomping, Isabel organized all the students into a big circle of chairs, spinning what had just happened to me as one of those lemonade-lemons lesson, like *When life steps on your face, get a refreshing ice pack.* I watch them out of my one good eye.

"Well, you stepped on my face," I say, trying to keep my voice light. "So, yeah. It might hurt a little."

"Have I mentioned how sorry I am about that?" Smiling apologetically, he pulls up a chair next to me to watch Isabel in the circle of kids. She's gesticulating wildly and they're eating it up, laughing as a group at something she says.

I motion to her. "She's great with them."

He pulls on the strings of his hoodie, watching her fondly. "Yeah, she is."

I hold the ice away from my face for a second, not sure what's worse, the throbbing or the cold. "Does she ski, too?"

He raises his eyebrows. "Oh, yeah. She skis." The way he says it, the way he watches her while he says it, tells me there's more to Isabel and Logan than just the Goggles after-school program. I've never wanted someone to look at me like that. Suddenly, I do. He leans forward, resting his forearms on his thighs. "Our girl over there will probably be heading to the Olympics someday."

"Really?" I can't keep the awe out of my voice. I rack my brain for Olympic terms but can't remember any for skiing. "Does she have an event?"

"Downhill. Mostly super-G."

I hold the ice pack back against my swollen cheek. "Sorry, ski newbie over here — I don't know what that is."

"Super giant slalom," Logan explains, making a squiggly motion with his hand. "Really fast. Lots of turns."

"I know nothing about skiing." Skiing. Meditation. Building fires. Clearly, in Tahoe, I'm an idiot.

He looks at me, surprised. "You don't ski?"

"Don't get too many snow days in San Diego."

He leans back in his chair. "I just figured, you know, with your parents and all."

It's strange to think he has certain information and ideas about Trick and Mom. "I just found out my mom used to ski and, well, I don't really know anything about Trick. Just that he used to be some sort of skier and got hurt. That's pretty much it. I mean, we've never been, you know, close." He shifts uncomfortably in his seat and avoids my eyes. Universal body language for *Please change the subject*. I set the ice pack on the floor and motion to the circle. "So, pretty nice kids you got here."

"Yeah." Logan frowns a little, watching them. "So many of them have these terrible lives. Seriously, Dad's in jail, or they're living in

60

their car, or their home life is just messed up in some way. It's intense." He motions to a shaggy-haired boy sitting with his back to us, wearing a Burton beanie. "Like Franco there. His dad died when he was six. Three older sisters. Mom works two jobs cleaning hotels around here. He sort of slipped through the cracks at school for a few years, but last year his teacher got him hooked up with Goggles and he's passing all his classes now."

My chest squeezes. "It's cool you guys do this," I say. When he doesn't say anything, I awkwardly add, "And it will look great on college applications."

He hesitates. "Actually, Isabel and I aren't going to put it on our applications."

"What — why?"

"This year our coach is on this whole mindfulness kick." Logan makes an apologetic face. "I don't know; he read an article or something. Anyway, he challenged each of us to choose something in our lives that we decide not to go public about." He smiles at my confused expression. "Look, it's not like Isabel and I won't get into college — we have plenty of other stuff. It's important to our coach that we try things like this." He stands, crosses to a table by the stage, and starts setting up snacks, opening bags of chips and Oreos and pulling a jug of lemonade from a cooler of ice.

Sitting here, it suddenly feels like more than just my face got stepped on.

After Logan finishes setting up the snack table, I watch him settle down next to a boy with straw-colored hair and a constellation of freckles across his nose who has just scooted his chair off to the side, his face long. They talk quietly, and in a minute, Logan coaxes a smile out of him.

Every kid in this place has a life that belongs on my Get a Grip List.

. . .

An hour later, we wait outside the school until Trick pulls into the driveway. The back of his truck is heaped with pillows, blankets, and quilts. "Hop in," he tells the three of us. "We can grab some burgers and go do some meditating." He winks at me.

"Sweet." Isabel hops into the back, pulling a soft patchwork quilt over her and resting against a mound of pillows near the cab.

I walk around the front of the truck and yank open the passenger door. "I have a chemistry test on Monday to study for," I tell Trick.

"Right, Monday." He taps his thumbs on the steering wheel in time to the low music on his stereo. "Good thing it's Friday."

I'm not convinced this is a good idea. "Are we even allowed to ride back there?"

"I'll take back roads." He squints at me. "What happened to your face?"

"The hazards of accountability triangles." I leave my backpack in the front with Trick and go around to the bed of the truck. Isabel has her eyes closed, the quilt pulled to her chin. Standing up in the back, Logan offers to help haul me into the truck, and I try not to notice my stomach jolt when he grabs my hand.

A half hour later, Trick parks in the middle of a meadow. Despite the cold, we're warm under the mounds of fleece blankets and quilts. My head propped on several pillows, I stare up at the glittery stretch of sky. Around me, the Tahoe winter night is still and silent and I want to relax into it, but instead, I'm making a list of the topics I need to study for my chem test. I try counting stars, but they blur above me as my mind shifts to the formulas I need to know for Monday's test.

A flash of light slips through the sky. "Shooting star," Isabel announces, her voice sleepy.

"Not actually a star, though," I say, remembering something from one of my long-ago science classes. "Meteoroids. Space dust. They make that flash when they collide with the atmosphere."

"Shooting star sounds prettier," she murmurs. "But that would explain why you're going to be valedictorian at your fancy-pants private school."

"Not anymore," I mumble, pulling the quilt up over my chin.

"Why not anymore?" Logan wants to know.

I swallow, saying the words out loud for the first time. "I got a B in calculus last semester. So, yeah, no more valedictorian for me."

"That's it?" Trick asks into the dark. "One class. That shouldn't matter. One B."

It mattered to Rebecca Song, new front-runner. We'd been neck and neck since freshman year when she came to Ranfield. I'm sure she ran a victory lap when she found out about my B. Of course, Josie would argue that Rebecca's run wouldn't be very fair considering she is clearly some government experiment made out of bionic, superhuman parts.

"So you got a B." Logan's voice floats into the mix. "That's normal."

Normal. At Ranfield, the goal is not to be normal. Quite the opposite. In every possible way, we're taught to want to be exceptional — winners, leaders, the cream of the crop. Just read the brochure. No one wants to be *normal*. At Ran, everyone has something special, whether it's sports or dancing or debate or ceramics. One kid at our school is a world-champion juggler. And even if you aren't currently the best at whatever that something is, you're *trying* to be. That's the point. We set goals and if we work our hardest and give our best selves, we can achieve anything. Ranfield prides itself on being a school community nobly built from each of its distinct achievers.

Seriously, that's a direct quote from the website. Go, Ravens.

And *my* thing has always been my academics — the tests and essays and the 100 books you're supposed to read before you graduate from high school (3 different lists cross-checked and compiled into a list of 216 books, of which I still need to read 47).

I have only, ever, gotten As.

My thing: to be the Ranfield valedictorian.

So what happens when you devote your whole self to a goal, you give your best self, but still fall short of it?

I couldn't possibly have worked harder than I did, not and actually sleep, so that's not it. People think it comes easily for me, but it doesn't. I'm not like Rebecca Song, bionic human. I work my butt off for my grades. I stay up late every night, spend every weekend studying, no exceptions. I have taken schoolwork on every family vacation since I started high school. If I'm not playing tennis or sitting in class or going to choir rehearsal or eating dinner with my family, I'm working on school because I don't know how to want anything else. To *be* anything else.

And then I had a very bad day and all that changed.

I fell flat on my YouTube-viral-video-worthy face. So it's occurred to me in these last few weeks that somewhere along the line, I may have been given faulty information. Apparently, you can do your best and *not* achieve your goal. Turns out, you can't do anything just because you set your mind to it. Which changes things, doesn't it?

"It's partly why I'm here," I find myself telling them, my eyes tracing the ribbon of the Milky Way across the night. Then I say something that surprises me.

"I would actually *love* to feel normal."

EIGHT

Sitting in Elevation, I check my watch again. Logan and Isabel should be done in another hour and the butterflies are starting to wage war in my belly. Stargazing last night, they offered to start teaching me to ski today when they finished their race. "You want to be normal in Tahoe?" Logan had asked. "We need to get you on the mountain."

Now List #1: Learn to ski.

My whole body feels carbonated at the thought of heading up onto that mountain. When was the last time I felt this excited and nervous about something I was probably going to be horrible at? Maybe when I was eight and tried to play basketball for a season, only to discover I clearly belonged in sports that involved a net between me and the girl who was trying to smash me in the face. Still, I liked playing basketball. I just wasn't any good at it. So Mom and Will thought it would be best for me to focus on tennis, where I at least showed some natural ability.

I tap my pencil lightly over my chem formulas, staring out at the winter light of Squaw Valley. It's strange to realize I haven't tried a new sport in years. I haven't tried much of anything new in years. Too risky. Stick to your strengths. Over the years, Mom and Will have encouraged me to focus on the things I'm already excelling in so I would have better chances for college scholarships. No time for dabbling. That would waste time and resources.

Behind me, Elevation's door opens and, turning, I see Beck Davis stroll in, his face flushed from the mountain. His eyes light up when he sees me and he heads for my table. "Hey, bookworm." Is this becoming a thing with him? The nicknames. *San Diego. Bookworm.*

I try not to like it. "Hi, Beck. You done racing for the day?" Maybe Isabel and Logan aren't far behind.

He slides into the chair next to me and helps himself to a piece of my cookie. "Oh, I don't race anymore."

"You're not on the ski team?"

Shaking his head, he wipes his hands on his ski pants. "Used to be. A bunch of us were on Squaw's development team when we were kids. That's the team they start you out on to see if you have the chops. I raced some gates for a few years, but it wasn't my scene. Racers are such jocks. I'm a freeskier now."

"I don't know what most of that means," I say apologetically. There it is again, Tahoe as foreign language.

He runs his hand through his tangle of hair. "Freeskiing is not traditional skiing. It's way chill. You do your own thing. Mess around at the terrain park, you know?

"So you're on a freeski team?"

He makes a sour face. "Nah, they have competitions and stuff, but I don't do any of that. I ski for the fun of it, not so some guy can hand me a medal and a ranking."

"Sure," I say, slightly unnerved to hear an argumentative echo to my earlier thoughts.

"Hey," he says, crossing his arms and leaning back in the chair. "How'd your Emily Dickinson paper turn out?"

Surprised he remembered, I say, "Good, I think. It was mostly just an analysis of five of her poems." I don't tell him how unhappy I was with it, how I couldn't seem to get the conclusion quite right.

Beck watches Finn across the room as he adds some wood to the fire. "I heard something cool once about Emily Dickinson, that she didn't really want her poems published."

Something warm moves through me. "Yeah, I read something about that, too. I'm not sure if it's true or not." I should research that.

He waves to someone walking by the window outside. "Still, it's a cool thought. Especially these days. To write for yourself. To not need other people telling you how great you are all the time, to not have people commenting on it or hashtagging or reposting it all the time. To just do it for the sake of doing it. Too bad more people aren't like that." His eyes drift over my shoulder and his face darkens.

Logan appears next to our table. "You ready to head up?" He nods, almost curt, to Beck. "Hey."

I gather up my books and binders, stuffing things out of order into my backpack. Something in the air changed when Logan came in, the heat from the café evaporating around us. "Logan and Isabel are attempting to teach me how to ski — wish me luck."

"Luck," Beck echoes, his chair scraping the floor as he pushes it away from the table, but before I can say anything else, he's leaning on the counter, his back to us, laughing at something Natalie is saying as she makes a latte behind the gleaming espresso machine.

•   •   •

Outfitted in some old red ski pants of Isabel's, my parka, and what feels like twenty pounds of random gear from Neverland, I follow

Logan toward the funitel building. "Isabel said she'd catch up," he told me. "She's still over at Northstar talking to our coach." Logan wears a pair of tan ski pants and a green plaid jacket. I clomp after him, my ski boots like cement blocks, noticing he clomps much less than I do. He motions for me to follow him through a gate, his goggles pushed up on his helmet, his hair curling around his ears.

"Is Northstar another resort?" I ask, moving up to the gate. It beeps as it reads the pass Logan's dad got for me, then lets me through.

"Yeah. We take turns racing at the different resorts around Tahoe." We step into the next available funitel car, the wide-windowed enclosed pods that carry skiers to the upper part of the mountain where we can catch some easier lifts.

"Your first funi ride," Logan says, stashing our skis and poles next to him in an empty slot by the bench, and scoots over so I can sit next to him.

My stomach lurches as the funi swings out and up, and I try not to think about being suspended from a cable high above snow and rock. We soar over people lounging by a fire pit at an outside bar, over hotel tops, and as we climb, I can see the Village parking lot and the valley beyond. We climb higher. Logan doesn't seem to notice my terror, pointing out the long, sweeping curl of the Mountain Run and, as we pass especially close to a jut of granite, three plastic flamingos someone has twisted into the netting on the rock. Two are pink, but the one in the middle is a sort of washed-out gray.

"Wave at the flamingos," Logan says. "The pink ones are Primp and Preen. I named the gray one Stan."

"Hi, Stan." I wave lamely at the disappearing flamingos.

"Oh — see." Logan points at the stretch of view suddenly emerging. From here, we see a triangle slice of metallic lake, the layers of mountains beyond fading into sky.

"Beautiful. Is that Lake Tahoe?"

"Yeah." He nods as we drop slightly and the lake disappears. Logan shifts on the bench. "Wait until we get up to the top of the Big Blue run. You can see even more of it."

"Is Big Blue a green run?" I pull off my backpack and extract my binder. "I read a few articles about learning to ski and they all said it's important to start with the green runs and feel really solid with those before moving to the blue runs. Also, it says there are different levels of green. Is this an easy green?"

He fiddles with our poles, giving me a funny look. "What's that you got there?"

I look down at the cover, now a snow-covered Swiss alp. Much more thematic than the Hawaiian sunset, I think. "It's just some research stuff." I hurry to push it into my backpack. "So is it an easy green?"

"Don't worry about it," he says. "I'll take care of you."

Right. *Don't worry about it.* One of those expressions uttered only by people who already know how to do it. Little does he know I have the ever-evolving worry list. So far on this funi trip alone it looks like this:

> the funi car unsnapping and us plummeting to our deaths
> getting stuck in this funi car for hours because of a power
>   failure
> not being able to get on the chairlift

falling off the chairlift once I manage to actually get on looking like an idiot in front of Logan Never

"Do I look worried?" I manage to ask. Why do I suddenly care so much what this boy thinks of me?

Before he can respond, the funi slips into a docking station inside an open-walled building. The doors slide apart, and I follow Logan into a blast of cold air, dragging my gear. Other skiers and boarders move past me, their skis easy over their shoulders, their snowboards held casually like you'd carry a library book. I drop one of my skis, my bulky gloves not able to grip it, and it clatters to the ground. Maybe this was a stupid idea.

"Here." Logan bends to help me, and with a quick flick of his wrist, locks my skis together somehow and sets them gently on my shoulder. "You'll get used to it."

I'm not so sure about that.

Outside, the sky is a shock of blue against the blinding white of the mountain. Logan helps adjust my goggles and makes sure my skis clip in properly and that I have a good grip on my poles. Watching him, I'm reminded of babysitting for three-year-old Aiden Simms, who lives down the street from me in San Diego. Whenever I take him outside to ride his Scoot bike on the sidewalk, I have to check him in the same sort of way.

Which, of course, makes me feel idiotic.

"Okay," he says, pulling his own goggles down. "I'm not sure what you've read, but skiing is about balance. To start, though, I want to make sure you know how to stop once you get going."

Yes, knowing how to stop seems especially important. Biting

my lip, I watch people whip down the mountain, barely slowing, even when they're near the signs that clearly read SLOW. My mind blanks on everything I've read and I try to keep my voice even. "You should probably assume that I will most likely be killed today on this mountain."

Smiling, he slides his skis back and forth in quick scissor-snap moves. "You'll be fine. Just don't think so much about it."

Did he not see the binder?

He takes me through a series of moves with food names, showing me French fries (skis parallel to each other) and how to make a pizza-slice shape with my skis.

"This is your snowplow," he says of the pizza shape. "It will allow you to stop anywhere, anytime, but you can also use it to slow down and turn. You never have to move faster than you want to." Looking at the mountain spilling out around me, I seriously doubt that's true. "We have to ski down just a little bit to catch the Big Blue," he says, his goggles reflecting the patch of sky behind me, swimming with white clouds. "Ready?"

I wave one of my poles vaguely in his direction. "Yes, yes, go ahead." He skis down the hill, and I push off, the way I might do on roller skates, and my skis slip across the snow. *Pizza slice, French fries, pizza slice*, I repeat in my mind over and over while I attempt to follow Logan as he curves down the mountain to the left. Off to our right, skiers zoom toward Gold Coast, a blue lift that glides up the mountain away from us. In front of me, Logan moves in slow, unfinished loops, occasionally skiing backward to check on me. Show-off.

Miraculously, we make it to a flat spot near a lift called Big Blue Express. Logan jams his poles into the snow so they hold, and skis over to me. "You did great! How'd that feel?"

72

Like certain death was zooming around every corner, I want to tell him, but instead, I say, "I'm not really sure what to do with my poles."

"Keep your core pointed toward the downhill and use your poles to navigate." He demonstrates a few short turns, his poles moving in sync beside his body. I attempt to follow, concentrating on copying his form, but my skis slip out from under me and I'm suddenly on my butt. By the way, falling on snow hurts. Logan skis back to me, showing me how to position my skis and use my poles to get up. Okay, so maybe I will need my poles.

"Let's grab the Big Blue and I can show you up on the run. It's a really mellow little bunny hill." He skis into line. Following him, I inch forward as the skiers fill the lift benches. When it's our turn, Logan helps me get in place, showing me how to look back to meet the lift chair that comes trembling around the curve. "Don't worry, they're slow and easy," Logan tells me, but it still catches me off guard and he has to practically yank me back onto the seat. Smooth. I will clearly not be impressing Logan Never today with my grace and skill. The lift lurches forward and my stomach drops as my skis leave the ground. But then, suddenly, I'm floating.

It's called a lift for a reason.

As the hum of the Big Blue line fades behind us and we move through the cold air, everything stills. I can't remember the last time I sat like this without doing something, without checking my phone or taking notes or reading a book or finishing an assignment or failing to meditate. Now, though, I just float.

I breathe out, a long sigh, and Logan says, "Feels great, right?"

Nodding, I look out to my right where ski runs disappear down the mountain, and much farther off, another building sits on a distant peak. "What's that?"

Logan leans into me, just slightly. "That's High Camp. You can take a tram up there and they have food and a skating rink and a pool."

Up ahead, I notice the spot where we get off the lift and my stomach pitches at the sight of a sloping mound of snow. "How do I, um, get off?" Logan explains that I need to keep the tips of my skis up and then just stand. We raise the bar and moments later I feel the snow connecting with my skis.

"Now." Logan stands, giving me a little tug so I slide down next to him. Forgetting my snowplow, I crash at the bottom. Logan hurries to help me up as other people exit the lift around me. "Not bad." Really? Not bad? I'm pretty sure I can add that to the list of the worst lift exits in skiing history. He motions to his right. "Here, follow me so we're out of the way."

I snowplow after him and, looking up, find myself on the edge of the world. Everywhere I look, miles of snow and pine and mountains. People zoom by, heading to other runs or stopping to take pictures in front of the blue wedge of Lake Tahoe in the distance. Without warning, I tear up.

"You okay?" Logan skis back over to me.

"This view," I say by way of explanation, glad for my goggles.

He studies me closely. "It's cool to watch someone see it for the first time."

"Let's do this," I tell him, motioning to the hill, trying to get quickly past the mushy moment. What is wrong with me?

Logan guides me slowly down Big Blue and I continue to fall.

And fall.

And fall.

At one point, halfway down, I throw my poles to the ground in frustration and sit, breathing hard. Logan skis over. "You want a break?"

Yes. But, a little embarrassed by the pole throwing, I tell him, "No. I'm good." I squint up at him. "Is it wrong that the ski lift is my favorite part of this process?"

He offers me his pole and pulls me up. "Not for long. You're catching on quick."

We finish the run.

After an hour, every part of my body starts to ache. Even with all my tennis training, I apparently have millions of unknown muscles throughout my legs and back that have banded together to collectively scream at the top of their little muscle lungs.

On our third run, Logan waits for me partway down Big Blue. "That looked better — no falls!" He holds his poles up in victory over his head.

I snowplow to a stop. I'm an awkward wooden puppet next to his fluid, graceful turns, but he seems genuinely happy for me. "Thanks," I tell him, still breathless. "That felt better." And it did.

No, wait. It didn't just feel better. At one point, my skis had smoothed out, I'd felt balanced and strong, and it felt . . . like what? Like flying. But without worrying I might fall from the sky.

"You're nice to take me out here. This can't be any fun for you at all."

"Are you kidding? I love introducing people to the sport." He smiles at me, and for the smallest moment, it seems like we're the only two people on the mountain. Whatever this weird energy is, he must sense it, too, because he clears his throat and leans heavily on his poles. "I wonder what happened to Isabel?" He pulls a glove off with his teeth and fishes his phone out of his pocket. "She's going to meet us at Gold Coast." Before I can respond, he skis off toward the funi building.

I follow him over to the deck at the Gold Coast building, where we leave our skis and poles in a rack. He motions for me to grab a seat at an empty table and takes off his helmet, stuffing his gloves inside it. "Be right back," he tells me, and I wait, setting my helmet and gloves next to his. He emerges a few minutes later with hot chocolates and a bottle of water. "Drink this first," he says, handing me the water. "You should stay hydrated on the mountain." I study his messy hair. Clearly, most of the bed head I've been noticing around the Village is more a by-product of the helmets these guys wear all day long than their morning grooming habits. Or probably a combination of both.

Whatever the reason, messy works on Logan Never, and I can't stop my mind from listing what else works on Logan Never:

> dark eyes
> great smile
> patience

Stop it, I tell myself. It's not like me to crush on another girl's boyfriend. I drink half the water to avoid staring at him. "Thanks." Then I stare at him some more:

> freckles
> easy laugh

Ugh. Like always, when I start making it a list, it seems to take on a life of its own.

Logan takes a sip of his hot chocolate. "So you're getting your ski legs. Wait until you tell Trick. I mean, he doesn't ski much anymore, but he'll be stoked to hear you got some runs in."

"Why doesn't he ski much anymore?" His limp doesn't seem bad enough to keep him off the mountain.

Logan looks uncomfortable. "I mean, he tools around and stuff, I guess, but, you know, the accident jacked up his leg."

Mom told me he'd had a bad skiing accident when I was little, but she'd never really elaborated. "Do you know what happened to him? With his accident?"

Logan swirls his cocoa. "Only what my parents tell me. I mean, we weren't even three when it happened. But it ended him."

The cocoa tastes too sweet in my mouth and I set it down on the table. "Ended him how?"

"He couldn't ski anymore. At least not like before. I mean, he was amazing. I've seen pictures, some old videos and stuff. He was incredible." Logan waves at someone over my head. "Oh, hey — Iz!" he calls out, and I turn as Isabel makes her way toward us. In that movement across the deck, she reminds me of Josie, with her blue jacket and long legs in tight black ski pants and with her easy, athletic grace.

"Sorry to miss your first day," she says, sliding in next to Logan and taking a long drink of his hot chocolate. "How'd it go?"

"She crushed it," Logan says, his eyes slipping from me to Isabel, who leans in to casually flick some snow from his shoulder.

Not crushing it now. Unless you count World's Biggest Outsider.

NINE

The next morning, Trick reads a ski magazine as he spoons huge bites of Fruity O's into his mouth. Outside, falling snow dots the gray light, but inside, the fire crackles and the smell of coffee hangs in the room. "Morning," he says, looking up, spoon halfway to his mouth. "There's coffee."

"Thanks." I pour some into a red mug, add lots of milk, and then grab some of his cereal. Putting the milk back in the fridge, I notice Trick has gone shopping; the fridge has actual food of the nonfrozen variety — some cold cuts, a loaf of bread, a sack of carrots. Three cans of chicken noodle soup sit on the counter near the stovetop, next to some apples and a box of Wheat Thins. I guess he finally noticed the half dozen Post-it lists I'd left on the fridge. And in the bathroom. And on his work boots.

I slip into the other folding chair at the table, smoothing out some wrinkles in the tablecloth I bought in the Village yesterday. Dark blue with tiny white snowflakes. Trick hasn't seemed to notice it. "So I went skiing yesterday."

"Oh, yeah?" Trick looks up from the magazine.

"Logan took me." I take a bite of cereal, working up my nerve. "Actually, he mentioned that accident you had when we were little." I try to sound casual.

Trick fiddles with the magazine. "That was a long time ago. I'm sure your mom filled you in."

"Not really."

"No?"

I pick at my cereal, trying to figure out how to say, *I don't really know anything about you* without adding too much more to the sudden change in atmosphere. "She hasn't really told me much. About you. About that time in her life. Just that you were a competitive racer."

"Freeskier," he says. "Not a racer."

Like Beck. "Right, okay, but then you crashed and, well, stopped. And you two . . . didn't, um, work out."

Trick rests his elbows on the table, folding his hands in front of his chin. "That about covers it, then."

I don't tell him she has also said, more than once, that he just wasn't into being a dad. Anytime he'd send a card for my birthday a couple of weeks late, she would say it in a sort of offhand way. The way you might say someone's just not that into eating sushi. Or hiking. My heart hammers and I'm certain he can hear it. Maybe he hears it asking, *Why didn't you tell me all this yourself?* "Do you still ski?"

"I get up there sometimes, soak in the mountain. But it's hard . . . with the knee, with this bum leg." The quaver in his voice makes me think the knee isn't the hardest part.

"Would you take me up sometime?" My heart thrums and I imagine he can hear it pushing the blood through my vessels.

He stands, clearing his bowl and turning to the small sink. "Sure, though I'm not a great teacher. Logan's a better teacher. You're really better off with someone else."

I've spooked him. Obviously, #11 on the Now List is going to be harder than I thought. "Right, okay. I just thought it might be fun to, you know, do something together." I've had math tests that weren't this painful. And, with my history, that's saying something.

He runs the bowl under the faucet for longer than he needs to, and I see the tips of his ears turn pink. He sets the dish carefully in the metal dish rack. "Sure, yeah, also we could grab dinner sometime."

I swirl my spoon in the colored milk left behind. "Yeah, dinner sounds nice."

He runs his hand nervously through his hair. "I better get to work. You need a ride into the Village?" He wipes his hands on a lemon-yellow dish towel. It's new, too; its tag still attached. He'd definitely seen the grocery list I stuck to the fridge:

dish towel
soup
milk
something resembling a vegetable

"I'm going to stay here. You know, mellow Sunday by the fire. Maybe I'll read a book or something. Cross a few things off the Now List."

"Of course," he says, visibly relieved to be at the end of this particular conversation. He pulls on his coat and beanie and, in leaving, lets in a swirl of snow. Sipping the rest of my coffee, I watch it melt into small pools on the mat.

Which totally counts as meditation.

•   •   •

I spend Monday at the cottage doing schoolwork: English, history, chemistry, calculus. On Home Hospital, I still have to do all the same assignments as my regular classes and there are some online lectures for me to watch. Still, this doesn't translate into a full school day — the lunch breaks, the passing periods, the after-school commitments, the classroom lecture time (where, if I'm honest, I sometimes just space out). In a typical school day, there's a lot of time occupied with the anatomy of those other parts. Teachers take attendance, we go to assemblies, spend time doing group projects or listening to guest speakers or researching things in the library. So, right now, it definitely takes less time to do the actual curriculum.

At this rate, I'll finish everything by midweek.

So much spare time makes me feel strange and defensive, like one of those puffer fish that blow up when they're threatened. I find myself sorting my socks and refolding my clothes, even getting a jump on assignments not due for another two weeks. I'm not good with downtime. It makes me feel unproductive and I've been raised to see unproductivity as a sort of disorder.

Josie texts me as I'm settling down for some quality time with my SAT Hot Words list:

how's the break?

My hackles go up.

what break? been buried in work all day.

A second later:

u r supposed to be kissing a cute snowboarder.

Me:

no boys — u know the rules.

Josie and I agreed freshman year that we'd watched too many of

81

our classmates fall into the boyfriend trap. Smart, focused girls who morphed into lovesick idiots because of some boy. Getting into the right college is hard enough without the distraction of all that ridiculous *Ooooh does he like me what did he mean when he said that?* drama.

She texts:

those rules only apply in certain zip codes.

I smile.

yeah, the zip code of my life — i'm working!!

Her text smiles back.

deep thoughts . . . work shmurk. more kissing!

I miss her.

Around one, my stomach starts rumbling and I make a sandwich. Ham, slices of cheddar cheese, white bread. It's like the food Will bought last year when we rented an RV and went camping at the beach. Come to think of it, Trick's whole world seems this way, like he's camping in his own life.

After I eat, I wander around the cottage, snooping. Trick takes minimalist to a new level, so the cottage itself is pretty empty — a couple of Warren Miller movies, a Burton sweatshirt draped over the dusty TV, and a VCR that looks like it might have voted for Bill Clinton. I find most of his things tucked onto shelving in the small closet by the front door. A down parka, two pairs of jeans, a pair of hiking boots, some long underwear, three fleece pullovers, four T-shirts, four rolls of ski socks, and, embarrassingly, five pairs of folded white underwear. Making a face, I start to close the closet door but catch a glimpse of pale yellow tucked beneath the short stack of fleece pullovers. A picture book.

Naked Mole Rat Gets Dressed

At the sight of it, tears sting my eyes. I pull it out, careful not to upset the stack of fleece, and read the inscription I'd written to him in blue ink on the title page.

Hi, Trick. I saw this and thought of our trip to the zoo! XO, Mara

Inside, he has also tucked two of my school pictures. My ten-year-old one with a big smile and some unfortunate bangs. And the one from freshman year of high school. Same smile. Slightly better bangs. Mom must have sent them. I quickly slip them back inside and return the book to its place on the shelf, my hands shaking.

In the bathroom, I find a couple of ancient-looking cleaners beneath the sink because, for some reason, I'd rather scrub the toilet than sit around wondering why he never wrote me back about the book.

•　　•　　•

That evening, Trick knocks on the door of my room even though it's only partially closed. "Come in."

His arms are full of ski gear. A helmet, some pants, boots, a jacket. "Um, I got you some stuff today. And I've set some skis aside for you at Neverland. They're used but in great shape." He comes in and dumps everything on the bed. One boot falls to the floor with a heavy thud. He grabs at it. "Or, you know, you can use this as a weapon." He mimes hurling it across the room.

I run my hand over the soft fabric of the gray jacket. "Wow, thanks."

He clears his throat and backs up a step toward the door. "It's better up there with your own gear. You'll see. Just let me know if anything doesn't fit. Matt helped me pick stuff out. Logan's older sister is about your size."

I hold up a pair of ski socks with flames running up and down their sides. There are visible chew marks on the label. "Um?"

He grins. "Oh, right. Piper chewed on those, but I checked. No holes in the socks. Matt said you could have them."

"Cool, nothing like slobber socks to get a girl going on the mountain." I start peeling off the gnarled label. "Are you sure you don't want to take me up?" But I don't know if he heard me because he's ducked from the room, and soon I hear him rustling with wood for the fire. I go to the bathroom mirror and try on the silvery helmet, smiling at how silly and round it looks on my head, the smile wobbling a bit when I realize it's the first real gift he's ever given me.

TEN

The next two mornings, I wake right at 8:05. #4 on the Now List has clearly become a regular thing. I can't believe how much sleep I'm getting in Tahoe. I'm like a bear. I hurry to catch Trick so he can drive me to the Village.

When we get there, he heads straight to Neverland, but I stop off at Elevation to buy Logan a bag of the cookies they sell by the register. "Which ones?" Natalie asks. When I tell her they're for Logan, she points out the kind with dark chocolate and coconut. "His favorite." She winks.

I hurry to explain. "He's helping me learn to ski — I just want to say thank you."

Five minutes later, the bell on the front door jingles as I walk into Neverland. Logan sits on the counter, wearing his Frost Boys sweatshirt and rifling through a stack of rental forms, but he looks up at the sound of the bell. "Hey," he says in that low, easy voice of his that makes you feel like a favorite friend. "Oh, Pipe, come here, girl, give her some breathing room," he calls to his golden retriever, who is showering me with love and fur.

Extracting myself from Piper's enthusiastic welcome, I hand Logan the cookies. "I got you these."

"Sweet, these are my favorite."

My limbs fill with warmth at his smile. "Thanks again for taking me skiing." As he unwinds the twist tie that holds the bag shut, I hurry to add, "I would have baked them myself, but Trick doesn't have baking stuff. Or an oven, for that matter." He has a frying pan, a soup pot, a can opener, and a hot plate. The next list I make him needs to be kitchen supplies:

> mixing bowl
> slotted spoon
> cheese grater
> frying pan that doesn't look like death
> (toaster) oven?

Logan pops an entire not-small cookie into his mouth. "Tasty, thanks," he mumbles through the crumbs, and holds the bag out to me. "Want one?"

"It's, like, eight-thirty in the morning."

"Power breakfast." His eyes slip to where Trick comes out through the shop door, followed by a taller, older man who wears a battered black Spyder soft-shell jacket and a pair of jeans with holes in both knees. Judging by his shock of silver-black hair, he's probably in his late fifties.

"Oh, hey, Oli." Logan nods at the man.

"Mara," Trick says, racking a pair of skis. "This is Oli. He's an old-time Tahoe boy. Been skiing Squaw since . . ." He squints at Oli. "How long now?"

"Since I could pee standing up." Oli's smile adds wrinkles to his face and animates his already bright cobalt eyes.

"Nice to meet you." I hold out my hand.

He flashes Trick a bemused look. "Good manners," he says to Trick, shaking my hand. To me, he says, "You can thank your mama for that, because I know you didn't get them from this guy." He hooks a thumb at Trick.

"Well, she withheld food if I didn't greet people properly," I deadpan.

Trick's mouth falls open. "Is that true?"

"Of course not!"

Trick laughs out loud, grabbing a pair of bindings someone has left on the counter. "Right, sorry — okay, so you said you want to keep learning to ski." He glances at Oli, adding, "All those years in San Diego, she never once skied." Under it, just a shadow, is an accusation. Then he adds, "So I thought it might be a good idea for you to spend some time on the mountain with Oli. You won't find a better teacher — no offense, Logan."

Logan waves him off, still working his way through the bag of cookies. "None taken."

I try to catch Trick's eye — I was hoping *he* would take me. But he doesn't glance up from the binding. "Logan has been teaching me," I explain to Oli.

Logan holds up the bag. "Will teach for cookies. Want one?"

Oli shakes his head but says, "Mara, let's go out tomorrow and take some runs. It's important to also learn some respect for the mountain."

"Thanks, Oli. Love you, too," Logan mumbles. His cookie bag depleted, he returns to sorting the pile of rental forms next to him.

Oli scratches at the gray stubble of beard on his chin. "No

offense. I was the same way at your age. Thought the only thing that mattered was speed." Oli leans down to collect a stray form that has fallen to the ground and hands it back to Logan.

I hurry to say, "Logan wasn't like that. He really made sure I felt comfortable on the greens." A hint of a smile plays at Logan's mouth, but he doesn't look up from his sorting. "Besides," I say, "it's just skiing."

Trick and Logan exchange sudden looks. "Uh-oh." Trick raises his eyebrows dramatically. "Now you've done it."

Oli stares at me intensely. "It is far more than *just* skiing."

"Watch it, Mara," says Logan, holding up his hands in mock alarm. "Next he's going to tell you the part about how the way you ski is the way you live."

Oli shoots him a sobering look. "Laugh if you must, Mr. Never, but I'm an old man and mostly an idiot about everything in the world there is to know."

Trick interjects. "You're fifty-eight — hardly *old*. Talk to me in twenty years."

Ignoring him, Oli presses on. "I may be mostly an idiot, but not about this. I know skiing. I know this mountain. And I know that how a person skis this mountain speaks volumes about how this person walks the good earth we live on."

Where did Trick find this guy? "Like if they go fast, they're a risk taker, you mean?" I ask.

Oli fixes those dark blue eyes on me. "Nah, that's just good fodder for ski documentaries. I'm not talking about black diamonds or out of bounds or any of the technical stuff. I'm talking about *listening* — about constant awareness and purpose and respect for the elements, for the shifting seasons and conditions, about knowing where you are in any given moment and the deep under-standing of what track you're meant to take. I'm talking about love."

"Love?" I glance at Trick to see if he's laughing, if this is a prank, but he's nodding as though listening to a familiar song.

"Aw, give it a rest, you old hippie." Logan grins, moving on from the rental forms to restock the lip balms and sunscreens in the spinning rack on the counter.

"It's a dance of love, skiing is," Oli says, affecting a Yoda voice. He moves a few steps toward me and I almost need to lean back. He's very tall, this snow oracle. "I'll take you out tomorrow, intro-duce you properly to the mountain."

I swallow. "Okay."

He nods at Trick and heads for the exit. As the door swings shut, Logan catches my eye. "Congratulations — you've got your-self your own personal snow guru." He yoga-bows at the closed door. "*Namaste*, Mountain Master."

I move to the window of the shop, peering out after Oli, but he's disappeared into the sea of people moving by with their skis and boards, getting ready for another day on the mountain. "Um, how exactly will I find him? Will he just appear? Maybe send a droid with hologram directions?"

Trick grabs a pair of skis to take back to the shop. "Well, he'll be parked in our driveway for the next few weeks, so you won't be able to miss him. And I don't know about the droid, but I wouldn't put it past him."

• • •

After meeting Oli, I head to Elevation so I can get some work done. I feel behind and I need to study for a history quiz if I'm going to

89

take part of the day off tomorrow to ski. After a few hours, I look up from my laptop and see Isabel at the counter, grabbing a cup of hot water from Natalie. Unwrapping her own chamomile tea bag, she dunks it, then carries it carefully to my table.

"What's up, buttercup?" She peers at my laptop. "AP history. That looks familiar."

I roll my eyes. "Fun with DBQs."

"Ugh, I know." She plops into the seat next to me.

"What are you up to?" I ask, wondering vaguely when she has time to take an AP history course. It seems like she's always training.

"I'm going to hit the gym for an hour, then I have to study for a test tomorrow." She sits up a little. "Do you want to come?"

"To study for your test? No, thanks." I tap on my history book. "Plenty of that right here."

"No, silly. To the gym. My mom could take us." She picks up her tea and takes a small sip. "I could show you some ski-specific exercises since you're learning."

It's tempting. And a change of scenery would be nice. My phone buzzes, flashing CHEM! on my Google calendar. "I would, but . . . I probably shouldn't. I'm supposed to be starting chemistry now. And I'm taking part of tomorrow off for some ski lessons."

She shrugs. "Suit yourself."

"I'm going with a friend of Trick's, actually. Oli."

She perks up. "Oli's in town?"

I frown. "Is he *not* normally in town?"

Isabel winds the string of her tea bag around the bag itself, draining the liquid off, before she sets it on the table. "Oli lives in his Airstream. So he lives anywhere he feels like. Sometimes he's here and sometimes" — she pauses — "he's not."

"Oh." He lives in his Airstream? I don't even know what that means. I picture someone hunkered down in a wind tunnel.

Isabel must see the confusion on my face, because she laughs. "His *trailer*. You know, those silver ones you tow behind a truck."

"Right, okay." Not a wind tunnel. That's what Trick must have meant when he said he'd be parked in our driveway. "He lives in it year-round?"

"Yep." She waves at a boy who comes through the front door. I've seen him before with Logan. One of the Frost Boys. "Hey, Bodie. Do you know Mara?" Bodie. The arm of the accountability triangle with the dentist appointment.

He nods at me, his blue-tipped hair falling in a fence in front of his eyes. "My understudy! How's it going?" He leans on the back of an empty chair. "Iz, your mom's waiting."

Isabel stands. "Gotta scoot. Come hang out with us sometime."

"Thanks, I will." I watch them leave. They pass by the tall glass windows, laughing, Isabel giving Bodie a playful shove at something he says. I'm distinctly aware of how much Tahoe belongs to them, and also how much of this place I'm just borrowing while I sort myself out.

My phone buzzes again. "Okay!" I say to it, my face flushing as the guy at the next table raises his eyebrows at me over his coffee mug. I shrug sheepishly, hoping to convey *Come on, it's totally normal to yell at your phone, especially one as bossy as mine.*

•   •   •

Later, I lean on the counter, watching Natalie make coffees for a group of skiers who just came in off the mountain.

"What's up?" She adds a dollop of foam to each tiny cup.

"I left something in Trick's truck. Can I leave my stuff here and run out and get it?" I motion to my table over by the fire, knowing if I pack everything up, someone will steal it.

"I'll keep an eye on it." She puts the four coffees on a tray and waves me out the door.

I run to Trick's truck. He never locks it, so I grab my chem textbook and start heading back toward Elevation, when I hear two people arguing in the next row of cars.

"This is ridiculous, Beck. You're going, end of discussion. Your mother doesn't get to make plans on my weekend." A man stands near the open door of a shiny black Range Rover, frowning at the boy in front of him.

Beck, his back to me, has his hands shoved in the pockets of his parka. "Since when do you care what I do on the weekend?"

The man folds his large arms across his chest. He has Beck's thick head of hair, but perfectly cut. "You will show up at that dinner and you'll leave that crap attitude at home. That's not a request." He's not exactly shouting, but he might as well be. His voice echoes through the parking lot.

"Sir, yes, sir," Beck mumbles.

The man's hand flashes out and grabs Beck's shoulder. "I'm not kidding, Beck. Lose the attitude." He gives him a shake, a pretty hard one, then gets in the Range Rover. Beck practically has to jump out of the way to avoid getting run over.

I hurry back to Elevation, hoping neither one of them sees me.

ELEVEN

Dressed in my new ski gear the next morning, I knock on the door of Oli's Airstream trailer, which Trick told me is named Powder. Oli must have rolled into our driveway late last night at some point, but I didn't hear him.

He appears in the doorway, dressed in a pair of ski pants and a flannel shirt. I have no idea what color his baseball hat used to be. I can just make out its barely readable JACKSON HOLE logo. "Hiya there," he says, slurping a cup of coffee.

"Can I see Powder?"

I follow him inside the coffee-scented space of the Airstream. Trick told me over breakfast that Oli has lived in Powder for as long as Trick could remember. He travels the country in it, crashing at campgrounds and RV parks and with friends. "How does he afford to do that?" I asked through a mouthful of cereal.

Trick's brow creased. "He lives simply. Takes on the occasional seasonal job. I guess he figures it out," he said, shrugging. After a moment, he added, "He's a master carpenter, so I suppose he makes some money that way. You should see the inside of Powder. She's a beauty, so much detail and so many salvaged things. It's a work of art, really."

Now, standing inside Powder, I can see what Trick meant. "Wow," I breathe, taking in the Airstream's cozy interior. It holds a

93

bed covered in a faded quilt, a compact wooden table with padded bench seats, a narrow kitchen counter with cabinets, and a stall for a bathroom, all rich cherry wood, meticulously crafted. Hard to imagine fitting a whole life inside this small space, but he's done it. Photos dot the walls and he seems to have a soft spot for vintage postcards from ski resorts. Or maybe they weren't vintage when he first got them. "This is really cool." My eyes rest on the row of paperbacks wedged into a built-in wood bookcase above one of the bench seats. None of the books from Ranfield's reading list.

"It's home," Oli says casually, but he looks pleased, like I'd complimented a favorite pet. "You all set to get on the mountain?"

•   •   •

A half hour later, we're riding up the funi, our skis tucked neatly next to us. It's cold today, but bright, and I'm grateful for the smoky lens of my goggles as the funi lifts us up the mountain. As we climb, Oli asks me questions about what I've skied so far, and I fill him in on the Big Blue runs I did with Logan.

"What have you noticed so far about yourself as a skier?"

"What do you mean?"

He sprawls his legs out in front of him. "What's your sweet spot? Some people like to go fast. Others like technical terrain. Some people want to feel the mountain beneath them, enjoy the ride up the lift."

"I just want to keep getting better," I say.

He studies me through his own smoky lens for a moment, then turns and points to a woman skiing swiftly down the mountain below us. "See her?"

I follow the shot of her body before she disappears around a curve. "Yes."

"Did you see how clenched up on her poles she was, how her whole body was bent and rigid?" He points out a man this time, with similar form. "See that tension?"

I don't really see any tension; they just seem fast. "Yeah, I guess," I lie.

"See how they ski — quick, aggressive? It's like a migraine on skis. Now see her?" He points out a woman in a sleek silver parka and teal ski pants, her jet-black ponytail flying behind her. She's fast, but moves with a relaxed waterlike grace. "She's not in a fight with the mountain. Look at that awareness."

I'm not sure I'm *seeing* any awareness. I study the skiers moving below us, all so different. Some zipping past, some falling, some making wide smiles in the snow. "And that's better?"

The funi bumps into the Gold Coast building, and Oli gathers his gear. "Not better. Just different. Who do you want to be on the mountain?"

"I would like to not fall on my butt every five minutes," I say, collecting my skis and poles and following Oli's warm laugh off the funi.

We ski Big Blue two times, and I'm surprised at the muscle memory from my day with Logan. I figured I'd be starting from scratch, but my body sinks into the glide over the snow; it remembers. At the bottom of Big Blue, after the second run, Oli stops me. "Remember, Mara, skiing is a dance between you and this mountain. And it's about listening. This time, as you ski down, really listen."

"To what?"

"To everything." As he skis into the lift line, I let a giggle escape. Is this guy serious? I think of Logan bowing to him as he left the store yesterday, and stop myself from calling out to him, *Yes, Mountain Master, listen Mara will.* But I follow him because, hokey or not, I feel completely at ease right now.

In fact, this whole time with Oli, I haven't made a single list in my head and I haven't once felt that jittery, tense feeling I get, knowing I have homework waiting for me on the laptop.

It's a feeling I could get used to.

.   .   .

"Skiing?" Josie frowns at me through the screen. "Sounds horrifying."

"You'd be amazed, Jo — it's really fun." I sit on my bed, my knees tucked under me, the night outside purple through the window. "Like flying."

"Flying's for birds. Are you a bird?" I stick out my tongue at her and she giggles. "Well, don't get hurt. I need my doubles partner back."

"Josie?" I hesitate, inspecting my nails. "Did you ever, you know, figure out who posted that video of me?" Before I left, sitting on my bed back home, watching me pack, Josie had said, her voice fierce and protective, *I will find out who did it, I swear.* I know people say things like that and most of the time they're just words to make you feel better at the time. But, with Josie, they might actually be true. The intensity in her eyes had even scared me a little. Like maybe she might find out and then dispose of the body.

Now she drops her gaze, revealing eyelids glazed in glittery silver eye shadow. "I haven't yet."

I hurry to say, "It's okay. I didn't expect you to. Besides, I'm not sure I even want to know." In bed at night, listening to the pop and crackle of the fire, I often wonder if it would be better to know or if it's better this way. I'm far away in the mountains where I can't see any of them anyway. But then I keep wondering, wondering, wondering. I can't seem to let it go, shake it off, not worry about it.

"Mara?" Josie peers into the camera. "It would be fine to come back. No one's even talking about it anymore. You know people around here have the attention span of a fruit fly. Besides, last week, Jaelynn Chambers cut off all her hair, dyed it magenta, and got an eyebrow ring. A hoop. Believe me, no one's talking about you anymore."

"Are you serious?" Jaelynn Chambers is student body president. Her dad is an important conservative congressman. He must be freaking out. Which, I'm sure, is the whole point.

"I think she looks great, but yesterday her *mom* picked her up." Jaelynn's mom never comes to school unless it's for a photo opportunity.

My phone buzzes next to me on the bed. A text from Logan:

heard you rocked it up there today. want to go up tomorrow? i'm no mountain master but i buy hot chocolate — thx again for the cookies.

He's attached a photo of the empty cookie bag superimposed on a picture of Cookie Monster.

Josie looks annoyed. "Um, hello?!"

"Sorry," I say sheepishly, pushing the phone away. "I should go and call Mom. You know how she gets."

"I do — talk soon." She signs off.

I stare at the blank screen, feeling like a lying jerk. I didn't say, *That was Mom on the phone, so now I have to get going.* But I implied it. Still, that's not why I feel guilty. It's that the whole time I was talking with her, I kept thinking about how I don't miss Ranfield at all. I miss Josie, but that's it. It's Tahoe. There's something about this place — the snow, the mountains, the dark green of the trees, even the cold bite of the air — that's acting as a kind of memory eraser. I felt it on the mountain today, like I'm being recalibrated by the uncomplicated pace here. By its simplicity.

And I like it.

Picking up my phone, I stare at the message from Logan. I text back:

time? place? I'll bring cookies.

A minute passes. Then,

funi. 10. nom nom nom.

I lie down on my pillows, my muscles already itching to be back on the mountain. Something else feels itchy, too, as if I'm forgetting something, but I can't place it. Should I have told Josie about Logan? Not that there's anything to tell. He has a girlfriend. Was I supposed to check in with Mom? I rack my brain. What else? I scan my phone, check my binders and lists.

Nope, nothing due today.

Whatever it is, it can't be that big a deal if I can't remember, right? I'm not going to let it ruin the melty weight of my tired muscles, and before I can even brush my teeth or change into my pajamas, I'm falling into the heavy sleep a day on the mountain gives you.

TWELVE

I get up early Friday morning to submit an assignment for AP chem. I probably should be working on my English homework today since I haven't even starting reading *The Great Gatsby* yet and the essay is due Monday, but I really want to go skiing with Logan. The book sits there on the coffee table, staring at me. "I need PE credits, too!" I say to its blue cover, its judgmental eyes following me out the door.

Outside, my breath makes patches of fog in the morning air. Trick sits in his truck, letting it idle. I move past Oli's quiet trailer and notice his truck's missing. On the way down the hill, Trick glances sideways at me and clears his throat. "So I got a call from that therapist guy, Dr. Elliot, yesterday afternoon — sorry, forgot to mention it last night before you turned in. Totally spaced it."

My stomach drops out. *My appointment.* That nagging itchy feeling that I was forgetting something last night. I missed my therapy appointment. "Oh, no," I breathe, my heart skipping.

"Yeah, he said you could reschedule or just come in next week. Whatever works. Maybe give him a call later?" Trick takes a right onto Squaw Valley Road, winding toward the Village.

Despite the cold, my hands begin to sweat. "I can't believe I did that. I went skiing. I completely forgot." My voice wavers in the cold air of the car.

Trick's eyebrows lift at the sound of it. "No harm, no foul. He's not even going to charge your mom for the session, which was cool of him." He pulls the truck into a parking spot.

What's the chance Mom doesn't know about it?

My chest tightens. "But is he going to *tell* Mom?" I fiddle with the latch of my seat belt. "Because that was part of the deal for me being here. That I see him. I can't believe I did that. I've never missed any appointment before."

He slides the keys from the ignition. "You've *never* missed any appointment before?"

"Not without calling first, without rescheduling." I tug more at the seat belt. *Why won't it unlatch?*

Trick leans over and unclicks me. "Wow, Mara versus the seat belt. Seat belt takes the first round," he teases.

I'm not in the mood. "Mom's going to kill me."

He gathers up his jacket and wallet. "I doubt that."

My phone rings. Glancing at it, my heart picks up pace. We both stare at the incoming name on the screen. "It was nice knowing you," I tell him. With a low chuckle, he pushes open the driver's-side door and leaves me in the truck to face the Wrath of Mom.

I answer the phone.

"You completely skipped an appointment," she states, her voice echoing in a way that tells me she's driving.

"I know, I'm sorry."

"You can't stay up there if you can't stick to your commitments. That was part of the agreement. It was in your calendar."

Wait. I had checked my phone and hadn't seen it there. My body floods with hope. Could I possibly get off on a technicality? "Mom,

I checked my phone. It wasn't there." I don't mention that I checked my phone about four hours after I should have already been at the appointment. That doesn't seem relevant now, right?

She turns her phone into a wind tunnel with her sigh. "Your brothers had the same thing yesterday. Their schedules were totally blank. I'm not sure what happened."

I love technology. "I'm sorry I didn't remember, Mom. But it wasn't there."

"You need to call Dr. Elliot. Today. Reschedule, okay?"

"I will." Guilt needles me.

But before I can confess, she says, "I have to run, Mara — I'm late," and then she's gone.

·   ·   ·

Logan is waiting for me outside the funi building, checking his phone. I hurry to meet him, or whatever hurrying looks like in ski boots, like a drunken robot, probably. "Sorry I'm late. Mom drama."

He zips his phone into his jacket and smiles at me. "No problem. I don't practice today until two and I already did my gym reps." He takes a closer look at me, his smile fading. "You okay?"

I try to look relaxed. "Oh, sure. Let's get up there!" We scramble through the gates and onto the funi. Logan leans our skis in the corner and stretches out on the bench perpendicular to mine. I try not to glance out the window as the funi lifts us out and up, my stomach clenching with that first swing out of the dock. I thought it would get easier each time, but it doesn't. Staring at my snow-caked boots, I try to shake off the list of our progress up the mountain that peppers my brain:

Now we're as high as a tree

Now we're as high as a three-story building

"What'd your mom want?" Logan tries again.

"I just missed an appointment yesterday and she was checking on why."

"Was it important?" He looks genuinely concerned.

"Not really." Logan Never does not need to know I'm seeing a therapist.

He watches me for a minute, waiting for me to elaborate. When I don't, he simply says, "Okay," and rests his arm along the back of the bench. We stare out at the white world below us. "But you can talk about it if you want," he adds.

"Thanks. It's really nothing." We're quiet, listening to the creak and shift of the funi. He's nice to even ask and my stomach gets swirly and strange watching him sit there, his long legs out in front of him. I clear my throat, trying not to think about how much I might like this boy. Because I definitely don't need to add *that* to the messy list of my life right now. A boy. A boy with a girlfriend. I try to focus on remembering some of the vocab for my French quiz on Monday.

How do you say *Pull it together* in French?

•   •   •

Even if I don't fall as much as the first day I skied with Logan, I start off sluggish. After a couple of runs, though, I feel my body loosen and I start to trust the feel of the skis beneath me. Of course, as soon as I start to feel a sense of ease, just as I begin to move faster down the mountain, I catch an edge of my ski and end up on my butt.

Logan skis over and offers his pole, but I don't reach to take it. "Turns out, I suck at this whole skiing thing. So much for genetics," I say, staring up at him. "Surprise!"

"Are you kidding? You don't learn to ski overnight. It takes years. You're picking it up fast." He offers his gloved hand, and this time I grab it. As he hauls me up, my skis slip out from under me and I fall into his chest. "Whoa, got ya." He steadies me, dropping his poles to put both hands on my shoulders. His closeness sends that unfamiliar shiver through me again, and I scramble to push away from him, launching myself backward. "Careful!" He tries to make a grab for me, but I end up on the ground again. He looks confused, but also like he's trying not to laugh at me. "Okay, not sure what just happened there."

"Lost my balance." *Because you're too cute and need to stop touching me*, I keep myself from adding. I take a deep breath, thinking about that confident line I'd drawn through "green runs" on my Now List a couple of days ago. Not sure I've earned it.

I follow him back to the Big Blue lift, wishing I could shed the feelings of frustration with each sift of snow that falls from my dangling skis. I'm not sure what's making me more frustrated, the skiing — or the way I can't stop thinking about how nice it had been to fall into Logan, to have his hands on my shoulders.

"Where's Isabel today?" I ask brightly.

He shrugs. "Not sure."

Maybe I should add *negligent boyfriend* to the list.

Which is when it dawns on me.

I'm still making a Logan Never List in my head. And it keeps getting longer.

The way he smiles with the corners of his mouth
How patient he is while he's teaching me to ski
How sweet he is with his dog
How hard he works at Neverland
How he never complains or seems stressed out
His face, in general — he just has a really nice face
And body

Stop it. I don't have time for Logan lists.

Or maybe I do.

Because it doesn't really count, right? I'm not breaking any rules. I'm not here very long and he's not available anyway. What was that thing Trick said this morning? *No harm, no foul?* I'm Tahoe Mara now. Be brave! (#9) I've never had time for a crush before. *Crush,* what a stupid word. What does it even mean? So what if I think he's adorable and sweet and looks really good in ski pants. I mean, who looks that good in ski pants? I'm allowed to *look.*

As he lifts the bar to get ready for another run, he says, "Seriously, Mara — you're doing great out there. Trust me, it just takes time."

It just takes time. Good thing I happen to have a little more of that these days.

• • •

Back at the top of the Big Blue, Logan and I are about to head down the mountain for a final run when someone calls out behind us. Beck slides up on skis. "Hey, bunny hill," he says to me, his voice carrying a dark voltage just under the surface. "You two want to hit Shirley with me?"

Logan kicks some snow from his skis. "I haven't even done Gold

Coast with her yet. I'm not taking her on Shirley Lake." He avoids looking at Beck, instead watching the light shift across the patch of distant lake. "And I have practice in a half hour."

Beck fiddles with his sunglasses. "Shirley's for toddlers. She'll be fine."

"Do you think I can ski Shirley?" I ask Logan, my heart quickening. "Is it a green run?"

"It's a blue, but you could handle Shirley." Logan bends down to adjust something with his bindings. When he stands, he says, "Most parts of it at least. I have to get to practice, but don't let me stop you."

Am I imagining annoyance in his voice?

The thought of skiing a more difficult blue terrifies me, but I don't want Logan to know that. "Okay, yeah — I'll try Shirley."

Logan's lips pinch together in a thin line before he exhales. "Just remember your snowplow and try not to get going too fast, and —"

Beck interrupts. "Pizza slice, French fries, pizza slice — she's got this." He tugs on my jacket. "Come on. Let's show you some real mountain."

"Later." Logan skis away, the familiar flash of his green jacket disappearing down the mountain. Wow, he's fast when he's not waiting for me.

I follow Beck down the catwalk, my stomach dropping out as we come to the brim of a run. Shirley Lake looks hard and half of it is in shadow. I'm sure it's nothing to Beck, but I might as well be jumping off a building. "Oh, wait," I say. "Let me get your cell number in case we get separated." That's what Logan had done with me. Beck pulls out his phone, and I send him a quick text so he has my number. Tucking my phone back in my pocket, I take a deep breath. "Okay, ready."

"This is an easy shoot," Beck assures me. "And it's actually better if you go faster. Just follow me, okay?" Before I can answer, he takes off down the mountain and doesn't seem to be stopping and waiting the way Logan always does. My body floods with a tingling blend of excitement and fear. *Pizza slice. French fries. Pizza slice.*

Chewing my lip, I push forward, my skis tilted inward. At first, I handle it, cutting across the mountain the way Logan showed me, carving a smile into the snow. Then I pick up pace, and suddenly it's too fast, too slippery. Halfway down, I turn too sharply, trees suddenly appearing ahead of me, a thicket of green in the blur of my vision. Too close. I can't stop, can't get my skis into a pizza slice in time, and end up yanking my body uphill to the right, the side of my helmet hitting the snow.

Ouch.

People speed by me, hazy impressionistic shapes.

"Awesome!" Beck materializes above me, blocking out the sky. "That," he says, grinning, "is what we call a yard sale!"

"A what?" I murmur, trying to sit up. I find snow everywhere. In my mouth, in my ear. Both of my skis have popped off. One is nearby, but I can't see the other one. Both of my poles stick out of the snow several feet away, and somehow I've managed to lose a glove.

Beck hands me my other ski. "A yard sale. Your stuff went flying — that was sick!"

"I think I broke my face."

Beck hoists me up, our faces so close our helmets almost touch. "Looks pretty great from here." There's that magazine smile again.

I hurry to reassemble my gear and put on my skis, and ski slowly to the bottom and over to the Shirley Lake lift, nestled in the deep bowl of the mountain. This is definitely a more challenging part of the mountain than what I've been skiing so far. Huge peaks rise around us, and the lifts carry skiers high up into them.

"Want to try again?" Beck asks as we move into the lift line. He leans his shoulder into me playfully, flushing liquid nerves through my limbs.

"Better not. I think something isn't totally right with my left knee," I hurry to explain. "Besides" — I wave at the mountains around me — "I've had enough trouble for one day."

"Aww, come on," he coaxes. "Take another run with me. If it doesn't look like trouble, it's not worth your time."

My stomach must house multiple flare guns. "Listen, peer pressure. I'm done for the day, okay?" But Josie's newest addition to the list is poking me as we inch ahead in line. I glance sideways at Beck, at his mirrored glasses and auburn hair that curls from under his ski helmet, wondering if *he's* the kind of trouble she had in mind.

"Do you snowboard?" I ask as we move into place to catch the lift.

"Sometimes. Why? You want to learn?"

"Just wondering." The Shirley lift chugs into view behind us, lifting us up, up, up and out of the snowy Shirley bowl to the place where I can head back down the front section of the mountain. I settle into the shiver of the lift, the cold wind on my tender cheek, watching as, up ahead, skiers and boarders cut down the steep first Shirley shoot, snow rooster-tailing behind them, like surfers against a blank white ocean. Beck leans into me, pointing out other parts of the mountain, and the strange prickly awareness at the nearness of him feels like the start of trouble to me.

THIRTEEN

Later Friday afternoon, nestled on the couch at Trick's with a bag of ice on my knee, I pull my binder onto my lap and read the essay prompt: "How does Nick's role as an outsider impact his exploration of Tom, Daisy, and Gatsby's world?" His role as an outsider. I should be able to answer that. If I'd actually read the book. Feeling the familiar creep of overwhelm, I toss the binder back onto the table and glance at my phone.

Four messages. All from Mom.

I click the fourth message and Mom's voice spills out, edged and frustrated. "Mara, I've been trying to get ahold of you all afternoon."

It doesn't even ring when I call her back. "Mara?"

"Hi, Mom."

"Where have you been?"

"I, well, I went skiing."

"You went *skiing*?" *Skiing* comes out as if I'd said *smoking*.

"I started learning a few days ago. Logan Never took me. I was on Shirley —"

"What were you doing on Shirley Lake already?! That's too hard for a beginner."

"Practicing my pizza slice, French fries," I try to joke, but she doesn't laugh. Remembering her dark look at Beck's exit that first day in Neverland, I decide not to mention him at all. I then spend no less than five minutes proving to her that I haven't turned into a ski-bum derelict.

When she seems more convinced, she asks, "Did you reschedule your appointment with Dr. Elliot?"

Oops. "I will."

"Do that right when you get off with me, okay? I'm not sure how much longer his office will be open today. And you have a *Gatsby* essay due Monday."

"This live Google reminder brought to you by Lauren James."

"Mara."

"Mom, it's due *Monday*. I have the whole weekend. I've always gotten my work done on time before. You don't need to remind me." But as I say it, I know that even with the whole weekend, I'll be pushing it. I adjust the ice on my knee.

"Have you at least read the book?" she presses.

"Yes," I lie. "Rich people behaving badly. Otherwise known as the view out any window in Squaw Valley."

"Okay." I hear the smile in her voice. "I'm just checking. You seem . . . different."

"I do?" She doesn't mean it this way, but she has no idea how good it is to hear that.

Maybe Tahoe is working.

•　　•　　•

Someone knocks at the front door of Trick's cottage later that evening. Oli pokes his head in, carrying a white sack of something that smells savory and delicious. My stomach rumbles on impact. "Is there a hungry skier in here who needs some lasagna?"

"Me!" I set the bag of ice I've been using for my knee on the floor and toss *Gatsby* onto the coffee table.

Oli moves around the kitchen, opening and shutting drawers and the fridge, and then, miraculously, I have a plate of lasagna and salad on my lap. He sits on the coffee table next to me. "That's April's lasagna — Isabel's mom. It's the best in the world." He motions for me to try it.

I take a bite. Wow. "Mmmmmm."

"Right?"

"This is incredible." I try not to eat like a wild animal who's been starved for days, but I can't really help it. What is it about skiing that makes me want to eat a house each time I'm done?

"I ran into Logan at Neverland." Oli folds his long legs gracefully between the table and the sofa like someone used to maneuvering his body into small places. "Heard you tackled Shirley today."

I wipe my face with a napkin before answering. "I'm pretty sure it was the other way around. And I might have done something weird to my knee."

He runs his hands through his hair, his blue eyes sympathetic. "Anyone can fall anytime. None of us is a stranger to icing a knee." Oli picks up the sloppy bag of ice and moves to put it in the sink. "But you were liking it up there?"

"I was." Saying it, I realize this is more than just a little true. Skiing terrifies me, but in a delicious, roller-coaster way. "I know I'm no good at all, but there's just something about being up there — the air is different, the sky. It's . . ." I search for the right word. "Magnetic."

Oli grins. "Yep, you've got it."

"What?"

"The ski bug." He pats my arm. "The mountain got under your skin."

And like that, I realize he's right, it has. And not just the mountain. Something else. Its *newness* appeals to me, too. And the fact that no one is grading me. I mean, there's no chance I'm going to the Olympics. Ever. I'll never even race competitively, so I can just fall into it on my own terms without some larger system clutching its clipboard and telling me *Yes, that's good* or *No, be better.* I can't remember the last time I put time toward something just to do it and not because it might look good on a college application.

Oli fills a glass with water and brings it back to me. I don't know what it is that makes him unusually easy to talk to. Unlike most adults. "Maybe you could take me up again? Teach me how to better handle the blues. I'm not sure Beck's the best teacher."

I don't miss his frown as he moves back into the kitchen, opens the fridge, and helps himself to one of Trick's beers. I hear the pop of it, then the clatter of the bottle cap in the sink. He holds it up to my water glass. "To getting back on the mountain."

I clink it against his bottle. "Cheers."

•   •   •

The next day, before he leaves for the shop, Trick makes me toast and hands me a mug of coffee with extra milk, his eyes drifting over my bruised cheek. I woke up this morning to a bluish-purple welt the size of a small peach. Trick zips up his jacket and pulls on his beanie, but hesitates, his hand on the door. "That fire should hold up fine." He frowns at my laptop. "You shouldn't be working on a Saturday."

"*You're* working on a Saturday," I point out.

"Fair enough."

"I have to get this essay done." Small bubbles of panic started erupting in my belly early this morning. Gone was the feeling of extra time, replaced with feeling madly behind in my schoolwork.

"Who am I to mess with a good system?" Trick nods good-bye and disappears outside, letting in the smell of fresh snow.

I sip some coffee and take a few bites of toast before pulling my computer onto my lap. I'd finished *Gatsby* in the small hours of morning, surprised to find myself sucked into the story, feeling a tie to Nick I hadn't expected — the outsider drawn suddenly into all the glamour and secrets of Gatsby's world. I'd jotted some notes for my essay as I read, so now I just had to write it. Except the page in front of me remains infuriatingly blank.

I study the quote from the first page of the novel. I scribbled it down yesterday, the advice Nick's father had given him: *"Whenever you feel like criticizing any one,"* he told me, *"just remember that all the people in this world haven't had the advantages you've had."* At first, I thought he meant money and privilege, but the more I page back through the book, the more I think Nick's advantage is his ability to really see people. Maybe an outsider has this advantage?

Maybe because he knows he'll be leaving soon.

My phone bleeps with a picture text from Will. His weekly Shells of Wisdom. The sight of them there, carefully arranged, floods me with homesickness. This time they spell out one of Will's favorite expressions, something he says to us to keep us going when we're on hikes or to remind us that the hard work will be worth it later on: DIG IN.

I mean to dig in, I plan on digging in, but I don't. I pop one of

Trick's Warren Miller movies into the VCR and watch skiers and snowboarders do crazy things on mountains around the world.

I can write the essay tomorrow.

• • •

Late Sunday afternoon, I give up and submit my not-very-good *Gatsby* essay. I feel a little sick that it's not better, but I'm tired of working on it. I stomp around the cottage, trying to wake up both feet, which have fallen asleep from my sitting so long on the couch. The cottage hums with emptiness. Trick is out somewhere with a friend. He never seems to bring his friends here, usually meets them in the Village.

Maybe he's avoiding me.

I can't believe it, but I actually miss my little brothers and their LEGO mine field in the hallway. And Mom yelling up the stairs for me to fold my laundry. And the smell of dinner floating through the house. My stomach rumbles at the thought, and I make some soup for dinner, crumbling Ritz crackers into it.

After doing the dishes, I Skype with Josie. "Your face belongs in a bad action movie," she tells me, which is Josie-speak for worried. "What did you do?" When she finds out I fell skiing, she says, "There better be a cute snowboarder involved."

"Skier."

Now she's interested. "Oh, *really*?"

Maybe she can't see my blush through the bruising. "It's nothing. He knows Trick."

"I want daily updates."

"There will be nothing to update you on, I promise."

"Don't make that promise." She sighs. "I hate to do this to you, but I have to go. I have sooooo much chem homework."

"Me too. Talk soon." Only I don't really feel like tackling my chemistry right now. Instead, I play some music on my laptop and re-sort both of the kitchen cabinets, moving all the boxed foods into one and all the canned foods into another. I alphabetize the cans: beans, corn, olives, tomatoes. Wait, should diced tomatoes go after corn? I set both cans on the shelf and back away from the alphabetizing. I'm starting to care a little too much about diced-tomato can placement. Wandering into the bedroom, I refold all my clothes onto their small shelf, organize my toiletries along the back of the bathroom sink, dab some of my relaxing lavender oil behind my ears (#5!), and poke needlessly at the fire.

I miss Josie. We used to study for chem together.

In my head, I make a list of synonyms for *alone*:

    deserted
    isolated
    abandoned
    solitary

They all seem sad and negative, and I wonder why I can't think of any positive words for *alone*.

Still no sign of Trick, I brush my teeth and crawl into bed. Falling asleep, I imagine I can hear a storm coming in, the wind stepping up a notch, bringing snow and dark purple air.

•   •   •

Turns out, I wasn't imagining the storm.

I wake in the dawn of Monday to Trick knocking about outside in the woodbin. Curled in my blankets, I scoot to the window and pull aside the shade. I'm met with a wall of snow halfway up the window and more still falling.

Congratulations, Mara. You now live in a snow globe.

After an hour of helping Trick dig out (Will had no idea how literal his shells would end up being), we head to the Village and I find a table at Elevation. It feels good to escape my solitude and settle into the sounds of other people working around me, but outside, the snow picks up, chasing most of us home by midafternoon. Trick pokes his head through the café doors at two and motions for me to follow him. We have to redig the path to the cottage we had made only hours ago.

People spend a lot of time in Tahoe just trying to get in and out of their houses.

·   ·   ·

Proving my point, Dr. Elliot calls Tuesday to tell me we'll have to reschedule our appointment because he actually hasn't been able to dig out of his house. Half-proud/half-sick, I let him know about the B+ I received on my *Gatsby* essay, without sharing the note at the end from my English teacher that my eyes immediately snagged on: *Not as fully developed as some of your other work.*

My first B of any kind on an English paper in high school.

"How'd that feel?" Dr. Elliot asks into the phone, and I imagine him sitting in his green wool vest by a fire somewhere.

I try to joke. "Well, I didn't spontaneously combust!" Afterward,

I realize that combustion isn't what worries me. I could have made that essay better, but I chose to watch ski movies and sort the cottage and stare out at the snow instead of making it better. I didn't put in the necessary time. Only that's not really what bothers me. What bothers me is that it actually doesn't feel as bad as I thought it would.

Spontaneous combustion would be easier because it would let me know I blew it. Bam! Disintegration for not trying your hardest.

This feels more dangerous, like erosion. And you don't really notice erosion until it's wiped out an embankment or something. And then it's too late.

·   ·   ·

On Thursday evening the skies finally clear. A pot of soup bubbling on the hot plate, I'm settling into the couch with my math homework when Beck texts. Attached is a picture of the gray-white haze of an incoming storm. It looks like it was taken at the top of Big Blue. Tahoe shines like a slice of nickel beneath its sleeping mountains. A scrawling script over the photo reads:

Most people are on the world, not in it. —— John Muir

I try to ignore my sudden sensation of falling as I text back:

wow, deep. you should post that on tumblr next to a photo of kittens wearing pajamas.

He texts back immediately:

brat.

Then sends:

just out of curiosity, is there a mr. mara in san diego?

My chest tightens.

i don't have time for boys.

Instantly:

is that a double-dog dare?

Nerves buzzing, I type but don't send:

i'm allergic to dogs.

My sweaty fingers leave damp prints on the phone. I've opened a door with Beck wider than I should have. Taking a breath, I remind myself, *Get in a little trouble*, and add a googly-eyed smiling puppy face to my unsent text, one that has little hearts for eyes, and hit SEND.

FOURTEEN

Saturday morning, I push through the doors of Elevation, inhaling the warm café air, the mocha-cinnamon smell of the place. I gaze around the packed room buzzing with people enjoying their late-morning coffees. With all the snow this week, the resort is crazy busy today.

Natalie sees me and gives me the kind of wave she reserves for locals. Leaning across the glass case that holds the pastries, she says conspiratorially, "You want a free latte? I made it with whole milk instead of nonfat. You'd think from the woman's reaction, I'd laced it with toilet bowl cleaner." Finn snort-laughs from behind the espresso machine.

I grin. "I'll take it, thanks." She hands it over.

Miraculously, I find an empty table near the bathroom and slide into a chair. I have a disturbing amount of calculus homework to get through this weekend and want to make sure I get some time to ski. Within minutes, Natalie appears at my side, looking almost apologetic. She holds a fruity-looking scone on a plate. "From him." She sets the plate down, rolling her eyes at someone over my shoulder.

Beck materializes, carrying his own chair. "Hey, Mara-velous."

"Clever." I start up my laptop, actively avoiding eye contact with him. I spent the last two days regretting the silly puppy face I'd sent him, which he'd never responded to, and secretly hoping it had been lost in some kind of emoticon, cyber-pet graveyard somewhere. I should never have texted him back. I blame Josie and her Get in a little trouble #12. "Not hungry," I tell him, pushing the scone away.

"Hey, it's the second-best thing for a" — he glances at my book — "calculus study session."

"What's the first?"

"Me."

Trying to ignore the buzz in my belly, I take this opportunity to look him straight in the eyes. His gorgeous hazel eyes. I take a breath to steady my nerves. "Just out of curiosity, do girls ever actually vomit when you say stuff like that? I have a really strong stomach, but, you know, some people are a little more squeamish."

He tips his head back and laughs. "Wow, you sure make a guy work for it."

Despite my assertion, I don't have a strong stomach at all. Quite the opposite. And I'm not a girl who makes guys do much of anything, except maybe move out of the way if they're standing in front of my locker. But he doesn't know any of this and my competitive side takes over. I shrug. "I'm an overachiever."

"So I've heard." Leaning forward in his chair, he tilts his head to the side, his eyes intense yet somehow still smiling. "Miss Perfects don't come along every day. Especially ones who can shred."

My body turns to liquid. He's seen the YouTube. My head swimming, I tell him, "I actually have some work I need to do." Game over.

He notices, and softening his voice, he says, "Listen, I think what you did was amazing."

"Right, sure you do." I shake my head, eyes on my screen, even though I'm not seeing anything there.

He leans on the table. "Seriously. And brave."

He's really laying it on thick now. "Don't you have somewhere else to be right now? Aren't you actually supposed to be *independently studying* something?"

"On a Saturday?" Scooting his chair even closer, so our knees touch beneath the table, he says, "This isn't a line, I swear. I do think what you did was brave. That whole world you're in? I looked up your school's web page. It's insane. All that stress, all that pressure, all those other people telling you you're not good enough unless you compete for their praise all the time? It's a judgment factory. Personally, I don't subscribe to that whole ambition paradigm we get sold from the time we're in preschool. It's garbage. You are who you are and you know what you know and everything else is one big first-world power party. It makes me sick. So, yes, I think what you did was brave. Laugh if you want. Don't believe me, whatever. I just want to hang out with you." He sits back into his chair, folds his arms across his chest, and waits. Your move, Mara-velous.

I wrap my shaking hands around my latte. Even if what he's saying right now feels like the truest thing I've heard in a long time, I still don't want to get sucked in. "Is that why you stopped racing?" I ask, setting down my coffee and closing the lid of my laptop.

"It just stopped being my scene, all that competition." He says it the way someone would say *toxic waste*. "So I got into freeskiing instead. Racing was too much like school. Everything's about winning and rankings and being the best. I *hated* it. I don't exist so my dad can brag about my résumé to his friends."

Frowning, I think about the argument with his dad I'd seen accidentally in the parking lot. I'm no stranger to this type of boy at Ranfield, the *I have nothing to prove to daddy* boy. Most of them spend their time watching obscure independent films, quoting dead philosophers they haven't actually read, and have no guilt burning through said dad's bank account. "But what about your own goals? Wanting achievements for yourself, not just because of your dad?"

He shrugs. "I live for the basic stuff, like being on this beautiful mountain with friends, or" — he breaks off a piece of scone and pops it into his mouth — "this scone. You should try it; it's delicious. I just want to enjoy the things I already have and not worry about all the self-imposed *Oh please let me be impressive and important* stuff because it's not actually as important as we all try to make it out to be."

I'm about to call him on his pretention, about to tell him that wanting to be successful in school or having dreams bigger than eating a scone doesn't make me a slave to some corrupt ambition system out there, but then again — does it?

He might have a point.

I want to ask him more, but suddenly Isabel's banging on the window of the café, sleek in her racer uniform, cheeks flushed and hair braided into a red rope. It's Beck's turn to roll his eyes. "Oh, goody. The morality police." Our eyes track her as she makes her way around the café windows, pulls open the door, and comes inside.

Isabel arrives at our table, her eyes just a little too wide as she glances between us. "Hey, Mara. Beck."

"Aren't you racing?" I ask, my voice light, trying to push back against some of the intensity she brought into the café with her. Maybe she's pumped up on race endorphins or something?

"Trick's fixing my binding. Lucky we're racing at Squaw today. What are you two up to?" She shoots a dark look at Beck. "Signing her up for one of your slacker seminars?" She tries to play it off as funny, but she's too amped and it comes out sharp-edged.

He takes it in stride, breaking off another bite of the scone. "If I offered seminars, that would be highly hypocritical of me, wouldn't it?" He grins up at her. "How's my favorite praise junkie?"

She rolls her eyes. "Nice. Mara, you'll find that for our friend Beck here, anyone who might want to do something in life, who might actually want to *try*, is a praise junkie. Sorry, am I interrupting the part where you tell her that we should just live life for the moment, enjoy this beautiful mountain and nothing else?"

Beck gives me an amused look. "I might have mentioned it."

"Being predictable and being laid-back are not the same thing," she tells him.

As they continue to argue, I stop listening. This clearly isn't their first time having this particular fight, and besides, something outside distracts me.

Logan.

He and some of the other Frost Boys walk past in their racing suits, laughing as one of the boys, obviously telling a story, gesticulates wildly. Logan catches my eye and gives me that relaxed wave of his, before his gaze slips back to his friends. I force my attention to Isabel, her hands on her hips, still arguing with Beck, and I flush with irrational anger. Not all of us can have laid-back adorable ski racer boyfriends, so maybe she should mind her own business. It's not like I'm going to marry Beck. I'm not even here very long.

I stand, interrupting them. "So Beck and I were just about to head up to High Camp. Want to come?" I start collecting my things. Beck hops up next to me, taking my new announcement in stride.

Isabel frowns. "I'm still racing today."

"Oh, bummer." Beck blinks at her, a look of mock disappointment on his face.

As I start to move past her, she tugs my sleeve, pulling me aside. "Be careful, okay? Most girls end up needing an emotional hazmat suit with this one." She glares over my shoulder at Beck, who blows her a kiss.

"Thanks for the heads-up." My voice is colder than I mean it to be.

Stung, she takes a step back. "*Your* funeral."

Beck and I push through the door into the wet winter air, and I force myself not to look back at where Isabel still stands, watching us leave.

●   ●   ●

As we weave through a throng of skiers, I try to study Beck without his noticing. Which probably makes it look like I'm about to sneeze. His moss-colored down jacket is almost the same color as his eyes, which I'm sure he does on purpose. It's clear he knows how good-looking he is, but it also strikes me that he seems harmless. As far as bad boys go, he doesn't seem very, well — bad.

At least he's not your generic brand of bad influence. No motorcycle, no piercings, no drugs, no loud parties trashing his parents' beach house (at least, that I know of). He doesn't do his homework and rambles on (and on) about society's messed-up systems, but as slackers go, he never seems stoned or out of it. He broods, sure, and when he rants, he sounds a lot like the coffeehouse hipster crowd at Ranfield with their heavy-framed glasses and obscure music interests. But he's not like them, either. I don't know where he fits, and something in me, something I'm trying very hard not to listen to, wants to know what makes him come with Isabel's warning label.

"After you." He motions me into the wide elevator that takes us to the tram, but he's quiet as we transfer the few short yards across to the car itself, finding us two spots against the wall of windows since the benches on the narrow ends are already taken. The tram operator announces that we will now be lifting from 6,200 feet to 8,200 feet and it will take eight and half minutes to get to High Camp.

My stomach lurches as we lift up out of the valley, and I see Beck watching the ski race over by the Red Dog lift, the sponsor banners bright against the white hill, the packs of racers moving about in their sleek uniforms.

"Do you ever miss it?" I ask, following his gaze.

He looks guilty at being caught watching it. "What? No, not ever."

I wonder if that's true.

"It's weird," he says, turning and leaning against the glass wall. "I can actually pinpoint the day it changed for me. It wasn't anything gradual; at least I didn't think so at the time." The tram carries us up through the sky, the wide snowscape stretching all around and below us, the parking lot of the Village growing small in the distance.

My body feels shivery and strange, suspended in too much air, and I want him to keep talking to distract me from the thought of plummeting to my death.

> Now we're as high as a tree
> Now we're as high as a four-story building

"When was that?" I manage.

He slips his hands into his jacket pockets. "I was fourteen. We were racing at Sugar Bowl and I'd just finished a particularly grueling round of gates. It wasn't my best run, but it wasn't my worst. I'd placed maybe third. But when I got to the bottom, I pulled off my goggles and looked around at all the people cheering, at all the sponsor banners, at all the other racers, and there was my dad in the crowd, standing with his arms crossed. And he just looked so . . . disappointed. Right then, a switch flipped. I took off my skis and walked away. That was it for me."

A shadow ghost of something passes through me. "Because of too much pressure from your dad?"

He shakes his head. "Nah, it was all of it. Never being good enough for him, sure. But also the whole scene — the busy weekends, the constant worry about times, the workouts in the gym, the practices, the other skiers and their intense attitudes, everyone competing with each other, backstabbing each other even though we were supposed to be teammates. The *stress*. It made me question everything, how driven we all are by these arbitrary goals. I was so sick of it." He pulls out a pair of mirrored Maui Jim sunglasses and slips them on against the glare of the bright day. "What changed for you?" he asks. "What made you go all Captain Paper Shredder?"

I try to chuckle at his joke, but it catches in my throat. It still makes me sick to think about that terrible day and the YouTube video. I stare down into the sweeping valley, the rooftops, and the wide snowy yawn of Squaw Valley beyond. Since sixth grade, I've spent all my time building my life at Ranfield, a life that would turn into a golden key to an unknown future door. It's crazy how quickly it has evaporated like fog behind me, how far I feel now from everything that had seemed so important and crushing and desperate.

"It was a little like what happened with you," I say.

We watch the valley spool away beneath us, swaying into each other with the swing of the tram as it passes the tower. We stay like that, our sides pressed against each other, pretending to listen to the tram operator talk about how Walt Disney, who was acting as the grand marshal of the 1960 Winter Olympic Games, saw these rocks beneath us and got the idea for the Thunder Mountain ride. The operator goes on to tell us that at the highest point of this trip, we will be 550 feet up, high enough to fit the entire Washington Monument underneath us, but I register his crackly voice as backdrop, my whole body fixating on the heat of Beck next to me, on how nice it feels to just float up the mountain with this boy who thought it was brave of me to rip up those tests. I even forget to worry about the car snapping loose and dropping to the valley floor below. Well, at least I mostly forget.

Finally, the car docks, the sliding door opening so we can exit to High Camp. I follow Beck out into a hallway, trying not to give away how nice it feels to be on solid ground. We move up some stairs and out onto a sundeck. He points out the pool, caked with snow, a few blue bits peeking through, and the circle of blue hot tub steaming. We dodge a pack of tiny ski-lesson kids, one sobbing, "There's a bug in my jacket," and I smile sympathetically at the young ski instructor who tries to get the little girl's coat off over her gloves, mumbling, "Probably not a bug, honey." It makes me miss Seth and Liam. Mental list:

> Skype with brothers
> send them Squaw stickers for their scooters

We pass a massive glass dome that spills light into the restaurant on the level below, and head to the railing, taking in the view of Lake Tahoe and the mountains beyond. From here, everything is rock and snow and pines and that wide blue lake. "You must never get tired of this view." I breathe deep, the wind catching my hair so I have to hold it back with one hand.

Beck shakes his head. "Never."

A woman walks over and leans on the railing near us. She wears a down jacket that shines pale pink like an abalone shell and has her back to the view, her glossy dark hair spilling out from under a fuzzy white hat that looks like someone fastened a baby polar bear to her head. She snaps her gum and fiddles with her phone. "Come here," she says to the guy with her, and they take a selfie with the view in the background. She fiddles with her phone again, probably posting the photo somewhere.

He stares out over the vista, his hands in the pockets of his designer jeans. "See, babe, it's totally worth it, right? Coming up here?" He tries to catch her eye, but she doesn't look up from her phone.

"There." She pockets her phone. "Ugh, this is boring. Let's hit the bar." The man looks disappointed as they head in the direction of the restaurant.

Beck frowns, his gaze following them, and even though I can't see them, I can feel his eyes narrow behind his sunglasses. "I hate people like that. They come up here, but they don't even *see* any of it."

The couple disappears back inside the tram building. I shrug. "Some people just don't think about things like views. They're probably not, you know, nature people."

"Idiots," Beck growls, his tone surprising me. "Just watch — because of people like that, we'll end up having to live on the moon in tiny metal boxes."

I turn back to the view and give him a small nudge with my body. Trying to lighten the mood, I tease, "Well, we should go push them off the tram. I have no interest in lunar condo living."

He gives his head the tiniest of shakes as if clearing an unwanted thought and tries to smile, but that shadow of annoyance lingers. "Sorry. But if you're going to be such a clueless moron, don't come to my Tahoe."

A burst of laughter and stomping feet fills the deck behind us. I turn just as a bride emerges from the side door of the tram building, her dress fluttering beneath a white down jacket. Already on the deck, the groom wears a black down jacket and tux pants and it takes me a minute to realize they're both in ski boots. They're surrounded by a pack of bridesmaids and groomsmen hauling skis and also dressed in ski-themed bridal outfits. Laughing, the group heads toward the slopes near Bailey Creek Run. "Hey, look." I tug at Beck's jacket sleeve. "*They* love your Tahoe."

"Awesome," he says, though without much energy behind it. *Awesome*, I'm learning, is a go-to placeholder word in Tahoe. Beck's mood seems to have diminished along with the oxygen levels.

"Want to show me around inside? Isn't there an Olympic museum?"

Inside, we wander around the small museum, squinting at the black-and-white photos and watching a short video about the 1960 Games. Near a wide window, we come across a life-size cutout of a man in an Olympic racer suit. I get an idea. "Hey, take a picture, okay?" I hand Beck my phone.

"What are you doing?"

I lean in and plant a big kiss on the cutout face of the skier. "Take the picture," I mumble through the smooch.

Shaking his head, Beck takes the picture, but he's smiling again. "What's that all about?"

"Now List number seven. Kiss a cute snowboarder," I tell him, grabbing my phone and texting the picture to Josie.

Beck tucks his hands in his pockets. "Um, that's Jonny Moseley. He's a *skier*. And, like, forty years old now."

I squint at the cutout. "He doesn't look forty."

Clearly enjoying this, Beck says, "Old picture."

Shrugging, I check the photo again. "Hmmm . . . So I guess I just sent a super-creepy picture to my friend."

"Little bit, yeah." He takes a step toward me. We're alone in the museum, the late-morning sun lighting up streaks of dust in its beams. "But if you're looking to kiss a snowboarder to, you know, check that off a list, I'm happy to oblige."

My mouth turns into a desert. "Oh." *Oh?* A boy wants to kiss me and I just said, *Oh?!* I try to recover. "I said *cute* snowboarder."

129

"Aww, be nice — I'm a little bit cute." He's very close now — I can smell his spicy soap. He tips his head down, waiting for me. My mind makes a ten-second speed list.

Reasons to kiss Beck:

> He's magazine cute.
> He has a good mouth.
> He smells like pine trees and spice.
> He's *offering*.
> #7!

But in the exact same ten seconds, the opposite list tries to scribble over it:

> Hazmat suit!
> I don't really feel like *that* about him — do I?
> He's not Logan (grrrrrr, stop thinking about Logan).
> I'm not a girl who kisses random boys.

And yet, maybe in the spirit of Tahoe Mara, I go with list 1.

So I kiss him. I grab him by his down-jacketed shoulders and pull him into me. Apparently, it doesn't matter how much I think I like or don't like Beck Davis, because kissing him feels like that moment right before falling on skis — that exhilarating stomach-dropping tug — and his warm mouth erases everything on list 2.

THE NOW LIST

1. Learn to ski: ~~green runs,~~ blue runs, black runs??
2. ~~Internet cleanse (no social media, no news, Skype okay!)~~
3. ~~Meditation —— at least 10 minutes a day!!~~
4. ~~Sleep until 8 on a school day when I'm not sick~~
5. ~~Essential oils to relax —— lavender, chamomile, orange~~
6. ~~Simplify & downsize!!~~
7. ~~Kiss a cute snowboarder!! (Josie's suggestion)~~
8. ~~Breathe! (obviously)~~
9. ~~Be brave (from Will)~~
10. Read for fun? (see attached suggested book lists)
11. Get to know Trick McHale
12. Get in a little trouble

FIFTEEN

Kissing Beck translates into an afternoon of manic energy at Trick's cottage. I do four homework assignments and make dinner, but I can't seem to stop picturing the moment I pulled Beck in to kiss me. Even with chem formulas swirling in my brain, I can't stop thinking about how soft his mouth was or the weight of his hands on my back.

I'd scratched out #7, but I'm pretty sure it was a bad, bad idea. I blame Josie.

On the other hand, I think this means I can cross off #12, too.

Trick comes through the door just as I'm spooning from-scratch minestrone soup into bowls. As he hangs up his jacket, I set out a plate of warm, sliced French bread with butter and a green salad.

"Whoa, what's all this?" He pulls his beanie off and tosses it onto the couch. "What's the occasion?"

I keep myself from shouting, *I kissed Beck Davis!* and slip into my chair. "In the real world, you don't need an occasion to make dinner. You just get hungry, go to the grocery store, and, you know, *survive*." I sprinkle parmesan cheese onto my soup, praying he doesn't notice my hands shaking.

He takes a slurp. "You *made* this?" I nod, and he adds, "Your mom taught you."

I look up at him, surprised. "She did, yeah."

"I remember this soup," he says, his head bent over the bowl as he eats. His words twist in me, and for a few moments, we eat without talking. I wait for him to say more, maybe tell me a story about Mom making this soup for him, but he doesn't say anything. Just eats his soup.

I'm still trying to read Trick like a map. The obvious stuff came quickly, the similarities in our eyes and the color of our hair. Mostly, though, I'm noticing myself in his quiet ways, how he seems more content to observe than to dictate a conversation. I've always been quiet like that. But this hush right now makes me uneasy. At home, dinner is never quiet. Mom always takes the lead, asking questions and getting answers. If we don't talk enough, she has a box of conversation cards that sit on our buffet to get the ball rolling. Will usually talks about work or sports during dinner (when he's not answering *What kind of domesticated pet would you be?*), and the twins are loud and rowdy. Labradoodles. Both of them. Trick's on the opposite end of the spectrum. If I don't say something, we'll pass the whole dinner without speaking a single word.

"You're one of those quiet cats who sits in the window of a bookshop," I blurt over our slurps and chewing.

He jerks his head up. "Huh?"

Oh, right. It helps to actually *intro* the card game. "If you were a domesticated pet, you'd be a quiet shop cat."

"Um, okay."

"Sometimes, at home, Mom makes us play games to get the conversation going at dinner. Like, what color of the rainbow would you be?"

He shrugs, reaching for some bread. "I don't know, blue?"

133

"Why blue?"

"Red?"

"You have to explain your answer." He looks pained. "Forget it." This isn't going well; our words seem wispy and fake, like whole rivers of other words swirl in the spaces between them. No more rainbow colors or bookshop cats. "Trick?"

"Yeah?"

"What happened after you got hurt? Is it why you and Mom split up?" It's amazing how certain words asked in a certain order can change the entire atmosphere of a room.

He sets down his spoon and rubs his eyes. He looks at me for perhaps the first time all evening. "Can we go back to that question about the rainbow? Blue, definitely blue." I stare at him, waiting. He picks up his spoon again, swirling it through the dregs of his soup. "I guess I was pretty messed up for a while after."

"You mean your knee?"

He sighs, looking hard enough at me to make me suddenly very interested in my own soup. "Physically, sure. I completely jacked up my knee, my whole leg. I shattered it in multiple places, so I couldn't compete anymore. I lost sponsors. I couldn't ski at all, really. Not for a long time." He takes a slurp of soup, dropping his eyes. "But that wasn't the main issue." I swallow, not wanting to move, not wanting to even take a bite of bread lest it upset this sudden flash of openness. He stares sideways out the window at the dark blue fade of late evening light. "When I couldn't ski anymore . . . when I couldn't ski like myself anymore, well, it just took everything else away with it. It's like I fell into a sinkhole I couldn't get out of. Your mom tried, she really did. I don't want you ever thinking your mom didn't try."

I know this about my mother. She's nothing if not solution oriented. "But then you both stopped trying?"

"Mostly me . . . a long time before she did." On the table next to me, my phone buzzes, startling both of us. I hurry to shut it off but not before I see it's a text from Beck. Looking relieved, Trick nods at it. "You should take that."

"It's nothing," I tell him, but he's already standing, collecting his dishes.

"Dinner was fantastic," he says, his back to me as he sets his dishes in the small sink. He's already gone, even before pulling on his coat and heading out to gather some firewood.

Frustrated, I check the text.

sick stars out tonight. come hang. i'm close by.

He includes directions to a house one street over. The thought of staying here in the silence makes my head want to explode, so I go into my room to change and brush my hair.

When I emerge, I find Trick reading a ski magazine on the couch. "I'm going to take a walk."

He looks up, one arm propped behind his head. "Now?"

"Just want to get some fresh air, maybe sit and look at the stars for a while." Avoiding his eyes, I wind a scarf around my neck and pull on my beanie. I hold my breath, waiting for the usual parental *Where are you going, who are you meeting, when will you be home?*

Or maybe even: *Are you about to kiss the wrong boy? Again.*

Instead, he says, "Take a flashlight," and returns to the pages of his magazine.

Outside, a wall of cold hits me, but the stars are spread out above like someone has spilled an entire bottle of silver glitter on the night. Totally worth the frostbite.

I start walking toward the next street, careful to stay in the center of the road to avoid icy patches. My boots crunch on the sanded streets. Most of the houses here are dark, their residents living elsewhere most of the year, so I can see the lights of a massive house up ahead glowing like a golden Oz.

Beck waits out front in the shoveled driveway, his hands jammed in the pockets of a silver down jacket, puffs of his breath illuminated in the air around him by the glow of the house. Seeing me, he breaks into a smile and holds up a folded blanket. I hesitate, my brain telling me to turn around and go home and do my math homework.

Funny how the heart can have a whole different checklist from the brain's.

"Whose house is this?" I follow him toward a row of stairs along the outside of the house that twists up to what looks like the third level.

"Just a guy I know. Watch that ice there." He holds the handrail as he climbs ahead of me. We reach a tiny deck and Beck settles onto a bench that has been converted from an old ski lift. From here, we can look out over the dark valley, the glittery sky immense and close.

Ski lift bench. Quilt. Starry sky. Trouble.

I sit down next to him, my teeth chattering. Noticing, he covers us with the blanket. "Better?"

"Trick thinks I'm taking a walk," I blurt.

"Does he know you're with me?"

I shake my head, looking sideways at his shadowed face. "He didn't ask, but I'm not sure he'd approve. Isabel doesn't seem to." I pull the quilt tighter, our bodies growing warm beneath its folds. "Why is that, by the way?"

His laugh floats out over the dark houses below. "My dear friend Isabel doesn't approve of my lifestyle. Thinks I'm wasting my opportunities."

"Are you?"

"I see it as doing the opposite."

"How?"

"Because I actually enjoy my life and don't care about setting goals or being perfect. Isabel gets annoyed because I don't try with school. But I read, I get an education — it's just my version. I think school makes you dumber, not smarter. It makes you conform to one set way of thinking. Isabel's all about getting approval from whatever system she's in — her skiing, her grades, her friends."

"School's about way more than being smart," I argue. "It's also about making sure we can get stuff done on time, following directions, building a work ethic so we can move on to the next step."

"It's jumping through hoops so we can go jump through more hoops." He shrugs. "Where does it end?"

I hesitate, my body tingling. He's hit on something I've been thinking about lately. Where does it end? When I stare out into the future, what I'm actually doing out there is hazy and blank. Because I work hard, people think I have some huge goal, like how Josie wants to be an oceanographer. But I don't know yet what sort of practical, day-to-day life I want after college. No driving force that wants to be a doctor or a professor or an attorney. The drive has always been the perfection — the grades, the awards, the test scores.

Still, I can't help but say, "You can't just spend your whole life winging it."

He slides toward me on the bench, and his hand covers mine. "Why not?"

137

My breath catches. "You need a plan."

He leans in, his face close enough for his breath to warm the cold air between us. "Oh, I have a plan."

I know I should leave, but my legs don't seem to work under the heavy blanket. It feels good to sit here, with someone who isn't demanding I work harder, do better, *improve*. Beck's like an antonym for self-improvement.

> self-deterioration
> self-destruction
> self-corrosion

"Your plan sounds a lot like instant gratification," I say softly, my lips nearly touching his.

He grins. "You should try it sometime."

"Instant gratification it is." I lean in, and his mouth, cold at first, warms quickly. He tastes like snow and peppermint gum, and as his hands move to capture my face, everything — the night, the stars, the snow, even my lists — evaporates around us.

•   •   •

Back at the cottage, I open the door as quietly as I can. The only light is the flickering fire. Trick is stretched out on the foldout twin bed, one arm tucked behind his head. As I tiptoe toward my room, his voice emerges from the darkness. "Nice walk?"

I start and feel a blush creep up my cheeks. "Oh, yeah — thanks. It's gorgeous out there. So clear."

"Be careful with all that ice." He sits up a bit in his bed. I can feel him watching me from across the room. "One minute you're on solid ground and the next you're flat on your butt."

We both know he's not talking about the weather.

• • •

The next morning, my phone buzzes on the bookcase next to my bed: morning, sunshine.

It all comes flooding back — the Olympic museum, the ski lift bench beneath the stars, Beck's peppermint kiss. My stomach twists and I double over. Maybe I'm not built for this instant-gratification-impulsive stuff. To make impulsive work, it's probably best not to feel crippling regret the next day. I'm guessing that's not really the point of it.

What am I doing? I came to Tahoe to sort out my head, to figure out where I stand with school, and maybe even with Trick and what happened between my parents. But certainly *not* to turn into some snowbound boy-crazed mess. It seems, though, this is exactly what I'm doing.

> giving Logan cookies
> taking off on skis with Beck
> kissing Beck — twice

Actually, in list form, it seems sort of exciting. Except that I feel like throwing up. I hurry to the bathroom, trying to take calming breaths. I'm always hearing how it's healthy to step outside your comfort zone, but I'm pretty sure #8 on my list did not imply gasping for breath next to the toilet.

Over the years, people have given me various definitions of my personality. Sometimes the spin can be positive: motivated, focused, productive. Or those qualities take on their more negative shadows: tightly wound, high-strung, stress case. Regardless, I'm tired of waking up tangled, regretful, and overthinking everything. Other girls I know at Ranfield would be posting about kissing a cute skier boy on Instagram, with hashtags like #hesjustthatcute or #studybreak!

My hashtag would read #peptobismolmoments!

I shouldn't have kissed Beck. It's complicating things. I reach for my glass vial of lavender oil on the sink, but instead of grabbing it, I knock it onto the tile floor, where it shatters, the scent of lavender instantly permeating the room. Not in a relaxing way. Gagging, I try to mop it up with a wad of toilet paper.

My phone rings in the other room. Standing, wobbly, I cross to my bed. Crawling back under the covers, I answer it. "Hi, Mom."

It's 9:04 on a Sunday. Mom has probably already run five miles, organized dinner for that night, and read most of the *Union-Tribune*. "Honey, I just spoke with Ms. Raff." And talked with my Home Hospital coordinator.

"Oh, yeah?" I take a sip from my water bottle, letting the cold water soothe my throat. I wince. It tastes like lavender.

"It's about chemistry." She sounds distracted. Probably measuring ingredients for dinner prep. *Never do one thing when you can do two,* she's always telling me.

I try to figure out which assignment I could have missed. "I'm pretty sure I turned everything in for chem this week."

"It's about the wet lab. They thought you could do it online, but now Ranfield says you have to find a lab locally or you can't get AP credit." I hear clinking and what sounds like rice against a glass cup. She's definitely prepping risotto.

"So I should wander around Tahoe until I can find a random lab to crash? That sounds likely." On the other end of the phone, the fridge door opens and shuts. "Are you making risotto?" I can almost taste the buttery rich grains.

She pauses. "Mara, maybe you should come home now." The only thing that surprises me is that it has taken her this long to suggest it. "I know they said you could stay on Home Hospital for this quarter and keep your scholarship, but, well . . ." I can almost see her mind sifting through all the possible ways to tell me she thinks I've overstayed my welcome, both in Tahoe and with the administration at Ranfield. "I think maybe it's time to come home."

It would be so easy.

No more Beck. No more Logan and Isabel, the World's Cutest Ski Couple. No more Trick the Enigma. I could slip back into Ranfield and remember the student I used to be, before I ripped up all those tests. The one who had her life on track. I'm so tempted to say, *Yes, please, come get me. I'm messing everything up here!*

Mom would set record time getting here.

But, for some reason, I don't. My voice feeling like something separate from me, instead I say, "I'd like to stay." Outside, sunlight glitters on the wet pines, the day clear, but I know it's nowhere near as warm as it looks. "Mom?" I ask, when she doesn't say anything. "Can I stay?"

She sighs, in that way she does when she takes the rare moment to stare out our kitchen window at the meticulously landscaped yard beyond. Finally, she says, "See what you can do about that lab, okay?"

After I hang up with Mom, I clean as much of the lavender spill as I can, but it still reeks. Then I curl up on the bed and start writing a new Now List.

THE NOW LIST II

1. Get Trick to talk more!!
2. Let my phone run out of power
3. Focus, Mara!
4. Be brave (thanks, Will)
5. Ski blue runs with confidence. Black runs?

SIXTEEN

I decide to focus on #3 on the Now List II probably because I'm just hardwired that way. Texting Beck, I tell him I'm going to be busy for the next couple of days, lots to do for school: you know me, the hoop jumper! I try to joke, but he doesn't text back.

I tape a sign to the bathroom mirror: *Sorry for the hazardous oil spill!*

I hole up in my room for the next twenty-four hours, barely sleeping, eating piece after piece of peanut butter toast, and turning in massive loads of schoolwork early. I keep an eye on the battery marker as it drains to dead on my phone (#2!). Beck doesn't text back. When the little red slash of the dying battery line becomes a sliver, I almost lose my nerve and plug it back in. I have never in the history of owning this phone allowed its power to completely drain. Which is ridiculous. Because it's not that big a deal. The Things More Upsetting than Running Out of Phone Power List I make in my head goes something like this:

poverty
drug addiction
sexism
terminal disease

Tiny subsets of my Get a Grip List. But they only make me feel worse and I start wondering if maybe I'm making the wrong sorts of lists.

When I start to feel like my phone is actually staring at me, pleading with me to *just plug me in, I'm dying!!*, I stuff it into the depths of my bag and tackle my calculus homework. Knowing it's in there, dead, fills my stomach with acid. That can't be healthy, that kind of attachment to a dead phone; it's not like it's a pet or something.

Even if I do spend more time with it than any pet I've ever had. Which is just sad.

· · ·

Early Monday afternoon, as I bask in the glow of the school report Ms. Raff emails me *(Best work yet! Fantastic insight!)*, Beck's words surface in my mind: *praise junkie*. Am I a praise junkie? Do I work feverishly like this, put all this energy and time into school, because I crave this kind of approval?

Or because I like the excuse it gives me to block out the world?

Are either of those reasons wrong?

Desperate to get out of my head and onto the mountain, I eye my ski gear hanging on the back of the door. My helmet sits on the shelf. An hour on the mountain couldn't hurt — I've gotten so much done already.

I knock on Powder's door, and moments later, Oli pops his head out. "What time do the lifts close?" I ask, staring up at him.

He grins. "We got time."

A half hour later, we're taking the funi up the mountain, the day clear and cold, but with a swirl of inky clouds moving in. The mountain seems empty, mostly locals. We're the only two people in the funi car and Oli leans back against the bench across from me. From my own bench, I watch as a man flies down Mountain Run, his form graceful and clean. I want to ski like that someday. Studying him, my body floods with a type of sadness, that feeling of already knowing that you'll miss something even before you've left it. Looking out at the snowy mountains above, I sigh.

"I believe they call that a heavy sigh," Oli says, stretching his long legs out in front of him.

"I was just thinking about going home." And trying not to think about the mess I've made of my time in Tahoe.

"You miss it?"

I watch the clouds, their varied layers of dark and light. We don't get clouds like this in San Diego. "I miss parts of it. Will and Mom and my little brothers. My friend Josie. The beach. Not that I ever had much time to go to the beach."

He looks surprised. "How is that possible? You're sixteen; that's all you should be doing."

We're almost at the dock, and I start to collect my poles and skis. "Ranfield keeps me on a pretty tight schedule. I don't really have time."

"We all have the same number of hours, kiddo," he says, standing as the car bumps into the funi building. I bristle at the *kiddo*, like I'm some dumb kid who doesn't know how many hours a day holds.

"Yeah, I learned the analog clock in, like, kindergarten," I mumble, following him out of the funi car. We ski down to the Big Blue Express. On the lift ride up, I tell him, "Ranfield is worth it, all the stress and time, for what it will get me in the end."

"Which is what?" Oli kicks some snow from his skis.

"It will help me get into the right college."

Oli looks sideways at me. "And what will the right college get you?" I know he's just curious, but I still feel defensive.

"I'm keeping all my doors open, but I definitely want a tier-one school." Looking over at High Camp, I add, "I just don't want to be ordinary."

Oli leans back into the ski lift, his arm draped over the side. "Everyone builds their own specific life. Nothing ordinary about any of us."

Oli's definitely not ordinary. But not all of us can whoosh around the country in a silver box, collecting postcards. As if reading my mind, he says, "My life wasn't always so different from yours, Mara. Busy, busy."

Okay, this guy might really be a Jedi. "What do you mean?"

He leans forward onto the bar. "I did the right stuff, too. Went to Berkeley. Became a banker. I spent most of my twenties that way."

"A banker? Like in a bank?"

"Yes, in a bank. In San Francisco. I had a suit and everything." He makes an overdramatic gasping sound and smiles with his whole face at my look of shock.

I eye the stubbly beard he clearly hasn't shaved in days. "What happened?"

"It was gradual, not some huge moment or anything. I kept looking around and thinking I had this gorgeous life, this lucky life, but instead of basking in it, I was fighting it. So I bought Powder. Fixed her up at a friend's. I wanted to cultivate something small and mine. But I built up to it. We all have to decide what's enough to fill up a life. And it's different for each of us."

147

The lift bumps toward the exit. We push the bar up and ski off to the right. Fiddling with his goggles, he adds, "But I don't want you to think it was an easy choice. Or an obvious one. It wasn't. It took time. For years, I got up early, slogged through my commute, sat with all those other suits at lunch, eyed the clock all the time. After a while, I just thought, *What am I doing here? This isn't where I'm meant to be.* Then again, some guys I worked with — they loved it, the game, the competition, the grind. Someone is always going to have more, someone is always going to have less. Eventually, you have to choose what's enough for you and not what's right for other people."

I stare down at my skis. "I don't care what other people think of me."

"You sure about that?"

Even though he said it gently, it feels like having snow dumped down the back of my jacket. Stupid Jedi Mountain Master. He doesn't know why I'm here; *I* don't even know why I'm here.

"Are we going to actually ski sometime today?" I ask glibly, fiddling with the straps of my poles, noticing the snow starting to fall, the bits of ice collecting on my goggles.

He belly-laughs loud enough to attract attention from passing skiers. "Yes, we are. Let's get a run in before this storm hits."

SEVENTEEN

I wake shivering in the muted Tuesday morning to no power and a steady snowfall adding to the pile outside. My fire died out during the night, so I wrap myself in my quilt and pad into the living room, where Trick has a camping lantern glowing as he stokes the wood-stove out here. "I'm out of wood," I say.

"I'll get yours going in a sec. Power's out at the store, too. All over the valley." He wipes his hands on his jeans and grabs an armful of wood for my stove. "After this, I'm going to snowshoe over to the store and help the Nevers deal with a few things. These fires should hold you until I get back." He motions toward the woodstove, where a metal coffeepot percolates. "There's coffee if you want it, but take that pot off soon or it'll burn." He's wearing the Santa Cruz sweat-shirt he wears often, the one he had on that first day I saw him in Neverland.

"Thanks," I say sleepily. Watching him disappear into my room, something shifts in me, squeezing my heart. I hear him in there, fiddling with the stove, crumpling paper, closing the little iron door, and I start to cry.

He emerges and catches sight of my tear-streaked face. Looking alarmed, he asks, "Oh, no — what?"

I shake my head, trying to blink away the gluey wave of emotion threatening to surface again. "Nothing, nothing. I just need coffee. This is my *I need coffee* face."

Shooting me an odd look, he grabs the pot and pours me a cup. He adds milk and hands it to me, which, ridiculously, brings on another hiccupy sob. Uncertain, he takes a step back. "Oh, well — are you sick or something?"

"No." I bury my face in the hot, sharp smell of coffee. How can I explain about the Santa Cruz sweatshirt and watching him build a fire? How can I tell him that him knowing I take milk in my coffee makes me miss all the years he didn't know what kind of breakfast I liked?

"You sure?"

When I nod, he heads for the door, casting me another funny, quiet look, before heading out into the falling snow.

• • •

An hour later, someone knocks on the door. I open it to find Isabel and Logan frosted with snow. "Put these on," Isabel says, holding up a pair of snowshoes. "You're coming with us." She notices what I'm wearing. "And you're very welcome to wear your pajamas, but you might want to throw on your ski pants over those so you don't get soaked."

I point at the books piled on the coffee table. "Oh, I should probably work —"

Isabel cuts me off with the raise of her gloved hand. "You should probably go put on your ski pants."

"And come with us," Logan adds, brushing some snow from his beanie. "It's a snow day."

Ten minutes later, I follow them awkwardly on snowshoes through the storm, the snow eddying around me. It's incredible how small the world becomes in a snowstorm, how quiet and still, like all peripheral vision has been erased. As we crunch along, it dawns on me that it feels nice to put life on hold for a day.

After what seems like an hour but is probably twenty minutes, we arrive at a house. We stomp up some stairs and onto a wide deck. Logan opens the front door, letting us into a fully enclosed glass-and-wood entryway with pale stone floors and hooks on the walls for our gear. We leave the snowshoes on the ground by a bench that looks like someone built it out of polished tree branches and hang up our pants and jackets. When we're ready, Logan pushes open another glass door and leads us into a great room, its lamps glowing warmly.

"Wait, you guys have power?" I ask, taking in the high ceilings, the living room with cozy couches and an enormous fireplace, and beyond that, a kitchen separated from the living space by a kitchen island with dark granite countertops.

"We have a generator." Logan heads toward the kitchen as Isabel settles onto one of the suede sofas, clearly at home here, and starts sorting through a pile of board games on the coffee table in front of her.

"Cool house." I join Isabel on the sofa.

Logan puts a pan of milk on the stove and opens a jar of cocoa powder, spilling some on the counter. "Thanks, we like it." He moves around the kitchen. Finally, he sets down three steaming mugs and a bowl of popcorn on the coffee table, grimacing when he notices that Isabel has set up a game called Chat Room. "Can't we just play Monopoly?"

Isabel flips up the first card. "This is a good starter game." She pauses shuffling cards to look out at the dense snow that has only grown thicker in the last half hour. "I don't think we'll be going anywhere for a while."

Logan fetches a beanbag from near the fire and flops into it on the other side of the coffee table. "Fine, but let's just play the talking way. I don't feel like writing anything down."

Isabel puts the little pads of paper away. "Well, we wouldn't want you to hurt yourself."

I sit cross-legged on the couch next to Isabel, glad I stayed in my pajama bottoms, and pull a fuzzy ivory blanket over my lap. With the fire glowing and the smell of hot cocoa and popcorn permeating the air, I could fall asleep. "How do you play?"

Logan grabs a handful of popcorn. "The way it works is, Isabel uses this game as an excuse to pry into your personal life."

"You're onto me," Isabel says, flipping up the first card. "Okay, here's the first question: If you could invent anything, what would it be?"

"A homework machine!" I blurt out. Then, blushing, I add, "I probably should've said something that cures cancer, right?"

Logan considers this. "How about a cancer-curing homework machine?"

"Yes, that! I would invent that," I say gratefully. We play through several questions, the game feeling a lot like a dinner with Mom.

What would you do with a million dollars?

What would you name a constellation?

Would you rather live in a house made of candy or gold?

"Well, that's obvious." I frown. "Gold. Candy would be so sticky and gross. Especially if it rained."

Isabel draws another card. "If you were a household appliance, what would you be?"

Logan immediately answers, "An oven."

"An oven?" I ask, the cup of cocoa warming my still-cold hands.

He shrugs. "I like to cook and I have a warm personality." He smiles in that way I feel down to my toes. He adds, "Isabel is an espresso machine."

"I get to answer for myself! But, yes, that seems right." This small affectionate exchange stabs at me, erasing the nice toe-warming feeling.

"My turn," I announce. I sift through possible appliances I could be. Refrigerator, hair dryer, washing machine. I decide: "Blender."

"Why?" They both ask at the same time.

"Because my life is a big mixed-up mess right now."

Isabel nibbles some popcorn, watching me closely. "Is that why you tore up all those tests?"

Ugh. *Everyone* knows.

Logan frowns at Isabel. "Pick another card, nosy. No follow-up questions."

"It's fine." I stare into my hot chocolate. "Okay, yeah." A log crackles and shifts in the fireplace, and I sit up straighter and put the mug on the coffee table. "I mean, I didn't plan it. I didn't wake up thinking, *Today I'm going to make a huge scene in calculus!* But I just got so overwhelmed and freaked out." My shoulders sag. "Kind of insane, I know."

"Oh, I don't know." Isabel passes me the bowl of popcorn. "I've always been a fan of a dramatic exit."

"But the thing is, I'm *not*," I tell her, helping myself to a handful

153

of popcorn. "I've always just been the girl who gets the work done." Studying the snow falling outside, I fill them in on what happened at Ranfield. "I just needed a break — from all the competitive, comparative intensity there."

Logan and Isabel exchange an uneasy glance. Great. I said too much. But then Isabel asks, "So you came to *Tahoe*?"

I nod. "It's just so much more relaxed here." Isabel cocks her head to one side, making a "huh" noise. Something in the sound of it makes me wary. "What?"

Isabel pulls herself into a cross-legged position on the couch. "I'm not sure it actually is. Don't let all the crunchy-hippie-mountain vibes fool you. People in Tahoe can be just as hypercompetitive as anywhere else." I must look skeptical, because she says, "Not about the same things, maybe, but they are. Here, it's all about how hardcore you can be as a skier or kayaker or anything in the outdoors, really. Or it's how hardcore you can be about yoga or organic food or your carbon footprint. You want to see some self-righteous intensity? Try talking to a vegan about why you eat cheeseburgers. Or, if you're a vegetarian, to some meat eater about why you don't eat cow. *Free-range, grass-fed* cow, of course."

I smile; San Diego has plenty of that. I think that's just California. "Well, it seems more relaxed to me."

She leans forward, lowering her voice. "It's an illusion. What's annoying is, everyone here wants you to think they're so chill, so mellow — so *inclusive*. But it's the same competitive crap as you've got everywhere. It's still the United States of Do It My Way. I don't care how much they talk about their chakras. At least at your school, it sounds like they're up front about it."

Nodding, I think about what she's saying. Did I assume life

154

would be so much easier in Tahoe because Mom always talked about Trick being such a slacker? Because he's not, really. A slacker. He works hard at the shop, shovels snow, chops wood. He just keeps things simple. I know I'd been hoping to find simplicity in Tahoe — original Now List #6! But nothing seems simple. Not really. I'm still confused. What I know for sure, though, is something wasn't working at Ranfield. "I just got so tired of playing the whole game. I thought a change of scenery would help."

"I get that." Isabel nods over the rim of her cocoa mug.

"Speaking of games," Logan says, clearing his throat. "We don't have to keep playing this one." He moves to pack up the cards.

"No, it's fine," I hurry to tell him. "It helps to talk about it."

And for the first time, it's true.

We play Chat Room for another half hour, almost quitting when Isabel and Logan get into a heated argument over the question of favorite superhero because, according to Isabel, Iron Man doesn't count. "He has no actual powers! And everything he does is for his own gain. Veto!"

"You can't veto my answer!" Logan's face flushes. "Batman doesn't have any actual powers and that doesn't stop him from being a superhero."

Isabel shakes her head, dead serious. "That's different. Batman's a superhero subcategory — vigilante. Everything he does is to make Gotham a better place. Unlike Tony Stark, who just tries to make Tony Stark's life better."

Logan leans back in the beanbag, crossing his arms. "I'm allowed to pick Iron Man. It's *my* answer. The suit he built made the world a better place."

Isabel shoots back, "He built his suit to save his own butt. Veto."

Logan bursts out laughing. "No veto — you don't get a ruling when your favorite superhero is Batman, the manic-depressive of Gotham City."

She chucks a playing card at Logan, who ducks, and it ends up in the fire, instantly engulfed in flames. She giggles. "Oops."

I crack up. "You two are so funny. Seriously, you're the cutest couple ever — it's revolting, actually."

Isabel sits up, coughing. "Wait . . . what did you just say?" She and Logan exchange a confused look. "You think we're *together*? Ewww!"

"Aww, thanks, that's nice, Iz. Feeling the love." Logan stands, gathering our empty cups and carrying them to the kitchen sink.

"Wait." My heart thrums in my ears. "You *aren't* together?"

Isabel shakes her head violently. "Oh, gross — he's like my brother. No offense, Logan. You're a total catch but . . ." She looks back at me, her body shuddering. "Ewwww, gross."

"I'm wondering if you could mention again how gross that would be," Logan says drily from behind the kitchen counter. "In case she didn't quite catch it."

"Sorry! But it is," she mumbles, putting the rest of Chat Room away and pulling another box from the stack. "Now, who wants to get their Monopoly on?"

Logan pulls lunch stuff from the fridge, making us another round of hot cocoa. At one point, he glances up, catches me watching him, and gives me a strange half smile. *Surprise*, it seems to say.

For lunch, we eat turkey sandwiches and share a bag of Doritos. The snow seems to be letting up a bit, but all the nearby houses remain dark, either unoccupied or the power not yet back on. When

I'm done with my sandwich, I push myself off the couch. "Can you point me toward the bathroom?" Isabel motions toward the long hallway past the kitchen.

On my way back to the living room, I stop to look at the dozens of framed photos lining the hallway. Most of them feature snow in some way: Logan and his older sister in racing uniforms; Logan's family snowshoeing; the family in front of the Squaw Valley Neverland, its windows trimmed for the holidays. There are other pictures, too: his parents standing in front of an old building that might be in Europe somewhere, a shot of the family on the bow of a boat with Tahoe's blue waters behind them, a picture of Logan and his sister dressed as Harry and Hermione from Harry Potter. This one makes me grin because Logan is the one dressed as Hermione.

My gaze falls on a group shot, with everyone dressed for summer — board shorts, T-shirts, sundresses. The kids sit on top of a picnic table, Lake Tahoe in the background, and the adults stand behind them, some in profile, clutching water bottles or beers. The shot seems half-candid, half-staged. The kids look straight at the camera, but many of the adults seem caught in conversation with one another. I can see Isabel right away, all that wild red hair and big smile. A woman who must be her mom stands behind her, her hand on Isabel's shoulder. Next to Isabel, a child-size Beck stares down the camera, looking annoyed, the same look he had staring after those tourists at High Camp the other day. Two or three other kids sit there, too, smiling while the adults chat behind them.

"We were ten in that picture. Fifth grade, I think." Isabel comes up beside me, studying it. "It's funny how many times I walk by this and never look at it. Look how cute we were. Look at Joy's hair!" She points out the girl from Elevation that first day, her oil-black hair in two high ponytails shooting out from her head like antlers.

I point at Beck. "Why so grumpy?"

Isabel squints at it. "That's just Beck's face. He's always looked like that."

I hear Logan rattling around the kitchen, the whirr of the espresso machine. Still studying the picture, I say, "You've known Beck a long time."

Isabel nods, moving down the line of pictures, examining each closely. "Since we were babies. Technically, *you've* known him a long time, too. And us." She points at a picture I haven't yet seen. "See? *Us.*"

I move to see the photo, my body tingling. It's a group of small children in ski suits, each with a bright yellow vest reading SQUAW KIDS SKI SCHOOL. We hold our tiny helmets, our hair mussed, our cheeks pink. I see Isabel, Beck, Logan, and Joy, and off to the side, I see almost three-year-old me with dark blond pigtails, holding a pink helmet in my starfish hands. Next to me, Trick stares at the camera, the word COACH embroidered on his jacket, his goggles pushed into his hair.

I swallow, unsettled, a whole world that might have been suddenly unspooling behind me. "I don't remember any of this. Any of you. Not you or Logan. Or Beck."

"Sorry." Isabel drops her gaze, her face creased with sympathy. "It must be really weird. This whole world that just went on without you after you left."

"It is." I lean in to look at three-year-old Beck grinning from under his too-big helmet. "Look, he's smiling in this one."

"Oh, he smiles," Isabel concedes, running a finger across the glass as if she could reach back in and touch our little-kid faces. "It just never lasts."

"What do you mean?"

She takes a step back. "Nope, no way. You made it pretty clear you don't want my thoughts about Beck Davis. So I'm going to stay out of it. You can kiss whoever you want at High Camp."

My stomach drops. "How do you know about that?"

"You kissed Beck?" I hadn't noticed Logan appear behind us in the hallway, holding a dish towel, but there he is, looking at me with too-wide eyes.

"Not really," I hurry to say. "Okay, yes. Accidentally. It's this stupid list I have —"

He interrupts. "Accidentally?"

I drop my eyes. "Twice."

"Oh." He takes the slightest step back. "Coffee's ready." He disappears toward the kitchen.

I officially hate snow days.

EIGHTEEN

The days following the crushed look on Logan's face morph into a list, informally titled: How to Tell the Boy You Like Way Too Much Is Avoiding You Because You Made the Wrong Assumption and Messed It Up. It's a working title. A little long, I know.

Every time you see him at Neverland, he suddenly has to "sort through an order" in the back. And disappears. Every time. No store has this many socks to stock.

When you see him at the café, he pounds his latte and leaves in under thirty seconds. Seriously, it hurts to drink a hot latte that fast.

He pretends not to see you on a ski lift. Three times.

He doesn't reply to texts. Eight of them.

The bag of cookies you leave him sits unopened on the shop counter. For three days. You're pretty sure Piper finally ate them.

You run into him (actually *run* into him) leaving Neverland and he turns and walks the other way, as if he hadn't just been heading into the store you were leaving, as if he hadn't just *run right into you.*

I can't really blame him, though. I've been doing the same thing to Beck all week. Not answering texts. Pretending not to see him. The latte strategy. Ouch. Seriously, I don't recommend it. The whole thing makes me think about how much time humans spend using avoidance as a general lifestyle strategy.

Just ask Trick. He's been perfecting it most of my life.

•   •   •

Late Saturday afternoon, Isabel texts to see if I want to meet for dinner at Ethan's Grill after her race. She and I find a table by the window and order some burgers. I start to ask, "How was your . . ." but trail off, my voice catching as Logan and Bodie push through the front door. Isabel sees them and waves them over. I don't miss Logan's hesitation before he follows Bodie over to our table. Isabel shoves over on her bench to make room for Bodie, and Logan, actively avoiding my eyes, slips into the chair next to me. When his leg brushes mine, my cheeks burn.

"Hey." Bodie nods at me, his mop of blue hair flopping over his forehead. He asks Isabel, "Did you order for us?"

"Why would we do that when we didn't know you were coming?" Isabel glares at him pointedly. Wait, did Isabel invite them?

Bodie's eyebrows shoot up. "Oh, right! We totally didn't know you were going to be here."

She looks quickly between me and Logan, her face hopeful. Yup, she invited him.

Logan pretends not to notice the mound of awkward between us. He motions to our waiter, who is en route with burgers for Isabel and me.

"Hey, Logan," he says, handing me my burger. "Get you something?"

"Two more of those? Thanks, Dex." He turns to Isabel. "Hey, congrats on the race today. You killed it out there."

Frowning, she makes room so Dex can set down her burger. "Still can't quite get the time where I need it to be." When she notices Bodie's eyes following the burger longingly, she pushes it to him. "Oh, you're so pathetic. Here."

"Seriously? Sweet. Thanks." He takes a huge bite.

Logan takes a drink from his Coke, then looks sideways at me. "Hey, Mara."

Figures he chooses to acknowledge me for the first time in days when I've just taken the World's Largest Burger Bite. "Mmmm, hi," I manage to get out through the mouthful. Swallowing, I add, "Did you get my texts?" I try to suppress an emerging ripple of anger with a mouthful of fries.

He drags one of Bodie's fries through some ketchup. "Yeah. I've been busy with skiing and school."

Too busy to answer a text? Weak.

Dex returns with two more burgers.

"Speaking of school." I put my burger down. "You guys don't happen to know if your school has a wet lab for chem, do you?"

Bodie chuckles, helping himself to some of Isabel's fries. "Wet lab. That sounds dirty."

Isabel elbows him. "Grow up." To me, she says, "Logan and I are in AP chem this year. We meet on Tuesdays to do all our labs. All the racers do. Well, not *all* the racers." She nods at Bodie, who shrugs good-naturedly.

I perk up. "Do you think they would mind if I came to it? It's just that if I don't find one, I might lose my AP credit for Ranfield."

"The horror, the horror," Bodie says in a whisper-ragged voice, bugging out his eyes.

Isabel ignores him. "Come Tuesday. Our teacher's really cool — you'll like her. I'm sure Logan's mom could give you a ride back to the valley after, if you can find a way to get to Truckee?" When he doesn't say anything, Isabel asks again, "Logan? Could she catch a ride back to the valley after chem lab?"

"What? Oh, yeah, sure — no problem." Only he says it like he might, in fact, have a problem with it.

"Don't worry about it," I say, trying to keep my voice even. "I'll figure it out."

•   •   •

Sunday morning, I wake up still annoyed with Logan, my body tense. Why is he being so distant and weird?

My phone buzzes. It's Will. Sending a whole sentence for my Shells of Wisdom photo this week:

Stop and smell the alpenglow.

I laugh so hard it brings Trick into my room, his eyebrows a question mark. I hold up my phone. "Will just told me to stop and smell the alpenglow."

Trick nods. "Good advice." He disappears back into the other room and I can hear the clink of his spoon against his cereal bowl.

Outside, small flecks of snow fall through the dark trees.

I take a deep breath and add his line to the Now List II.

•   •   •

163

Tuesday, I borrow Trick's truck and drive to Truckee on my own for the first time. I turn left at Monster Taco and wind up a street until a brown building resembling a loaf of overbaked bread (Isabel's description) appears at the end of the narrow road, its roof sagging under mounds of snow. The parking lot has been cleared, and I pull Trick's truck into an open spot and shut off the engine, which rattles and coughs at the end, like it always does.

The building doesn't look like a school. With the exception of a small wooden sign reading CREST CHARTER SCHOOL, at best it looks like a dentist's office. I push open the heavy door of the truck and head toward the building entrance. Isabel is waiting on the other side of the glass and waves when she sees me, scurrying to push open the door. "I give good directions, right?"

"Excellent directions." Inside, warm air greets me, and Isabel gives me a ten-second tour. "Okay, student lounge, classrooms over there, chem lab this way," she says as she heads down the dimly lit hall, clad in jeans, Uggs, and a teal sweatshirt. The walls are covered with pictures of students, all of whom seem to be doing something athletic — snowboarding, skiing, hiking, rafting. In one picture, a girl poses in black martial arts robes and glares fiercely at the camera. "Are all the kids who go here athletes?" I ask, squinting at a small, faded picture of a snowboard team.

"Not all of them. We've got artists, musicians, math geeks, and, you know, your occasional stoner." She turns and winks at me in a cryptic way. I've never seen Isabel so much as sip a beer, so I don't really know what all that winking is about.

"But you only come a few days a week?" I try to keep the judgment out of my voice, though I'm not very successful.

"Classes are two to three days a week depending on the class, but you're assigned an advisor and build the rest of your schedule with them; you can pick and choose from different options so you create the program that works best for your schedule."

Scratch camp, this school sounds like a salad bar. Um, would you like croutons with your French class? But I'd never really thought about anything other than the schedule we have at Ranfield. School has always just looked like, well, school.

She glances curiously at me as we turn down a hallway. "You probably get some flexibility in your school — I mean, all those rich kids. Seems like they would want a little more say."

I'm not sure how much say we get. We're basically told what we should be doing so that we have the best possible transcripts. "It's rigorous," I tell her. "But we have one free period a day." Which most of us spend taking an extra elective.

She gives me a look like I'd just confessed they force us into dark basements once a day and feed us worms. "I would hate that, too rigid. But, you know, everybody's got to do what they got to do." I've heard Trick use that expression before. It seems like the kind of thing you can say and not have to mean anything by it. I try to ignore it, but something about this school makes me bristle. It's not like I haven't been working hard while on Home Hospital. I get that this schedule is more like college, but still, it seems like a vacation compared to going to school every day and then doing all the work. It doesn't actually seem fair that other people can make this the whole high school package.

I follow Isabel into a small room that smells sharp and citrusy. She waves to Logan, who is standing with another girl and a boy who is so tall and thin, he seems like a human pencil. They all wear lab aprons and safety glasses. A young woman comes through the door. She wears a Patagonia vest and jeans tucked into glossy black boots and can't be more than twenty-five. "Okay, all — let's get this party started." She pauses when she sees me. "Oh, you must be Mara. I'm Malika, the AP chem teacher."

We call her by her first name? I shake her hand. "Thanks so much for letting me come."

She waves as if to say, *It's nothing*, and grabs an apron off a hook, handing it to me with a pair of safety glasses. "No problem. Someone actually *asking* to come to lab? It's fabulous."

"Should I, um, join a group?" Isabel seems to have joined Pencil Boy at one station, while Logan stands with the blond girl at another.

"You can jump in with Logan and Amanda." She motions toward them.

Great.

"Hi, I'm Mara," I say, walking over and standing across the counter from them.

"Amanda."

Holding up a graduated cylinder, Logan explains, sounding overly formal, "We're determining the molar volume of hydrogen gas at STP."

Amanda waggles her eyebrows. "Thrilling stuff." She seems sweet.

"Are you a ski racer, too?" I ask her.

"Nah, I snowboardcross." She twists at her ponytail, her eyes large and green behind her safety glasses. She has that tan glow of snow athletes who spend so much time on the mountain.

I vaguely remember that event from watching the last Winter Olympics with Will. "Is that the one where they knock each other off course?"

Amanda nods enthusiastically. "Not on purpose — okay, sometimes on purpose — but, yeah, it's rad." She goes back to her lab notebook, which is decorated with snowboard stickers and photos.

For the next hour and a half, we work through the lab, the atmosphere relaxed and peppered with jokes, but I'm hyperaware of Logan avoiding my eyes.

I try to concentrate on the lab and finally lose myself in collecting data. Malika watches and guides us. I like the way she explains things; she's clear and obviously loves her subject. Her enthusiasm infuses the whole process and I find myself caring a lot more about molar volume than I imagined I could. A ribbon of energy moves through me and I realize that I've missed this, working on a project with other students. The classroom. And this is extra nice because everyone seems to want to be here. In AP chem at Ranfield, my lab partner, Branson Tucker, never stopped reminding me that he was only taking the class because he was applying to Princeton and you couldn't get into Princeton without it. But even though Branson Tucker said *Princeton* about ten times a day, all he seemed to do during our lab time was try to light his hoodie strings on fire with the Bunsen burner.

As we finish cleaning up, Malika signs the form Ms. Raff emailed me this morning, verifying my time in the lab. "Good job today," she tells me, handing it back to me. "See you next week?"

I'm already looking forward to it.

"You guys want to get coffee?" Isabel suggests, hanging up her lab coat. Amanda declines. She has an essay to finish for English and wants to get it done so she can get enough time on the mountain tomorrow. She gives a little wave as she leaves, pulling a beanie over her ponytail and grabbing a huge red down jacket from a hook.

Logan has his back to us, sorting through his backpack. He doesn't say anything.

Clearing my throat, I tell Isabel, "I actually brought Trick's truck, so I'm up for it."

He turns. "So you don't need a ride?" His voice has that same odd clipped tone he used to talk about molar volume. I shake my head. "Cool — later, then." He disappears out the door.

I catch Isabel's eye. "He's been like that since the snow day."

She searches for something in her bag. "Maybe he's just busy. The store is crazy this time of year."

We both know it has nothing to do with the store. "Yeah, maybe. Hey, is there a drinking fountain?" I return my glasses to their white plastic bin and hang up my lab coat.

"By the student lounge," Isabel says. "We can do coffee another time if you're not feeling up to it."

"Maybe that's better. I have a ton of schoolwork to do and I should send in this lab form before my mom freaks."

We say good-bye and I find the fountain against the wall in the hallway running the length of the student lounge. Next to it, a glass window looks in on the lounge. A dozen or so kids sprawl on the four worn couches and a few others sit at round tables, textbooks open in front of them.

I almost miss him because he's sitting in profile. Beck. He's kicked back on the sofa that comes out perpendicularly from the wall, reading from a book to a small group of girls sitting cross-legged on the floor in front of him. I can't make out the title, but it's a paperback and has a picture of a man on the front, a philosopher-bust type of picture. His listeners stare at him, rapt, and behind the couch, a girl with short pink hair massages his shoulders in a steady rhythm, nodding at whatever he's reading aloud. She tips her head back, laughing, and leans to kiss him quickly on the cheek. I duck away before he can see me and hurry from the building as quickly as possible, welcoming the cold blast of outside air.

It shouldn't bother me, seeing him like that. *I'm* the one who has been avoiding *him*.

But it does.

NINETEEN

Mom calls the next afternoon and the first words she says are, "Did you connect with Dr. Elliot about your next appointment?"

"Not yet." I pick at some fuzz on the edge of Trick's couch. "Actually, I'm thinking I don't really need to have any more meetings with him."

Silence.

"Mom?"

"Meeting with Dr. Elliot was part of the deal, Mara. You agreed."

I take a breath. "I don't really want to go."

Sounding tired, she says, "This isn't about what you want. It's about doing your job. Life's not fair." Two of Mom's Core Principles: Do your job. Life's not fair.

It's that last one I catch on. I know she means sometimes things don't work out the way we want, but lately I've been thinking about how my life seems more than fair. I've been born into a privileged world. Expensive school, parents with important jobs, beautiful San Diego. It's amazing, actually — my luck. Yet so much of what I hear from everyone at Ranfield is *I'm so busy, I'm so stressed, my life is harder than yours*. Kids brag about getting no sleep, that the homework took six hours, that they *barely made it out alive* from that French test. Is it just human nature to be constantly competing for the suffering award? How much of it is just manufactured to seem like legitimate struggle?

I think of Oli with his simple life, his choice to leave the pressured world behind. Not that I want to live in an Airstream, but how much of my stress is environmental? I've come to Tahoe, but I'm still trying to win at the Ranfield game. All I did was change the view.

The realization hits me. For all my listing and living in the now, I'm still trying to impress the place I left behind, the place that wrecked me.

"Mara?"

I spaced on Mom. Clearly *not* doing my job right now. "Sorry."

"I'm meeting a client. Reschedule today." She hangs up.

•   •   •

Walking through the Village late Thursday afternoon, I see Logan come out of the frozen yogurt shop with a heaping sundae. He notices me and freezes. "Oh, hey. You caught me. Fro-yo addiction." He holds up a tub topped with what looks like a pound of candy. "Want one?" He motions back over his shoulder with his spoon.

"No, thanks, but I'll take a Sour Patch Kid. A red one." I help myself to one of the many sugar-drenched clumps on top of his yogurt, taking an overly long time to chew because the air feels strange between us. "I'm still not used to the blue Sour Patch Kids," I announce, just to have something to say. "Not sure I'm a fan. I think they're supposed to be berry flavored, but they taste like acid."

"Because you know what acid tastes like?" His chocolate eyes seem guarded.

"I'm just saying."

"I think it's fun to try out new flavors. But I'm more a fan of the orange ones. And I like that they get more chewy when they're cold." This could be the most detailed discussion of Sour Patch Kids in the history of conversations about sour candy.

"Logan?"

"Yeah?" He fiddles with his yogurt but doesn't eat any. His expression seems halfway between panic and interest. I'm hoping for interest.

"Um, so about what happened with Beck." I stuff my hands into my parka pockets and look anywhere but at Logan. "I thought you were with Isabel and, well, I —"

"Don't worry about it," he interrupts. "You're free to kiss whoever you want. Not up to me." He takes a big bite of sundae and makes an overexaggerated face, as if to imply *Nothing matters when you've got fro-yo!*

"Okay." Maybe he wishes we were still talking about Sour Patch Kids. Or Skittles, maybe? Junior Mints? Even with my stomach churning, I know I shouldn't let him off the hook like that. "It's just . . . well, you seem sort of mad."

He shrugs. "I'm not."

"Great," I manage. "So we're good."

"Of course." He waves me off. "Friends." But he still won't really look at me, stares instead over my shoulder at the ebb and flow of the Village.

"Sure, friends," I echo. "Awesome."

• • •

My schoolwork done for the week, I catch a ride to the Village with Trick on Friday morning. I'm meeting Isabel for a quick coffee when she gets done with the gym and then I'll find Oli on the mountain at ten when she heads to practice.

My phone rings. Josie. With a pang, I realize I haven't talked to her in forever.

"Hi," I say, standing in a patch of sunlight outside of Elevation.

"Where have you been?" she asks. "I texted you twice yesterday!"

"I'm sorry, Jo. Just busy." Ugh, there's that word again.

She sighs. "Tell me about it. You wouldn't believe the number of SAT words we have to memorize for English." Something in the way she says it makes me imagine the white tape of a finish line, both of us struggling to cross it first.

"Yeah, me too." Ms. Raff sent me the list yesterday. My 500 Must! words for the SAT, with the overbearing exclamation point. I haven't even looked at it yet. Josie chatters on — something about junior prom, which she assures me is going to be *totally lame* because they picked the *dumbest theme ever*. I'm only half listening. Through the window of Elevation, I see Beck sitting at a window table. I take a few steps back into a little shadow. He texted me earlier this week about hanging out, but I haven't written back. His head bent over his phone, he hasn't seen me standing outside yet.

The Ski Lift Bench seems like a year ago.

"Mara? Are you there?"

I start. "What? Oh, sorry — the theme. Yeah, it sounds totally dumb. See, this is why I don't go to school dances."

"Seriously, right?"

Beck looks up from his phone, his eyes catching me watching him through the window. He gives a short wave. No avoiding him now. "Um, Jo — I have to run."

"Oh — okay." She sounds hurt, but recovers quickly. "Well, call me soon."

"Definitely." I head into Elevation and cross to Beck's table. "Working hard?"

He shows me the game he's playing on his phone, something with brightly colored blobs that seem to be flinging other brightly colored blobs at each other. "I make it a habit to never work hard at anything." He tries for charming but mostly just seems tired, his hair even more disheveled than usual, bruised dark patches beneath his eyes.

"Everything okay?"

He leans back in his chair. "Okay, sure." Drained of his normal swagger, he seems smaller somehow. "Had a fight with my dad, so, you know, typical Friday morning."

I think of that day in the parking lot, his dad's too-aggressive grab. I glance at his nearly empty coffee cup. "You need a refill?"

His smile doesn't make it to his eyes. "Sure." Just then, Isabel and Logan come through the door, stopping when they see us. Beck leans forward, his forearms resting on the table. "Great. The model citizen brigade." He goes back to his game.

I grab his cup and, at the counter, refill his coffee. Isabel comes up behind me. "Someone looks crabby," she says, her eyes flicking to Beck.

"Fight with his dad."

"Ah." Isabel nods. "So just your average Friday." She hands her mug to Natalie. "Can I get some hot water, Nat?"

I order a latte, then take Beck's coffee to his table. "Do you want to come sit with us?" I motion to where Isabel and Logan huddle at a far table, whispering.

"I think I've had enough behavioral modification lectures for one morning." He takes a sip of his drink. "Thanks for the refill, though."

"Sure." I hesitate, then add, "Sorry about your dad."

"Give me a call sometime," he says, his voice flat, "or keep avoiding me — your choice." He returns to his phone, his shaggy hair falling into his eyes.

•   •   •

I meet Oli at the top of Big Blue. Something about being up here, the slight wind in my face and the stretch of Tahoe scrolling out in front of me, lightens the heaviness of seeing Beck. Oli motions for me to follow him down the catwalk to a Shirley Lake shoot. I take wide turns until I snowplow to a stop at the bottom, grinning. I'd managed the whole run with ease, that light feeling I had at the top intensifying.

"Look who's skiing blues like a star!" Oli waves a ski pole in a victory loop. "Take that, Shirley Lake!"

"Miss Perfect rocks Shirley Lake," I blurt out, feeling like an idiot the second the words emerge. Where did that come from?

The wind flutters the sleeves of his jacket. "That whole video thing really got to you, didn't it? Those dumb kids putting it on the computer."

I poke at some built-up snow on my skis with one of my poles, watching skiers move past in the deep bowl of Shirley Lake. "I guess." I brace myself for whatever version of the *You shouldn't let other people bother you* advice that will now undoubtedly come my way.

But Oli just sighs, studying the lift carrying people back up the mountain. "It must be tough these days, what you kids deal with. It's hard enough to be a teenager, but with the Internet now . . ." He whistles through his teeth. "I actually don't even know much about that MyTube Tweeter stuff. It all seems so brutal."

I burst out laughing at his botching of the names. "YouTube and Twitter, you mean."

"Whatever." He shrugs. "Bunch of nonsense."

"I shouldn't care what other people think of me."

"Hard not to," Oli says. "But I think the important thing to remember is that most people *aren't*."

"Aren't what?"

"Thinking about you." He scissors his skis back and forth. "In my experience, most people are just trying to find their car keys."

He skis off toward the Shirley lift.

TWENTY

I blink twice before I register her. Josie. Standing on our porch, the twilight deepening the charcoal of her down jacket. "Wait — what?!" I manage before she engulfs me. Her brother, Reuben, and a petite woman with short black hair stand behind her, grinning. "You're here?" I keep repeating into her down-jacketed shoulder.

"Inside! I'm freezing!" She pushes me back into the cottage, introducing me to Reuben's girlfriend, Lucy. Josie's eyes sweep the room. "Wow, Mar, this is *tiny*."

"Cozy," I remind her.

"It's darling," Lucy says, her pale blue beanie bright against her dark skin.

They stand like mirages in my living room. "How did . . . what are . . . ?" I stammer.

"We're surprising you, silly!" Josie tucks some hair behind her ears. "I was calling to tell you this morning, but you rushed off the phone. For the weekend! I even took the last three periods off from school today. Reuben and Lucy have been wanting to take a ski weekend up here and I convinced them to let me tag along! We're staying at a fancy hotel! Are you excited?" Josie can seem to talk only in exclamation points or question marks. "Come have dinner with us! Are you surprised? We just got here!" She squints at me.

"Trick didn't tell you, did he? I made him swear he wouldn't tell you."

Her energy like a tidal wave, I take a step back. "You talked to Trick?"

"We called him at his work — at Neverland. He didn't tell you, right? You're not just *pretending* to be surprised." She stares at me intently, decides I'm authentically surprised, and hugs me again.

"*Tranquilo.*" Reuben comes up behind his sister and puts his hands on her shoulders. "Give a girl some air." His brown eyes are warm. I've always adored Reuben. Best big brother ever. "Mara, would you like to join us for dinner? We're staying at PlumpJack."

I'd never been inside the hotel, only walked by it. "Yeah, great!" I say, still feeling breathless but trying to match Josie's energy. "Sorry, I just can't believe you're here."

●　　●　　●

Later, Josie and I sit on one of the queen beds in their hotel room, giggling over our cheeseburgers and fries. Reuben and Lucy decided to eat downstairs in the bar, but they ordered us room service. Reuben claimed they wanted to talk about "boring oceanographer stuff," but I know he wants to give Josie and me time to hang out in private.

Josie finishes a story about a party she went to last weekend with two of the other girls from the jazz band. She drags a fry through some ketchup on her plate. "The cops had to come and tell us the music was too loud, but they said it was the first time they had to tell a bunch of teenagers to turn down *jazz*. So funny."

"Sounds funny," I agree.

She tilts her head, her eyes suddenly serious. "It's so great to see you. When are you coming home?"

I take an extra-long sip of Diet Coke. "I'm not really sure."

"But you'll be back in time for our first match, right? First week of March? I want Coach to sign you up for doubles with me. Should I tell him?" She pulls out her phone.

"I haven't been playing at all," I say, but she's already texting Coach Jeffers.

"Catch me up," she says, taking a huge bite of her burger. While she eats, I tell her about skiing, about getting into a rhythm with Home Hospital, about finding the chem lab at Crest Charter, but mostly I talk about Isabel and Logan. "I spent the first few weeks thinking they're a couple, but they're not — isn't that funny?"

She gives me an amused look. "Is it a good thing for *you* that they're not a couple?" she digs.

I flush. "What? No, nothing like that." I take an unnecessarily large bite of burger.

She looks unconvinced. "If you say so."

I wipe my hands on the white cloth napkin and find myself telling her something that's been niggling at me for weeks. "Anyway, the craziest part of being here is that I'm getting to see this whole other life that got swapped out for the one I actually ended up living. It's so weird."

"Because you almost grew up here?"

"Yeah. This could have been my life. And, I don't know, don't take this wrong, but there's part of me that wishes it was."

Josie frowns at her half-eaten burger. "Maybe your mom wanted you to have a better life than you could have had here?"

179

"People have good lives here, Josie. It's not all beer and ski parties." She looks doubtful. "There's just something about it that sometimes feels like it fits me better than San Diego." I feel like a traitor for saying so, but it's the truth.

Josie sips her soda, carefully choosing her words. "It seems like a lot of people up here are on the fringe, like they're hiding from something. I mean, Trick works at a place called Neverland. There's a reason that's funny." She shakes her head. "I'd go crazy here."

"Don't you think you're being a little judgmental about a place you don't even know?"

Josie looks surprised. "I'm sorry. I don't mean to be. It's just, this place. It kind of *is* Neverland. It's a *vacation* spot, here so people can take breaks from their real lives." I start to argue with her, but she holds up her hand. "Okay, okay, I heard the judgment on that one, sorry. I'm sure people have great lives here, but you've worked too hard to just toss it all away to be a ski bum."

I dunk a fry in my ketchup. "Wow, talk to my mom much lately?"

Her voice soft, she says, "Your mom knows that part of the reason you've worked so hard is because you have a fire in you. It's not just Ranfield causing that fire — it's in you. You're one of the hardest workers I know. Seriously, you have been the whole time we've been at Ran."

"Yeah," I agree, my body deflating with a realization. "But what if that's not such a good thing?"

• • •

"Welcome to Neverland." I stop in front of the shop with Josie, Reuben, and Lucy the next morning before the slopes open. "Let's get you some gear," I say, my voice over-bright. I'm trying too hard.

Josie notices, shooting me an odd look as I hold the door open for them. After our conversation last night, I'm sure it seems like I have something to prove. "I'll get Trick."

I wave to Mr. Never as I pass him at the counter. Pushing through the door to the shop, I find Trick waxing a pair of expensive-looking skis, Piper snuggled in a curl near his feet.

"Oh, hey." He stands, Piper also jumping to her feet with her tail wagging. He wipes his hands on a tattered rag. "They here?"

I nod, wondering what they'll see when they look at Trick, if they'll search him for signs of me.

Of course, maybe I'm the only one looking for these small signs that connect us because he still feels so far away, still a blurry constellation I can't quite make out but know is there.

• • •

"He's nice," Josie says as we take the funi up. She sits next to me on a bench, and Reuben and Lucy sit across the funi from us, talking softly in Spanish. "You kind of look like him."

"I do?" My skin tingles.

She nods, staring out at the expanse of snow. "In the eyes. Not the color. The shape." She looks down at her boots. "So, not a huge fan of these cement blocks, but if you like 'em, I'm game to try." She studies the snow-covered mountains and trees. "Wow, it's freezing, but it's beautiful."

I reach over and squeeze her gloved hand. "Thanks for coming here."

I take Josie, Reuben, and Lucy on Big Blue. Lucy's already a good skier, but it's fun to show Reuben and Josie how to make wide smile turns and pizza slices with their skis. I find myself telling them things Logan and Oli have taught me, passing along hints about balance and turning.

At the bottom of Big Blue, Josie snowplows to a stop near me. "Wow, you're *good*."

"Thing is, I'm not," I tell her. "You should see these kids I ski with up here. Logan's amazing and Isabel might make it to the Olympics someday. Actually, they're racing today — I was planning to go watch them if you want to come?"

Josie nods, and says, "Sure, of course," but there's a trace of annoyance beneath it. I know I've been talking about them too much, my new friends, and she must be sick of hearing it.

I change the subject while we wait for Reuben and Lucy to catch up. "Are you entering the science fair again this year?" I ask, knowing full well that barring some sort of catastrophic event, she wouldn't miss the science fair.

Speaking of natural disasters, she tells me her idea in a spill of words, something about a simulation of the oceans and hurricanes and temperature change. "Reuben's getting me a special measurement program for my computer." She beams. "So I can geek out on all that data."

"That's great, Jo."

·   ·   ·

After a quick break for lunch, Reuben and Lucy head back out to the slopes, but Josie comes with me to watch Logan and Isabel race. "We don't have to go," I insist. "I can see them some other time at a different resort. This just might be the last time I can watch them race at Squaw."

"Sure, let's go." I can't read her eyes behind her mirrored glasses, but she shrugs. "I'm done for the day anyway — my muscles feel like jelly."

We shiver at the bottom of the race hill, the day cold, the sharp metal smell of snow permeating everything. The red and blue flags that dot the downhill racecourse snap in the wind. People mill around us, mostly spectators, but there are also a few of the younger racers in their sleek spandex outfits. Josie nods in the direction of a boy in a liquid-blue suit. "What exactly is Aquaman over there wearing?"

"A racing suit."

"Attractive." Josie jumps up and down in an attempt to stay warm. "Explain again why this is fun. And why there isn't coffee."

I point a gloved hand up the hill. "We'll just stay long enough to see Isabel and Logan."

Before I can say more, the crowd seems to buzz as a whole organism, their combined whispers boosting the level of energy in the space all around us. Isabel must be about to race. Logan told me it's easy to tell when she's about to race because everything around you — all the attention, hope, and energy — suddenly cranks up a notch. It's a good description. I squint up the mountain, through the steely air of the day, watching as the slate-gray streak of Isabel takes form. She shifts and bends around the flags, her body almost parallel to the snow on certain turns. Even from where we stand, it happens fast, and like flash lightning, she crosses the finish to a whooping cry from the collected spectators. I shiver but I'm not cold. Josie doesn't realize it, but I've never seen Isabel race before. Not live. I've seen video clips and heard stories.

Like most things, it's different live.

"Whoa," Josie breathes, clutching my arm.

Whoa doesn't begin to describe it.

We watch a few more racers, none of them with the same grace and speed as Isabel. At a break in the race, as they move from the girls to the boys, Josie leaves to find us mochas and returns with two steaming cups. "Hot beverage?" I take it gratefully.

Soon, it's Logan's turn to race. He barrels down the mountain, his body in rhythm with the red and blue flags, his movements clean, but something goes wrong. An overcorrection of a turn or a split-second catch of an edge, maybe? Whatever the reason, he goes down — hard — his body skidding down the mountain like a stone skipped across a pond. The audience gasps. I see a woman, probably Logan's mom, rush forward, grasping the arm of a guy with a walkie-talkie.

Logan doesn't get up.

I don't realize I'm chewing the plastic lid of my cup until Josie gently nudges me, saying, her voice concerned, "Mara, he'll be okay," and pulls the cup away from my face.

I nod, feeling ill, a liquid stomach-dropping-out-from-under-me sick, and I have to consciously tell myself to focus, to watch, to wait. *Be okay. Be okay. Be okay.* In that moment, I'm certain that time is elastic, that there is no way it always moves in the same ticking sixty-second minute we've been taught to believe in.

Finally, a murmur moves through the crowd, morphing into a cheer. With help, Logan walks off the course. "Wind knocked out," someone says. "Nothing broken," says another voice behind me. I pick up my stomach from the snowy ground, my knees wobbly, my heart beating as if I'd been running.

Josie tilts her head, an amused smile playing at the corner of her mouth. "Yeah, you're right — you don't like this Logan guy at all. Oh, wow, Mara, if you could see your face right now."

•   •   •

That night, Isabel invites us to a party at a friend's condo in the Village. She gives us directions through the maze of buildings and doors and we end up on the top floor. Isabel waits for us in the hallway outside the condo door, leaning against the wall, texting. She hears us coming. "You found it!" She leads us inside to the main room. Music pulses and a couple dozen people mill about, the wide windows showcasing views of the mountains and the purple sky. A fire flickers in a stone fireplace, casting an orange warmth into the room, and Isabel waves to a girl sitting curled in a beanbag near it; she's knitting and talking animatedly with two other girls sitting on the floor in front of her. "That's Kelsey," Isabel tells us. "She races with me. This is her parents' place."

Josie squints at her. "Is she knitting?"

Isabel nods. "Oh, she's always knitting. Actually, she knitted this hat." She points at her own sea-green beanie. "Cute, right?" We nod in agreement, as if everyone knits hats in their spare time. Isabel smiles. "You two want a drink?"

As Isabel heads toward the kitchen, Josie whispers, "Okay, I've changed my mind. You should live here forever. Right here. In this condo. I'll bring you food while you learn to knit."

"Yeah, I just happen to have spare millions here somewhere." I pat at the pockets of my jeans. Probably because we're so nervous in this fancy space, we find this lame joke hilarious and collapse into giggles.

185

Isabel returns with two icy cups of red punch. "Oh, good, you're having fun." She pushes the cups into our hands. I take a sip. Ick. Fruit punch and vodka. It tastes like someone spit in it. Isabel waves to someone across the room. "Let me know if you want something else," she says before moving away to talk to a guy I recognize as one of the Frost Boys always hanging out with Beck. His name sounds like a pharmaceutical company. Bayer? Bristol? Something like that.

I sniff my drink. I know it's not cool, but I prefer fruit punch to be the only thing in my fruit punch. Josie leaves to empty her cup into the kitchen sink and refill it with water.

When she comes back, she says, "So spill it."

"My drink? Gladly." I pour it into an empty cup someone's left sitting on a table.

"Logan," she clarifies.

"It doesn't matter, Jo. He just wants to be friends." I let the words out the way you let air out of a balloon, and it's stupidly painful to hear them out loud.

She shakes her head. "You're going to need to give me the lead-up to why you think that."

I fill her in on the details, leading up to "and then he found out I kissed Beck."

Josie's eyes practically pop out of her head. "Wait, what?! Who?"

As if summoned, Beck materializes from somewhere upstairs. If he had a caption, it would read ADORABLE SKIER BOYS WE LOVE TO HATE. He even pauses to run his hands through his tousled hair before moving smoothly across the room.

"Meet Now List number seven." I nod in his direction.

I have struck Josie dumb, left her gaping at Beck as he moves through the room. He waves at someone, flashing his white smile, and a different girl from the one I saw at their school squeals when she sees him, attaching herself to him like one of those gooey rubber toys my brothers are always throwing at the windows of our house, the ones that slowly unstick and then creep down the wall.

When he's out of view, retreating into a shadowy nook of the kitchen with Sticky Girl, Josie finally peels her eyes away and turns to me. "Who are you?"

"Tahoe Mara," I explain weakly.

She holds up her water in a cheers. "Well, it's nice to meet you, Tahoe Mara. And what have you done with San Diego Mara?"

I stare glumly into my empty cup. "Oh, she's still here, botching things up."

Josie puts an arm around me. "We can go if you want."

I lean into her. "Yes, please."

·   ·   ·

The next day, I say good-bye to Josie, Reuben, and Lucy out in front of PlumpJack. They have to leave by two to catch their flight in Reno, but we got a couple of good skiing hours in this morning and ate lunch at Ethan's.

"Thanks for coming," I say, hugging Josie. "And for — you know."

After leaving the party last night, we'd gone back to Josie's hotel room and I finished filling her in on what had happened with Beck and Logan.

"I can't believe I had to pry this out of you." She'd changed into her pajamas and sat cross-legged on her bed, running a brush through her dark hair. She pointed the brush at me accusatorily. "You should have told me. Especially because it was *my* list number."

"I was embarrassed. He's, well" — I grimaced — "as you saw, he seems to always have a different girl attached to him. It's like he needs them for life support or something."

She tossed the brush into her suitcase on the floor. "There are plenty of guys like that at Ranfield. And girls. You should have told me." After a minute, she asked gently, "And what about Logan?"

"We're just friends."

She pulled her hair into a rope and started braiding it. "Yes, you keep saying that. But I'm asking you how you *feel* about him."

"It doesn't matter. Besides, we're taught from birth not to make any choices because of a boy. To not let some guy influence us, right?"

Her expression was hard to read as she wrapped the end of her braid with an elastic band. She sighed. "That doesn't stop it from happening."

Now, standing in the wind outside PlumpJack, she holds on to me a little longer than she normally would. "See you soon, okay? Enjoy the rest of your time here. But then come *home*."

I nod into her shoulder as I hug her back.

TWENTY-ONE

I wake the next morning, my mind cloudy from dreaming about that horrible day in calculus, the way I looked in the video, my peach-pit face, the confetti of tests. Sweating, nerves buzzing, it takes a moment to remember I'm here in Tahoe, far north of it all.

The dream fades, replaced by warm blankets, the sight of snow floating past my window, the hot wood smell of the fire. More than a month ago and it's obviously still bothering me. What had Oli said? Most people aren't even thinking about you — they're just looking for their car keys. Is that true? That most people don't even notice what happens to everyone else?

It seems like the whole world watched that video.

I sit up and rub my eyes, feeling suddenly sad that we live in a world where most of the time we're practicing detachment exercises just to get through the day.

I push the covers back, get dressed, and catch a ride to the Village with Trick. I want to buy cookies for Logan at Elevation. Isabel texted last night to tell me he was going to be fine after his fall, but that he'd bruised his hip pretty badly and had to stay off the mountain for a few days.

Later, cookies in hand, I push through the door to Neverland, and Piper greets me with her slobbery kisses and flurry of golden

189

hair. "Hey, sweetie," I say, petting her. Satisfied, she trots back to where she was sleeping next to a space heater. A woman stands behind the counter, flipping through a catalog, her tangle of dark curls pulled into a loose ponytail. Logan's mom, Jessica Never. I recognize her from the photos at Logan's house and from Saturday at the race, only her face is no longer furrowed with worry.

Chewing the end of a pencil, she looks up. "Mara!"

"Oh, hi." I hang close to the door.

"Sorry, I'm Jessica." She hesitates, then adds, "We haven't officially met yet, I guess. Even if I did change your diapers."

What is with these people and diapers? "Oh, right," I say, chewing my lip and wondering if it would be rude to just turn and flee the building.

She shakes her head, looking uneasy. "Sorry, that was a totally weird thing to say."

"No, it's fine." It *was* weird. It's been strange to have so many people squint at me the way you would into a grainy old photo album. "Um, is Logan here?" I hold up the dark-chocolate coconut cookies. "I wanted to see if he was feeling better."

"That's so sweet!" She tugs absently at the end of her ponytail. "He's not here. Do you want to leave them with me? He's at the other store with Matt."

"Um, no — it's fine. I'll catch him some other time." I turn to leave.

"Mara?"

"Yeah?"

Jessica has both hands flat on the counter and she's studying me with Logan's dark eyes. "How . . . well, how's it going up here?

With . . . everything?" Her eyes flick to the counter once before adding, "Are things going okay with Trick?"

My stomach evaporates, like it's suddenly trying to float away from the rest of my body. "Um, I think so."

She fiddles with the catalog. "I know it's none of my business, but I just want you to know . . . he never meant, well, he thought it was for the best, okay? Your mom had a plan and he was just trying to honor that."

What is she talking about? What plan? "Okay."

The bell behind me jingles, and I turn to see Trick standing there, looking strangely at Jessica. "Hey," he says, rubbing some snow from his hair.

"Cookies!" I blurt, holding up the bag.

"Sure, thanks." He takes them.

Jessica stares intently at the catalog.

I mumble something about school and this time flee the store for real.

Walk it off, let it go, don't worry about it.

I owe Logan some cookies.

• • •

Dr. Elliot called me yesterday afternoon, leaving a sweet-voiced message on my phone — *Give me a call if you think it would be helpful.*

If I think it would be helpful.

So even though I actually like Dr. Elliot, I don't call him back. He seems perfectly nice in his mountain-hued, fountain-humming office, but I can't bring myself to drag myself up those stairs. Of course, Mom will not appreciate my taking advantage of his generous *if*, that tiny two-letter word of wiggle room. Now I'm just deliberately not doing my job.

On Tuesday, I go to chem lab, and afterward Isabel and I walk to the Second Story, the restaurant her mom manages on the actual second story of an old building just off the main stretch of downtown Truckee. Logan didn't come to lab today, so I have another bag of cookies jammed into my backpack. "I thought his hip was better?"

Isabel looks sideways at me, her breath making patches of fog in the freezing air. "Why don't you text him?"

I shift the weight of my backpack where my chem book is digging into my spine. "I don't want to bother him if he's recovering."

She shoots me a funny look but doesn't say anything as we climb the stairs. The restaurant has an old glass door, its name etched into the glass over an emblem of an antique typewriter. Inside, its books-and-writing theme hits me. Poster-size copies of famous novel covers line the walls, and a bookshelf crammed with endless titles takes up a full wall. Even the napkin holders look like books.

"Oh, I get it. The second *story*. Cute." I pick up a menu, my eyes scanning the literary-themed sections: Brave New Salads, As I Lay Frying, The Catcher in the Pie. There is even one whole section just for burgers and hot sandwiches under the heading To Grill a Mockingbird. I point this out to Isabel. "This does not sound appetizing at all."

Isabel surveys the semi-full restaurant, waving to a gray-haired man reading a newspaper at one of the corner tables near the window, in front of an open laptop. "The woman who owns this place is a total book nerd."

"Clearly."

She leans in close, nodding at the gray-haired man. "That's her husband. He writes creepy murder mysteries."

I stare at the man's kind face, his casual jeans and sweater. "Really?"

From the back, Isabel's mom emerges, checking a clipboard. Looking up, she sees us. "Hi, girls!" She tosses the clipboard on top of the glossy wood bar. Her hair is a carbon copy of Isabel's, only with streaks of white shooting through it.

Isabel slides into a chair at a table near the bar and flips through a paperback someone has left on the table. "Can we have some fries?"

"You must be Mara. I'm April." Isabel's mom comes out from behind the bar.

"Hi." I smile awkwardly at the same knowing look she has that Jessica Never was wearing when I went into Neverland yesterday. I guess Tahoe is full of Ghosts of Diaper Changes Past.

She nods at the menu in my hand. "You hungry?"

I set it down. "Oh, I'm fine."

"We'd love some *fries*," Isabel mentions again, reading the back of the book.

"Yes, we know." April shakes her head, heading back to the kitchen. "Only I missed the part where you said please and told me how nice I look today."

Isabel flashes her mom an overwide smile. "Great hair day, Mom! How about those fries, pretty please?"

"Your sincerity is staggering." April disappears through the kitchen door.

I slide into the chair across from Isabel. "Your mom seems nice."

Isabel sets the book down. "She's a good mama bear." We don't say anything for a minute, the air around us peppered with the conversations of the other diners, the clinking of utensils on plates, and the swing of the kitchen door as a server brings us a basket of fries and some ice waters. Nibbling a fry, Isabel studies me.

Uncomfortable with the stare-down, I ask, "What? Why are you looking at me like that?"

She shakes the ketchup bottle, looks annoyed at the lack of its progress, then beats the back of it until a small trickle of ketchup emerges. Isabel will *not* be bested by a ketchup bottle. Victorious, she sets it down. Chewing at last, she points half a fry at me. "Why don't you talk to Logan? You clearly like him."

"What?" I sputter. "No, I don't — I mean, he's fine. Whatever." It's my turn to battle with the ketchup bottle, which might be the exact color of my face now.

She cocks an eyebrow. "Convincing."

April returns to our table, rescuing me from further interrogation, and sets down a small oval platter of sliders. "You need some protein, too."

Isabel and I each grab one. "Lord of the Sliders," I say, holding up the tiny cheeseburger.

April laughs. "That's good. We should change the name." She disappears back into the kitchen.

Isabel does not release her death stare at me until I say, "Okay, look, Logan's great, but it doesn't matter anyway. He said he just wants to be friends."

"Oh, did he?" She snorts into her slider. "That figures."

"Why?" I press, but then hurry to say, "Never mind, it doesn't matter. I should just focus on getting my life back on track."

She leans a bit forward. "But I thought you came up here to take a break? Have some fun?"

"Right, fun." I stare at the mystery writer. He has put his paper away and is typing intently on his laptop, maybe killing off a character. I haven't read a mystery novel since Nancy Drew. I think of all the things on my first Now List I crossed off when I first got to Tahoe and then never did again. "I sort of suck at having fun."

Finishing her slider, she nods, her mouth full. "Yeah, Trick told us that."

"Wait, what?"

"When you first got here. He told us you were this super-serious workaholic and that we should show you some fun while you were here."

My head starts to throb. I set down my half-eaten slider. "Wait, so he, like, told you guys to hang out with me?"

She sees my face. "It wasn't like that. He was looking out for you. I mean, you'd just had that huge meltdown and he was worried."

My skin prickling, I say, "Well, he doesn't exactly talk to me, so I really wouldn't know." Clearly, Trick talks to other people, though — just not his own daughter.

She bites her lip. "Don't be mad. He was worried. He said that video really messed you up. Actually, he thinks that school is messing you up. Wait," she pleads. "Don't tell him I told you that."

I fold my arms across my chest, my heart racing. "You wouldn't have to if he'd try talking to *me* about it."

Isabel frowns. "I'm sorry I said something. He was being sweet, seriously. He's a good guy."

I don't say anything, just pick at the basket of fries. I can't believe Trick told them to hang out with me. How humiliating. Like I'm in preschool or something and he's setting up a playdate.

Watching me, Isabel swallows hard but then brightens. "You know what? Bodie was in a YouTube video once that got a bunch of views. His pants fell down during a race, tripped him, and it was a complete shot of his butt." She holds up her hands like a director surveying a shot for a movie. "Full. Moon."

She succeeds in getting a smile out of me. "Knowing Bodie, that sounds like something he would be proud of."

She nods. "True. He was. But it got, like, ten thousand views or something."

I play musical salt and pepper shakers, my smile fading. "That's the difference, then. He was proud of it." Outside, the Truckee sky starts to darken, that purple stain like grape juice soaking into cotton that starts early here. It must be close to four-thirty. "And mine had over six hundred thousand."

She looks shocked. "Seriously?"

I guess she hasn't seen it. "Miss Perfect's Epic Meltdown. After it happened, reporters called to interview me." I put on a mock interviewer voice. "Was the pressure of being a driven teenager too much for you? Do you think you're a casualty of the perfectionist teen culture? How did you *feel* when you ripped up all those tests?" I shake my head and toss my uneaten fry onto the plate. "It was mortifying."

Her sympathy takes its most common form, the head tilt. "Listen, Trick was just trying to watch out for you."

"Well, that would be a first."

Isabel hesitates, then digs through her bag. She pushes a polished, red-orange stone across the table to me. "Here."

I pick it up, its smooth red surface streaked with pale orange and almost translucent, like glass. "What's this?"

"It's a carnelian stone." At my puzzled expression, she explains further. When she was in eighth grade, she went on a trip to Carnelian Bay on Lake Tahoe, which was named for all these red-orange stones on the shore. That day, the guide told them how these stones held protective and healing properties, how they were used to ward off difficulty or evil. "I know it sounds a bit lame and hippie-ish, but I give them to all my friends — Logan, Bodie, Joy, Amanda — a bunch of people. Only I think Bodie lost his. Because he's an idiot. Anyway, they're to protect you from other people, mostly from how selfish and jealous people can be and how that can spill over onto us all the time if we're not careful. Believe me, I know. So I keep my carnelian with me like an amulet." She pulls a small stone from the pocket of her jacket and holds it up. "I don't race without it." I must look unsure, because she shrugs. "I know, I know, it's superstitious and weird but it works. Anyway, I got you one. For you to keep with you because, you know, it seems like you might need it."

I turn the glossy stone over in my hands, my eyes welling. "Thanks, Isabel." Tucking it safely in my pocket, I blink quickly. "What are you up to this week? Want to try to ski a little on Friday or something? I mean, I know I'm terrible, but Oli says I'm getting a lot better."

Her face falls. "I can't — we're leaving Thursday for Mammoth. We have a race there this weekend."

"Oh, right — okay." I try not to look disappointed. "Well, have fun!"

There's that word again.

TWENTY-TWO

Wednesday morning, I stare into a latte at Elevation and think about having fun. What do I do for fun? I guess I'd always thought tennis was fun, only the last year or so, it has kind of felt like one of my jobs. School used to be fun. I was that kid in elementary school who earned all her monthly STAR STUDENT! buttons (which I still have in a shoe box under my bed). And sometimes learning is still fun; it's just that there's too much of it. Too many essays and tests and SAT words and reading and studying and starting all over again each week. At what point do we reach a saturation point and there's no room left?

Not that Ranfield's not fun. We have a hyperactive student government who are always creating dances, activities, charity drives, festivals. But I don't go to many of those because I'm busy trying to keep afloat in the school part. And also because most of their events feel stressful and competitive. How many cans of food can you bring for the needy? How many laps can you do to raise money for the homeless shelter? How many pages can you read to earn books for the library downtown? Everyone's always trying to win at everything all the time. Even when it's for a good cause. It's exhausting and really doesn't feel that fun at all.

Or maybe I just don't know how to have fun.

Could I be having fun right now? I look around the café. It's sort of fun to study here by the crackling fire, with a steaming latte, listening to that new indie band Natalie has playing low on the speakers. Maybe I should buy a chocolate chip cookie? Cookies are fun. I stare at my AP history textbook. Fun's not so easy when I'm supposed to be reading a section called "America Chooses Imperialism." Maybe it would be fun if it were *American Imperialism: The Musical*, featuring the songs "Three Cheers for Oppression!" and "Just Give Me That!" Actually, that gives me a good idea for the next project.

I'm scribbling notes when I feel someone standing over me. "Hey, San Diego." Beck slides into the seat across from me. "Still avoiding me?"

"Obviously not very well." I give him a quick smile but make a show of flipping a few pages of my history textbook.

He pouts. "You didn't even say hi at the party the other night."

"You had something attached to your face." I pretend to think about it. "I think her name starts with an *M*. Madison, maybe? I don't know. Do you even keep track?"

He laughs in that charcoaly way of his that I'm sure he practices in front of a mirror. "Wow, jealous. A nice color on you."

"Not jealous. Concerned. I know how you don't like to work too hard. And keeping track of all of your girlfriends seems like a time management issue for you."

"Not really." He stands up, waving to someone outside. Not a girl, for the record. "And I always know where to find the ones I like best." He gives my shoulders a little squeeze and saunters out.

Can it count as fun to love-hate someone? I open my Now List II where I'd carefully written *HAVE MORE FUN* in all caps as #7.

(I'd also added "Be more spontaneous!" as #8 for good measure. And "No boys!" for #9.)

I'm totally crossing off #7.

•   •   •

A few hours later, I'm almost done with my AP history notes when suddenly someone is hiding under my table. "Um, hello?" I peer beneath it.

Logan crouches there, a finger to his lips. "Shhhh. Look like you're studying."

"I am studying."

"Shhhh."

Someone's feeling better. I return to my notes. Minutes later, Bodie flashes by outside the window at a run, looping back when he sees me. Jogging in place, he mouths, "Logan?" I shake my head, shrugging a *haven't seen him*, and he takes off at a run again around the corner of the store.

"He's gone," I say in an overexaggerated whisper.

"Give it a minute." Logan's voice floats out from his hiding spot.

He's right. Bodie flashes by the window one more time, going in the opposite direction. I dutifully study my notes, but who am I kidding? No way am I absorbing any relevant information about the Progressive Reforms of Theodore Roosevelt when Logan Never has wedged himself beneath my table, his back pressed into my shins.

Logan pokes his head above the table. "Okay, that's plenty of time."

I smile at his hair, messed up from the table. "What was that about? You're lucky you don't have gum in your hair."

He checks for it anyway. "Snow tag." He slips into the chair next to me. "What are you up to?"

"Nothing as fun as snow tag." I close the book. "Which is what, by the way?"

His eyes slipping to the window again, just in case he needs to duck at any moment, he explains that he and some of the other Frost Boys created this elaborate game of snow tag years ago and it kept evolving into an ongoing thing they play. They hound one another all over the mountain, following clues from people they know who are willing to rat someone out, until they tag someone who needs tagging.

"But that could take days."

"Sometimes," he agrees. "But mostly not." He looks at my closed book. "Want to come?"

Have more fun. "Do I need to be in my ski stuff?"

"It helps."

•　　•　　•

"I don't think I like this game," I say, peering over the edge of the chairlift into a wide canyon. Logan talked me into taking the Red Dog chair over to the Squaw Creek resort, and it feels way sketchier than the other ones we've been on as it shivers and creaks over a deep ravine. "Yeah, I don't like this lift at all."

Logan kicks back in the chair. "It's fine."

"That doesn't look fine," I say, pointing down. "That is what death looks like."

Chuckling, he slings an arm across the back of the lift, his glove just brushing my shoulder. "You worry a lot."

201

"Wow, Logan Never with the insightful observations." My nerves don't let the tease come out lightly and instead I sound defensive.

He notices and lets his gloved hand fall to my shoulder, giving it a reassuring squeeze. "I won't let you die on Red Dog."

Not convinced, I study a ski patroller who glides by beneath us in his red jacket, wondering how many people he's had to pull down the mountain today in one of those little sleds I've seen zipping by. "Is it much longer?" I try to look ahead to see the end of the lift, but suddenly, the whole chair shudders. Then stops. I seize the bar in fear. "What's happening? Why are we stopping?"

Logan looks behind him. "Don't know. Sometimes they have to stop the lift because someone falls off."

One hand on the front bar, I clamp my other hand on the side rail for support. "What do you mean, someone *falls off*?"

"Not from up here. Usually when they're trying to get on or off. Or they had a mechanical thing. It happens." He is way too casual about dangling up here midair.

"How long?"

He shrugs, craning his head to see up ahead, where the lift in front of us sways, the two guys on snowboards jostling each other. To distract myself, I take off my gloves, pull out my binder from my backpack, and flip it open to the Now List II. I scribble a huge star by Will's *Be brave*. Then I add another star next to it. I've earned at least two sitting up here. I also cross off *Be more spontaneous!* because this totally counts.

"What's that?" Logan motions at the binder.

"Nothing." I try to jam it back into my backpack, but Logan's too quick and he grabs it. He has the whole not-scared-to-be-suspended-above-a-ravine thing going for him, which makes him agile. You'd think he was sitting in a porch swing.

"Please don't read that," I say without much heart behind it. Maybe fear makes me docile.

"'The Now List II,'" he reads. "'Be more spontaneous!' Crossed off." He flips a few pages. Grinning, he looks up. "Wait, you made checklists? For living in the now?"

I tuck my poles farther under my legs. "It helps me."

"'Be more spontaneous!'" he reads again. "You know, writing it down is actually the opposite of being spontaneous."

I take a shaky breath. "Can I have my binder back, please? Ack!" The lift trembles and starts to move forward again.

"See, we're going again." He flips through the rest of the binder, the scratched-out former list, the articles and highlights, and all my notes. "This is . . . well, I've never seen anything quite like this before, Mara." But his voice is affectionate. He closes it and holds it up. "Nice cover. Very *now*." A picture of one of the Squaw Valley fire pits.

I try not to laugh. Seeing him there, holding it, it all suddenly seems a little silly. I shrug. "It works for me."

"To be more spontaneous?"

"Sure."

Then Logan Never tosses my Now binder off the ski lift.

"WHAT DID YOU JUST DO?!" For a second, as I watch it sail through the air and hit the snow below, where it slides and then comes to a stop, I forget I'm scared and lean heavily forward on the bar, rocking the lift back and forth. I stare at Logan, stunned. "You did *not* just throw my binder off a ski lift?!"

He feigns a look of surprise. "I was being spontaneous."

Shaking my head, I sit back, my body flooding with nerves and disbelief. "Like I don't have a backup copy."

· · ·

We spend an hour skiing into the Squaw Creek resort area. Exhausted, I collapse into a wide chair near a large glowing bonfire. A few minutes later, Logan brings me a hot cocoa, setting it on the arm of his side of the chair.

A flash of red catches my eye. I sit up, my cocoa sloshing on my sleeve. "Hey! I think that kid is sledding on my binder!" I point to a group of three kids in ski bibs taking turns sliding down a snow bank. The youngest one, in a white-and-chocolate-brown suit that makes him look like a s'more, clamps his small hands on the edges of the binder as he zips down the bank.

Logan leans in and says in a teasing whisper, "He's living in the now."

"Oh, forget it," I say, leaning back to sip my cocoa and let the bonfire warm my face. "Good for him."

Without warning, Bodie springs out from behind us. "Tag!" he shouts, grabbing Logan's shoulders.

"Oh, no! He found you because you were sitting out here with me instead of hiding." I watch Logan mop hot cocoa off his pants while Bodie does a victory dance that compels the couple next to us to actually get up and leave. Probably because he's making noises that sound like a sick rooster.

Logan glances up and meets my eyes. "Totally worth it."

· · ·

Mom Skypes with me on Thursday night as I'm settling into bed with my laptop, which is weird because she hates to Skype. It doesn't let her do twelve other things at the same time. "You're not answering your phone?"

My phone is currently dead at the bottom of my bag. "Hi to you, too."

"Hi. Why aren't you answering your phone?" She's sitting at our kitchen table. I catch a glimpse of the granite island behind her and can hear the low whoosh of the dishwasher.

"It ran out of power. Hold on, I'll charge it now." I throw off the covers, dig it out, and plug it into the wall.

When I'm back in front of the screen, she asks, "Did you reschedule with Dr. Elliot?"

My body's sore from a day of skiing, and with the warm glow of the fire, I could fall asleep in about five seconds. "Not yet."

"Mara!"

I burrow deeper into my pillow, watching the flames twitch and shift through the glass door of the woodstove. "Dr. Elliot said I should only come in *if* it felt helpful."

"How Tahoe of him." No one does patronizing quite like Mom.

I try to distract her. "How're the twins? Can I say hi to them?"

"It's nine. They're in bed," she says, as if I've asked to fly them to the moon in a helicopter made of cheese.

"Oh, yeah. Bedtime."

I listen to her report on the twins' science projects taking up half the kitchen, the difficult case keeping Will up all hours of the night, and the condo she just sold near where we live in North Park to the most annoying hipster couple ever. Finally, she says, "Okay, I won't bug you anymore about scheduling."

"Really?" A log shifts in the woodstove, sending the shadows on the ceiling dancing. "No more Google calendar alerts?"

"You're obviously not using them." Mom clears her throat, then says, "Actually, I'm mostly calling because I wanted to let you know I'll be coming up tomorrow."

"Tomorrow?" Who needs a Google calendar when you can monitor at close range?

"I'll be flying into Reno in the late afternoon. I should be there by dinnertime if it doesn't take a million years to get my rental car. Will you make reservations for dinner?"

"Valentine's Day's not until Sunday. We probably won't need reservations tomorrow." I hesitate, then bravely add, "What's this trip about?"

"Maybe I want to see my favorite valentine?"

"Right." But there has to be more to it than that. I should have just rescheduled the stupid appointment.

"Make reservations for dinner, okay? Somewhere in Truckee; let's get you out of the valley for a bit. You must be going stir-crazy."

"Not really."

Her silence hums with disappointment. "Okay, then — wherever you want to eat. A place with *vegetables*. I don't even want to think about what you're eating while you're there."

"I had vegetable soup for dinner."

She exhales a wind-through-a-shell sigh. "Probably from a can. Listen, I have to go. I have contracts I need to get out to people." Leaning into the screen so her face seems to swell dramatically, she says, "Mara, when I'm up, we need to talk about how to best reintegrate when you come home."

Reintegrate. It sounds like something someone dressed in khaki does with a wild animal.

After we hang up, my stomach blooms with nerves, making it almost impossible to concentrate on the imperialism essay I'm finishing. My history teacher had vetoed my *American Imperialism: The Musical* idea. Apparently, he didn't think it was very appropriate to make fun of something like imperialism, and I didn't have the strength to argue the power of satire with him via my Home Hospital coordinator.

Throwing back the blanket, I wiggle into some jeans and zip a parka over my pajama top. As I slip into my Uggs, I grab a beanie, gloves, and a scarf and walk into the main room. Trick sits on the couch, watching a ski movie. I know enough now to see it's a Warren Miller film he's watched a million times. "I'm going for a quick walk."

"Now?" He sits up a little, scratching his stubbly face. He leaves a little smudge of ash on his cheek, his hands dirty from the fire.

I yank my beanie down over my ears. "Just for, like, ten minutes. To clear my head. I'm having a hard time on this paper I'm writing."

"Was that your mom?"

"Yeah." I wind the scarf around my neck. "She's coming up tomorrow."

A flash of panic crosses his features. "Tomorrow — why?"

I make a face. "She claims she misses me, but I think she wants to talk me into coming home." I hold the words out to him almost like a litmus test.

His eyes lock with mine for a moment, but he only says, "Well, take the flashlight. It's pitch-dark out."

Outside, the air might actually have teeth. I'm shivering before I even pull my gloves on. I walk down the sanded street, moving as quickly as I can without slipping. Questions pulse through my brain, forming a list of the things I can never quite bring myself to say out loud to Trick:

Do you want me to go home?
Why did you think I couldn't make friends on my own?
Why haven't you taken me skiing?
Where have you been all my life?

A flash of anger warms me. Why should I always have to ask the questions? Doesn't he have anything to ask me? To *say* to me? Like, for example, *Gee, biological daughter, what have you been up to for the last thirteen years?*

At the end of our street, I stomp up a sloped hill that leads to a view of Squaw's famous KT-22. Reaching the crest, I stop, my breath making puffs in the air around me. Clouds obscure the moon, leaving it a glowing smudge against black sky. Up on the mountain, far away, a single groomer moves in lonely sweeps across the slopes, its light cutting a swath across the face of the mountain. I can just make it out, sailing like a ship along the dark mountain, and it's nice to know I'm not the only one out here tonight. I watch its sluggish light until it starts to snow again and I can barely feel my face before heading back.

TWENTY-THREE

The snow stopped sometime during the night, but there is enough of it that we need to dig ourselves out this morning. Mom will be here tonight and Trick wants to make sure she can get in the driveway and up the path to the house. I notice he's doing an especially detailed job. I bundle up and join him. He hands me a battered wide-mouth shovel that has clearly seen years of use and shows me where to begin on the path. Then he heads back to the driveway.

Trick was asleep last night when I crept back into the house, his heavy breathing even and measured — not worried at all if I'd frozen to death outside on my walk. The covers pulled to my chin, I'd missed my mom terribly as I fell asleep, even with all her spreadsheets and Google calendars and seashell sighs through the phone. *She* would have waited up for me to come home.

Now I shovel snow off the path, heaping it into a berm on the side of the driveway, the shovel scraping against the stone pathway. My cheeks flush and my breath quickens as I hurl shovelfuls of it to the side. I think about all the things I don't know about my life when I lived here, how as a three-year-old I was just whisked away and life here went on without me. People skied and Logan and Isabel went to picnics by the lake and Trick worked at Neverland and buried my naked mole rat book beneath a pile of fleece pullovers. And I went to Ranfield and melted down in front of a classroom of teenagers, one mean enough to film it so more than six hundred thousand people could watch it.

But it could have all been different.

I could have been living here, picnicking by lakes and skiing down mountains and tucking carnelian stones into the pocket of my jeans. It was a kind of theft, what was taken from me. This could be my life right now if two people had decided it was worth it to figure it out. I wouldn't just be taking a break.

It would be my *whole life*.

"Hey, Mara — not so high on that —" Trick starts to say, but I whirl on him, sending snow flying, and he ducks, shocked at what must be the rage on my face.

"What happened with you and Mom? What could possibly have been so bad that you couldn't work it out? Your stupid skiing career? That was more important than knowing your own daughter?"

"Whoa, wait — what?" He holds his hands up in defense, as if I might hurl more snow in his direction. Or throw the shovel at him.

"And then — what? You just gave up? You just said, oh, well, the kid's gone now . . . and what? Shoveled the driveway? Got a beer? Thirteen years and I saw you once! What is *wrong* with you?" I toss the shovel into the snow and storm back to the house.

"Hang on — Mara!" Trick tries to follow me but slips on the icy unsanded drive.

I track snow into the room and grab my phone from the coffee table. Isabel and Logan are gone — in Mammoth. I might be in Mammoth right now if my parents weren't so selfish. My eyes land on Beck's number. With shaking fingers, I text him.

you have to come get me at trick's! i'm freaking out!

He immediately writes back.

be right there.

I stomp into my room, slamming the door, but Trick doesn't come inside. Fifteen minutes later, an old Jeep Wagoneer in mint condition pulls into what's cleared of the driveway. I hurry outside to it, wading through snow to my knees in places. Trick sits on the pile of snow I'd made earlier, his face in his hands. Seeing him, I have a stab of guilt, so I try not to look at him as I move around to the passenger side of the Jeep and climb in. I'm not even supposed to be driving with Beck. California law. But I don't care right now.

Beck studies Trick sitting there. "Where to?"

I snap my seat belt into place. "Anywhere."

"Gotcha." Beck backs out of the driveway. We drive in silence down the hill, turning left onto Squaw Valley Road. Finally, as we turn right on Highway 89 toward Tahoe City, he asks, "You okay?"

We sail past the turnoff to Alpine Meadows and the River Ranch. I study the heaps of snow clogging the Truckee River as it snakes alongside us on the right, a silent, wintry yawn. "Not really." Occasionally, I see a house on the other side of the river, footbridges arching across a stretch of winter water. I wonder who lives in those houses or if they're empty like so many of the others.

"I'm glad you called," Beck says, driving through an intersection that leads us into the main stretch of Tahoe City, passing the Tahoe City Neverland store on the left. "You can always call me." He puts a warm hand on my knee. Or maybe the warmth is from the guilt

211

washing through me. I wouldn't have called him if Isabel or Logan had been in town.

Beck finds a parking spot on the street in front of Syd's Bagelry. I get out of the car, momentarily struck with the wide expanse of Lake Tahoe suddenly in view. "Wow," I breathe, my eyes drinking in the inky whitecapped water, massive against the distant snow-covered mountains. The water is empty of boats; only white buoys here and there dot the surface near the shoreline. Beck joins me, his hair whipped by the wind, and tugs me toward the door of the café.

We head inside and I find a table while he orders coffees. Beck checks his phone, cursing at something he reads there, then crosses to our table, sliding into the seat next to me. "You're a sight for sore eyes. I've had the worst week ever."

"Oh — I'm sorry." I stumble at his sudden shift of mood.

The waitress brings out steaming coffees for us, both black. I head to the counter and pour a generous amount of milk into mine. As I sit back down, he launches into a story about his parents, how they fight all the time, how even though they got divorced last year, they still can't stop constantly screaming at each other. Mostly about him. About what a huge disappointment he is to both of them. He leaves twice to refill his coffee. Sitting back down, he blurts, "And I just found out if I don't pass math, I can't graduate a year early like I planned. Some stupid requirement." He stares glumly into his already half-empty mug.

What happened to *School is just a system of tyranny*? "I thought you didn't care about society imposing standards on you or whatever? Wouldn't that include a high school diploma?"

He looks at me sharply but tries to hide it behind a shrug. "I don't. It's a stupid system that only rewards rule followers. It's the

212

opposite of an education." I've heard this argument before. "But my dad says I have to graduate or he's cutting me off."

But this detail is new. "What math are you in?"

"Geometry."

I sip my coffee. "I can help you with that."

He sits up. "Seriously? That'd be great. Just enough to pass. I mean, a diploma is a totally arbitrary piece of paper, but it's part of the deal I made with Dad the Despot." He finishes his coffee in a long gulp. "Four more months and then I'm out from under it all. On my own." He leaps out of his seat and I see him hurry to his car, open a back door, and pull out a backpack.

I can't help but think that he will *not* actually be on his own if his dad continues to bankroll his life, but I'm pretty sure he won't be interested in that particular observation right now. He returns, dumping a geometry book on the table.

"Wait, now?"

He flips open the book. "Sure, why not?"

"Oh, I just, well, I —" I almost tell him about Trick, about our fight, but he doesn't really seem to be listening. Instead, I opt for "My mom's coming to town this afternoon, so I'm not sure I have time."

The barista walks by, carrying a sandwich to a table, where she chats with two guys in beanies and ski pants. Beck eyes their plates. "Whoa, that looks great. Want one?"

He jumps up again. He's jittery and weird, not his usual calm swagger. No more coffee, Mr. Davis. I deposit his mug in a nearby busing tray while he's at the counter.

We sit in the café as the late morning turns into afternoon and it starts to grow dark outside, storm clouds clogging the sky again, the air holding just a few glints of snowflakes. Our empty sandwich plates pushed away and two chapters of geometry later, I sit back and study the paintings on the wall by a local artist, mostly abstracts.

One is called *Sorrow.*

I tell Beck about a site I used to follow. "It's called The Dictionary of Obscure Sorrows. Have you seen it?" He shakes his head, rubbing his math-bleary eyes. "It's all these made-up words for emotions that don't have names. One I really liked was *nodustollens*: the realization that the plot of your life doesn't make sense anymore."

He looks up from the problem he's working on. "Does the plot of your life not make sense?"

"Not really."

"Bummer." He returns to his scribbles on the page.

Bummer?

Outside, the snow is floating in thick flakes past the window. The tangle in my stomach begins to shift. "It's starting to snow pretty hard. I think we should head back."

He looks over his shoulder at the snow. "It's not bad. But if you want to leave, we can."

"I should go. My mom's coming soon and she's already furious with me. One more thing and she might pack me on a plane back to San Diego tomorrow." *And I really don't want to sit here with you anymore because you only care about yourself, you big jerk*, I don't add. Standing, I carry our plates to the busing tray.

We head out into the storm and climb into the Jeep. Beck makes a U-turn and heads back toward Squaw Valley. The snow picks up, swirling into the windshield. We pass only one or two other cars. Beck leans the Jeep into the oncoming snowfall, moving us faster and faster along the silent highway.

He's going too fast and I feel the Jeep slipping on the fresh snow beneath the tires. "Maybe you should slow down?"

He looks surprised. "You don't need to worry — this isn't fast."

"It's just the weather seems bad." I hold the seat beneath me with both hands.

"I've been driving in snow since I was twelve. This is nothing." He pushes harder on the accelerator, his eyes intent on the road ahead. We fly down the highway, the car slipping and skidding through the storm. My heart hammers and my stomach drops.

It's too fast.

"Beck, slow down."

"It's fine." But it's not fine. He overcorrects around a turn and the Jeep skids to the side. He catches it, but we both know that, for a scary moment, he'd lost control.

He slows down and we make the rest of the trip to the Squaw intersection in silence. As we wait for the light to turn green, he looks at me, his expression sheepish. "I really wasn't going that fast." Clenching my jaw, I ignore him. When I don't say anything for a minute he adds, "Seriously, you need to relax. You'll end up being afraid of everything with that attitude."

Not turning to him, I say quietly, "I'm not sure I need a lesson in bravery from you."

He doesn't respond, winding the Jeep through the valley as outside the world grows heavy with snow. Finally, as we near Trick's place, he mumbles, "It wasn't that fast." He tries to pat my leg, but I angle my body away from him, a new made-up word flashing through my mind.

Cherk: a charming jerk. Beck Davis is a cherk.

I stare out at the snowy world and don't reply. As he pulls into Trick's driveway, my stomach drops for the second time. Mom is already here, getting out of her rented SUV. Her eyes go wide when she sees me pull in with Beck, her mouth falling open. She takes the distance between our cars in huge strides, and before I can unbuckle, she whips the door open. "Out of the car."

"Mom, I got it."

"No, Mara. You clearly don't *got it*. Out of the car." She keeps her voice low, but her anger vibrates more intensely than if she'd been yelling.

I get out of the car.

• • •

Later, I sit across from Mom at a back table at Ethan's (where I had *not*, she noted, made a reservation). After she seats us, Maggie looks worriedly in my direction and brings us a free fried zucchini appetizer. Mom's still mad; it radiates off her like those heat shimmers that rise up from hot pavement in the desert.

Finally, she says, "I'm trying to understand, Mara, I am. I'm trying to find a reason why you thought it was okay to get into that car today with Beck Davis. Not only did you break the law, worse — you put your life in danger driving with him in this kind of weather." She shakes her head. "It's not like you to cause this kind of trouble." *Get in a little trouble.* Check. Only, the funny part is I'm no good at it. I try to focus on what Mom's saying across the table. "You're not going to your counseling sessions, you're pulling stunts like today. This is obviously not working."

"It is working," I mumble, more to the plate of zucchini than to her.

216

She rubs the skin beneath her eyes with the pads of her fingers, something she always does at the end of a long, exhausting day. "Okay, then, why don't you explain why I should let you stay in Tahoe when all you make are bad choices?"

As if I've been making heaping piles of them. "What other bad choices have I been making?"

She taps her fork on the napkin. "I'm concerned about your schoolwork."

"Ms. Raff told me my last AP history DBQ was the best so far." My mouth feels like sand. Where is Maggie with my Diet Coke? "And I found that lab all on my own. My schoolwork is fine. Better than fine, because I'm getting it all done but I'm not so stressed out. I'm getting enough sleep. And best of all — no one has posted a humiliating YouTube video while I've been *here*." Maggie sets down a glass of white wine for Mom, who is overly showy about thanking her, taking a long sip of it to delay responding to me. "You know what's funny, Mom?" I ask when we've exhausted the avoid-talking-by-drinking option.

She raises her eyebrows. "I would love to know what's funny right now."

"I can't even really get into trouble. That was on my list, you know. From Josie. Get in a little trouble. Number twelve."

"Great." She swirls her wine in the glass. "Great advice."

"It doesn't matter because I can't do it. You know what happened today with Beck? What terrible awful things happened?" She holds up a hand as if to ward off a shot to the face, so I lean in dramatically. "I ended up tutoring him in math and telling him not to drive so fast. I really let it all hang out there." I drop my head onto the table.

She sets down her glass and runs her slightly shaking hand over my hair. "Oh, honey."

I peer up at her. "Still, you don't even trust me. And you should. Because I don't get in trouble, don't you see? Even when I try. But don't worry, if I did, I'd feel sick about it for days, so you win."

"This doesn't feel like winning," she says, removing her hand, dropping it into her lap. "Mara, I just . . . I don't want you involved with the Davis family."

I sit up. So this is about *Beck*. Not my schoolwork. Not even my appointments with Dr. Elliot. If I'd climbed out of that car with Isabel or Logan, would she have reacted the same way? Still, she's not giving me credit for seeing through him on my own. Which I have. "Mom, you don't need to worry about Beck Davis."

She frowns. "I'm not sure how much you know about Beck yet or if Trick's told you anything." I shake my head at that. She hesitates, then says, "Let's just say it's much easier to be a rebel when you have nothing to lose, when you have his father's bank account as a safety net. You're on scholarship, Mara. And Will and I do fine, but we're nowhere near the Davises' league. You don't have the luxury of making Beck's brand of bad choices." Her brow furrows as she picks the breading from a zucchini stick before dropping it, uneaten, onto the plate. "But it's more than that. It's that family." She stares into her wine. "The Davises don't care about anyone. I'm not sure if narcissism can apply to a whole family, but if it could, they'd be the poster family for it."

Hadn't I felt that exact thing earlier today when Beck launched into his geometry drama? "Trust me, I don't care about Beck. He has nothing to do with what I'm feeling about being in Tahoe."

She looks skeptical. "Really? And how are you feeling?"

I'm not sure I can even articulate it, but I try. "You know what I love most about Tahoe? I'm not made up almost entirely of knots. Which is how I feel in San Diego at Ranfield. All the time." She winces, but I need to tell her this, to try to make her understand, even if it's hard to hear. "The best part of my time here is I actually have just that — *time*. And I'm figuring out that I don't want all the same things you and Will do, that I don't want to be stressed and busy and competitive all the time —"

"You wanted to go to Ranfield," she interrupts. "We've been supporting what you wanted." But even as she says it, she can't meet my eyes.

"You want me there, too." I try to keep my voice low. "You love having a daughter who's at a school like Ranfield. I hear you talk with your friends. With your clients. And now you're upset because I might not want the life you designed for me. But that's just it. I'm not some renovation project — put the stone wall here, put the atrium there. I'm not a project at all, I'm a person!" Now she just looks confused again. I let my point get away from me and I'm just rambling in weird house-remodeling metaphors. "It's hard to explain," I end lamely.

To my surprise, though, she dissolves into tears. Big tears. Mom is not a crier, especially not in public. She drops her face into her hands, her hair falling forward in a blond fringe. I have never spoken to her like I just did and my stomach lurches as I watch her cry. "Mom?" I reach tentatively toward her.

"Um, can I, um, set this down?" Maggie, eyes wide, holds our pizza aloft. She glances from Mom to me, apologetic.

"Here, set it here, thanks." I move my Diet Coke out of the way. Mom has not emerged from behind her hands. "Thanks," I say again. Maggie hurries away. The smell of the pizza makes my mouth water, but I don't take a piece. I let it sit there and congeal until Mom finally takes a shaky breath, wipes beneath her eyes with a napkin, and takes a piece for herself, as if she hadn't just sobbed in the middle of Ethan's, as if we hadn't said anything to each other at all.

"Mom?" I try again.

She concentrates on eating. "I'm really tired, Mara. Let's just eat our pizza."

TWENTY-FOUR

The next day, Mom and I drive into Tahoe City, not talking. She hums along to the radio, no sign of last night's tears, but the air in the rental car feels dense, as if I could actually scoop out chunks of it and roll it in my hands. The storm has blown out, leaving a blue-bird day, and my stomach tugs, wishing I could be up on the mountain. Geez, maybe I *am* turning into a ski bum?

We pull into the empty parking lot at Commons Beach and get out. Snow covers both the park and the beach, and the lake is caked at its edges with ice, making the bits of blue jagged fingers look like broken pieces of mirrored sky. We pick our way over the icy parking lot to the snow-covered shore and stand watching how the white gives way to the indigo water of the lake.

"I think you should come home, but I'm not going to decide for you," Mom says finally. Surprised, I swipe at the hair the wind whips into my face. Mom tugs her beanie over her ears. "You think I don't understand, but I do."

Over the years, Mom has told me bits of her childhood, how she lived in Colorado with my grandparents, how she didn't end up going to college because she got involved with real estate. Even as successful as she is now, Mom has never hesitated to tell me she wished she'd gone to college. "You know that's a regret of mine," she tells me again now, watching the choppy water. "One I don't want you repeating if I can help it."

"I still want to go to college," I say. "This place hasn't changed what I want; it's just put certain things in perspective. Besides, I won't be going to college if high school kills me first. That's not a good strategy."

She shakes her head. "I just wish you would have talked to us, to Will and me, about how stressed out you were. Why didn't you talk to us?" Her voice sounds young and afraid.

I study the snowy mountains out beyond the water. "I'm not sure I even knew, Mom. I just wanted to do my best. You always tell me and Seth and Liam — *Do your best*. Be your *best*. Then, I just collapsed under all that best, you know, and suddenly I was at my worst." I bite my lip to ward off tears.

She slips an arm around me and pulls me to her. "I love you so much I think it sometimes makes me a crazy person." I can't remember the last time Mom held me like this; not in a long time. "But being your best doesn't mean being perfect. It means doing right by yourself each day. It means having goals and being a good, hardworking person. That's what Will and I want for you kids. We don't expect you to be perfect."

"I might have missed that distinction," I mumble into the collar of my jacket.

"I know how much pressure you've been under. All you kids at Ranfield. I know how hard you work," she admits. "I just thought you were handling it."

"I wasn't." How can two small words be filled with so much shame?

She hears it and gives my shoulder a squeeze. "Honey, you have to learn to self-regulate. You can use your snowplow, even in San Diego. You didn't have to run away."

I bristle. "Why does wanting a change have to be called that?"

She looks apologetic. "I'm sorry — it's just *this place*." She sighs, staring out over the water. "It's hard to be immune to its siren song."

"And you're worried it's going to dash me against the rocks." She squeezes me tighter as if she could be like Odysseus's crewmen, lashing me to the mast to keep me safe. I guess tying us to masts is part of a mom's job description. It just feels like mine forgot to keep loosening the knots as I got older.

"I have a lot of memories here." She sighs. "Good and bad."

We watch the water for a few minutes, and from somewhere deep within me, a memory of my own surfaces. I'm not sure what reminded me, maybe the wide stretch of inky water, but suddenly the memory appears as if it happened yesterday.

"Mom?"

"Yeah?"

"Remember when we were in Maui a few years ago? At the Hula Grill in Kaanapali?"

She stiffens against me as if the memory comes suddenly to her, too. Every other year, we take a short trip to Maui. Just five or six nights because Mom and Will don't like to be away from their work much longer than that. This particular trip I was thirteen, I think, and it was April. We'd spent most of the day snorkeling in the turquoise water near Black Rock, eating lunch by the hotel pool while Seth and Liam made trip after trip down the water slide, and then

223

resting in our room until dinner, the boys watching a Harry Potter movie on Will's iPad. At dusk, we had meandered down the slim promenade in front of the hotel to the Hula Grill. I walked ahead with Mom, and Will had Liam and Seth in tow, sunburned and tired from the day. We'd just been seated in the outdoor patio when we heard a voice behind us.

"Lauren?" An auburn-haired man with broad shoulders and mirrored glasses approached. "I thought that was you." He nodded amiably to Will but I noticed, before Will turned on his lawyer smile, that his face had darkened. He stood and shook hands with the man, his gaze slipping to Mom, who was watching the man coolly.

I noticed she didn't shake his hand. "Jason, you remember Mara. And these are our twins, Seth and Liam." Mom motioned to each of us in turn.

Jason's eyes settled on me longer than on my brothers. "Well, look at you, all grown up." He pushed nervously at his sunglasses as if they were slightly big and turned again to Mom. "Life in San Diego seems to be treating you well."

"Yes," Mom replied, her voice businesslike.

"Mom, I have to pee." Liam wiggled in his chair, clutching the crotch of his board shorts.

Looking relieved, Will hurried to pull his son's chair out. "I'll take him. Let's all go."

"I don't have to," I started, but then noticed the pointed look Will gave me and followed my stepfather and brothers toward the bathrooms, leaving Mom to talk with the man.

"Who was that guy?" I asked Mom when we returned from the bathrooms, the man nowhere in sight.

Fiddling with the straw of her mai tai, she intently studied the menu. "Oh, just someone I used to know. Don't the fish tacos here look amazing?"

Now, leaning into her down jacket, the view of Tahoe in front of us a glacial and indigo mass, I say, "That was Beck's dad, wasn't it? That guy in Maui? That was Jason Davis. I saw him once here. He was fighting with Beck in the parking lot."

"That was so random," she breathes, uncurling her arm and stuffing her hands into her pockets. "I'm surprised you remember it."

"I didn't really, until just now. You and Will were both acting so weird. What happened with him?"

She jumps up and down in place. "It's freezing. Let's go get brunch somewhere."

• • •

Over brunch, she fills in some of the gaps she has never shared before. She skied growing up in Colorado, even raced on her high school team for a couple of years, but had plans to attend college in Southern California. "I wanted to be a nurse," she tells me, examining the tomato she'd speared on her fork. Senior year, she and her parents took a ski trip to Squaw Valley, and she had met Trick, a sponsored freestyle skier who had spent his childhood racing. Her expression turns dreamy. "He was three years older and just so cute and funny and . . . *fun*, you know? That week we went to parties and he taught me some tricks on my skis and we just, well . . ." She blushes, brushing a strand of hair out of her face. "We just had to be together." For a minute, I can see exactly what she must have looked like when she was my age.

225

Like me. She must have looked so much like me.

"At the end of that week, my parents had to drag me back to Colorado," she says now. "But the second I graduated, I was on a bus to Tahoe. Forget college. Forget being a nurse. I had my skis and I had Trick waiting for me in one of the most beautiful places in the world."

My mom threw away her plans for a boy? She would have surprised me less if she'd confessed she had once joined the circus. "I had no idea. Grandma and Grandpa have never said anything." We see my grandparents at least twice a year, but they'd never mentioned a word about Tahoe.

"I asked them not to. Not that it was all bad. Bad things often start out great." At first, she tells me, they had the best lives she could imagine — sleeping on people's couches, skiing all winter, kayaking in the summers. "Trick trained a lot and I'd train with him. We were in great shape. And we had a blast. I mean, we had no money and that sucked. But we had fun." But then, she says, she had started to realize what she'd thrown away. She started to think about enrolling in college.

But when she was twenty, I happened. "You . . . surprised us." She takes a bite of salad and chews thoughtfully. "You were such a beautiful baby, of course, but we were idiots about being parents. We didn't even know who we were yet as people. We definitely weren't ready for a baby." She has told me this part of the story before, never hesitating to advise me, *Don't be stupid and have a baby too early like I did.* Which feels awesome, naturally, even if she assures me she'd never trade me being born for anything.

I set my fork down. "When did you meet Beck's parents?"

"When you were about six months, Trick and I met the Davis family in a baby group along with Logan's parents." As she picks at an egg in her Cobb salad, Mom explains that even though the other two families were much older and more professional, they all became fast friends, all of them skiers, all of them with a new baby. "And the Nevers already had Logan's sister, so Jessica was so helpful. The expert." She remembers it all for a moment, then frowns. "But we had a falling out with the Davises. You were almost three." She gazes out at the water.

"What happened?"

She looks back at me. "Beck's dad was doing really well in real estate up here, and he approached us and the Nevers with this no-fail opportunity. That's how he sold it to us: *no-fail*. My parents had given us some money for a down payment on a condo." She taps her fork nervously against the side of her salad bowl. "I told Trick no way was I going to use that money for something like that — so uncertain." She looks ill at the memory. "But Trick gave it to him anyway. And we lost everything. The Davises weren't even sorry. I remember the way Jason told us, like it was nothing. *This just happens sometimes in real estate*, he said." She stares glumly into her salad. "The Nevers were lucky they didn't lose the store."

I reach across the table and grab her hand. "I'm sorry, Mom. I didn't know."

She stares out the window at the windy lake. "Trick got hurt a few months later." She runs her hand through her hair. "Wow, that was a terrible year. But I met Will when he was visiting Squaw Valley on vacation and, within a few months, I moved to San Diego and put things back together. I got lucky." She squeezes my hand. "We both did."

Untangling her hand from mine, she signals for the waitress. I eat the rest of my pancakes while Mom silently pays the check. Trick had gone behind Mom's back and lost all their money. He'd gotten hurt. More than that, though, something broke between them that she couldn't fix. My mother, the fix-it queen, couldn't make it right. Watching me here must make her want to reach back in time and yank her former self out of harm's way. I don't blame her. Because I would do the same if I could.

TWENTY-FIVE

Josie shouts, "Hello, valentine!" and holds up a shiny red heart that fills the laptop screen. But it's not just any shiny red heart. It's been decorated to look as hideously overdone as possible, with bows and glitter and curlicue ribbons shooting out from all parts of it. She has also attached a tiny stuffed cat with pink jeweled eyes. So it doesn't even look like a heart anymore. It looks like the cat is exploding with maniacal valentine glee.

"Oooooooh," I breathe. "That's a good one." Starting in seventh grade, Josie and I had agreed to be each other's valentine every year by giving each other the most extreme valentine heart we could create in thirty minutes or less. That was the rule. "Are you sure that was under the time limit?"

"Twenty-eight minutes, thirty-six seconds, thank you very much," she says proudly.

I hold up mine. "Okay, so supplies were limited, but, still, twenty-two minutes, eleven seconds."

She claps her hands together. "Very nice. Very . . . alpine." Late this morning, I'd smothered a heart cut from a brown grocery bag with pine needles and cones and dozens of random ski stickers that Trick didn't want anymore. Then I'd sprayed the whole thing in silver paint Trick found in the Stones' garage.

Josie sets down her heart. "How was the visit with your mom?"

"Enlightening."

She frowns. "Good enlightening or bad?"

"Both." I fill her in on some of the things Mom shared with me. "And I got snacks and some cute pj's." I hold up a box of my favorite chocolate and the snowflake-spattered flannels Mom had given me for Valentine's Day before she left this morning.

"I'm glad you two talked." Josie shifts on her bed and I notice a huge bouquet of red roses sitting on the dresser behind her.

"Um, hello, roses!"

She flushes. "Oh, well, no — those . . ." She waves her hand. "Whatever."

"Wait, Jo — those are from your parents, right?"

She picks at some lint on her blue sweater. "Not exactly."

"Then who?" My heart is beating too fast. It shouldn't matter *who* they're from, but for some reason, it does. "You're the color of a stop sign — tell me!"

"Chris Locke." She gets very close to the screen, her inky eyes huge. "I was going to tell you."

"Um, I hope so, because you got super mad when I didn't tell you what happened with my crazy Tahoe boy situation." There's a metallic flavor in the back of my throat. Whatever this is I'm feeling — confusion, hurt, frustration — tastes like swallowing loose change.

She settles back away from the screen, tucking her knees to her chin. "I know, but you always get so intense about that deal we made. You take that stuff too seriously, Mara. And this whole thing with Chris is brand-new. I wanted to make sure there was something there before I even mentioned it."

What is she talking about? We both made the deal. "I don't take it too seriously. I know things change. You don't see me wearing those green overalls I was obsessed with in sixth grade anymore even though I told you I'd never grow out of them."

"That's different." She sighs. "This feels different. You and I don't always, I don't know, do that normal giggly girl stuff. We mostly make fun of girls who do that." She's right. We do.

I struggle to find the right words. "How did . . . it happen? How did Chris happen?"

"I went to that twenty-four-hour dance-a-thon to raise money for Costa Rica." Now she actually giggles. "And he was there. We just started . . . talking. He's pretty great."

I stare at her dresser. "Those are some nice roses for just talking."

As she studies them, she can't stop smiling. "Look, Mara. I'm just going to see where it goes." She shrugs. "It's fun."

My list brain racks up questions and they spill out: "Is he being casual, too? Is that the plan — to just see where it goes? Is it going to change what you want —"

"Mara," she interrupts, annoyance fading her smile. "I don't know. I'm not making plans. I haven't made a pro and con list or a spreadsheet for all possible relationship outcomes." *Because I'm not you*, she doesn't add. She doesn't have to. I hear it.

I take a short, clean breath. "Okay. Well, if you're happy, I'm happy," I say, trying to mean it.

Her eyes brighten. "Really? Thank you. Because, well, I am."

I give her the best version of my smile I can muster. Sometimes being the friend you're supposed to be in a certain moment is harder than any chemistry equation.

231

She unfolds her legs and leans toward the screen. "So . . . are you doing anything tonight?" she asks. "Like with Logan, maybe?"

"He's not back from Mammoth yet." I fiddle with a loose string on the bedspread. "Not that we would do something if he was."

"The lady doth protest too much."

"Thanks, Shakespeare. This lady doth not need a boyfriend complicating an already overly complicated life."

"Maybe you should text him. Ask how his race was? You guys could hang out when he gets back. Lately, I've been going to more stuff here at Ran and it's really nice to just hang out with people. Your most meaningful relationship shouldn't be with your history textbook." Her cell buzzes next to her on the bed. She picks it up and the goofy look she gets gives away the caller.

"Say hi to Chris for me," I tell her, motioning for her to take the call. I shut my laptop and look around me. The fire shifts with its dim glow, my clothes sit in even rows on the bookcase, and the pile of books beckons me from the floor.

Happy Valentine's Day.

·   ·   ·

Trick and I move awkwardly around each other for the next few days. Like so many things with him, our fight before Mom got here just melts into silence, becoming part of the past. Trick might have once been a sponsored freeskier, but he's an Olympian at avoidance.

Early Wednesday morning, my phone buzzes. Isabel.

check your email.

I pull my laptop onto the bed. The subject line reads: Isabel has sent you a playlist! I click it open.

Get your gear, download this playlist, and get your
butt on the mountain. We'll meet up after practice.
Start this playlist right when you get on the funi and
play it all the way through at least three times before
taking a break!!
— Isabel and Logan

I push off the blankets and grab my ski stuff.

On the funi, I click track one, a mellow indie-edged song with a nice beat. I listen, my head bobbing along to it as I watch people sail down the mountain. I might be rocking out a little too much, because the guy next to me, a middle-aged snowboarder in duct-taped Burton pants, grins at me and gives me the peace sign. I give it back.

As I ride the lift up Big Blue, I stare at the winter landscape, all that graphite on white, gray sky and mountains layered with snow, and in the floating beat of a new song, I think about what fastens me to the world. Maybe, all those years at Ranfield, I stayed busy as a way to not float away into the atmosphere. Each piece of home-work, each activity, each club meeting was a way to staple me to a life, to say, *I am here, I am here, I am supposed to be here* . . .

But, honestly, I partly worked as hard as I did to avoid a lot of the social stuff. I never truly felt a part of things at Ranfield, always felt like I was borrowing someone else's life. The only thing about Ran that ever felt like home was Josie. I hadn't applied for the scholarship — it had been offered to me. Sitting in my fifth-grade public school classroom in the late spring light with my mom and Will, my teacher, Miss Kelly, had beamed as she handed us the invi-tation letter. Because of my test scores, my academic performance,

I'd been singled out for this amazing opportunity. I loved Miss Kelly, and she and Mom and Will had looked so *proud* of me. Maybe all these years I've worked hard simply to be worthy of their expressions, of being chosen like that.

I've worked to be the best.

But is it what I *want*?

Now all the hard work feels attached with Velcro. Which freaks me out. Because Velcro tears away so easily, just that ripping sound and then empty air. Moving down the mountain, it feels so easy to imagine staying here forever. For the next few hours, I fasten myself to the mountain, skiing up and down Big Blue and Gold Coast, the new playlist looping in my ears. Each song seems to be about finding something — a place, a love, a dream.

Back behind the music, though, two competing lists keep trying to form on the dark, hidden walls of my brain. Reasons to stay: the ease of Tahoe, Trick, Logan, friends. Reasons to go: Josie, my brothers, everything I built at Ranfield.

Pushing away the anxious rumblings that threaten to grow out of the lists, the mountain lets me ignore them both, even if just for now.

•   •   •

That afternoon, my body exhausted from its hours on the slopes, I slide into a booth at Ethan's across from Logan. "Where's Isabel?"

Logan slips his phone into a pocket. "Talking to Coach. She's bummed about the way she skied at Mammoth. She'll be here in a few minutes."

"Did you have a good practice?" I ask. He almost never talks about his own skiing.

"Fine. I just hope Isabel snaps out of it. She's too hard on her-self." We order a pizza and some drinks from Maggie. Passing her our menus, Logan asks me, "Did you get your playlist?" Maggie ducks away, but not before I see the smile playing at the corners of her mouth.

I can still feel the mountain in my body, the feeling of gliding over snow with their music in my head. "Yeah, thanks. I played it all morning while I skied. By myself!"

He high-fives me. "How'd it feel?"

"Like flying."

He nods knowingly, running a hand through his shaggy dark hair. "Always nice to just get on the mountain, plug in, and tune out. It's my happy place." Grinning, he catches my eye. "I'm glad you liked the list." When Logan smiles like that, I can see the little boy in him, all mop-haired and toothy and adorable. I fiddle with my napkin and avoid his dark eyes.

His phone beeps. Checking it, he frowns. "Isabel's not coming. She said she's going to go home and scream into her pillow."

"Was it really that bad?"

"She crashed. And today she kept falling. Her confidence got rattled. It happens."

"But she's okay, right?"

"She's not hurt." Frowning, he moves the ketchup and mustard bottles around in front of him to make room for Maggie to set down our drinks and some empty plates for our pizza. "But she was so close to having her best time last weekend and I'm sure she feels like she messed that up."

I pull out my phone and text her, sending five hearts in a row and the message:

don't go home! i need to thank you for my playlist!

It's buzzing before I set it back down, but it's Beck, not Isabel.

still mad at me?

He's like a virus I can't get rid of. A broad-shouldered virus.

Logan asks, "What'd she say?"

I hesitate. "It's actually Beck."

Logan rolls his eyes and helps himself to a slice of pizza.

I put my phone in my bag. "You don't like him, do you?"

He just shrugs, concentrating on pulling a piece of pepperoni from his slice. "What's to like?"

"I feel a little sorry for him. His dad's pretty awful."

Logan grimaces. "Yeah, but that's just become part of his act, you know? Yes, his dad is the worst. He's this big developer in Tahoe, and he's involved in a bunch of deals here in Squaw that make him *very* unpopular with the locals. My family included. He's not a good guy. But Beck uses it, you know? Makes him out to be this sinister supervillain."

I picture Beck's dad with a huge black mustache and a cape. Wait, do villains usually have capes? "Does he dwell in his mountain lair making evil weapons designed exclusively to torture his unsuspecting son?"

Logan grins. "Right? It's so melodramatic. I mean, he *is* a jerk. He's rich and aggressive and intense. He owns, like, three houses in Squaw Valley alone. And nothing is good enough for him. When we all skied together, they always had these crazy screaming matches in the parking lot or on the mountain." He shudders a bit, remembering. Wiping his mouth with a napkin, he adds, "But Beck just keeps it going. Everything is always so *difficult* for him." He grabs another slice. "He's such a drama queen. It gets old."

I swallow a bite of pizza. "I thought he seemed interesting at first — all his ideas about school and society. But mostly it's like he tries to be the biggest possible screwup just to get back at his dad. Nothing original about that. There are dozens of guys like that at my old school."

My *old* school. As if I've already moved up here for good. He hears it, too. I can tell by the look on his face.

He plays with his napkin, not meeting my eyes. "He must be doing something right with all the girls following him around."

Leaning my elbows on the table, I say quietly, "I only kissed him because of my stupid list. Josie told me to kiss a cute snowboarder. So I did. But *someone* I know threw that list off a chairlift."

He grabs another piece of pizza. "Someone who's a genius, you mean?"

"I think so."

He catches my eye, about to say something, just as Isabel flops down next to me, her face dark. "Okay, I'd love to hear about someone else having a good day. Because mine stank up the mountain."

·   ·   ·

That night, curled on my bed, I squint into the screen at Josie, who's in the middle of telling me how hard the AP chem test was today. I nod sympathetically. "Sounds brutal."

"You have no idea," she groans. I do have an idea since I took the online version an hour ago. She's sitting on her bed, too, and her dark hair falls around her face as she rubs lotion into her legs. "You're so lucky you just get to chill in Tahoe." She sighs. "Maybe I should have a meltdown in math class." She freezes, looking up at me, her eyes huge. "Oh, whoa. Sorry, Mar — I didn't mean that."

My skin shivery, I try to play it off. "It's not all it's cracked up to be."

"Still, I'll be honest," she says, capping the lotion. "I *am* the tiniest bit jealous. I'm so sick of school."

"I still have to do all the work."

She hesitates, looking pained. "Yeah, but, it's not like *school* school. It's not as hard."

Translation: *My life's harder. I win. You lose.*

"Why does everything have to be hard to count?" I think about what Logan said about Beck making everything so difficult. Do we all have different versions of doing that? "Maybe most of us make things harder than we need to. I don't think being stressed out lets you get more out of anything, including school."

She doesn't say anything, just makes little clicking sounds with her tongue as she inspects her manicure. "Yeah, you're probably right." She's being generous. She doesn't think I'm right at all.

TWENTY-SIX

It's Ski Week in Tahoe.

Or, as Logan and Isabel call it, the Week Everyone in California Remembers They Ski.

Because of the swell of tourists, the resort kicks the fun activities up a notch. Today it's Eighties Saturday on the mountain. Trick almost spits out his cereal when he sees me emerge from my room. "Oh, no way — sweet."

I'm dressed as Madonna. Mid-eighties Madonna with the teased blond hair, the layered messy skirt, the lace shirt, the bracelets. All of this over my ski parka and pants. I'm meeting up with Isabel and Logan after their race this afternoon. I twirl so Trick can see the full effect of the skirt. "Isabel and I went to the thrift store yesterday. She's going as Cyndi Lauper. Girls just want to have fun, right?"

He nods, impressed. "Very nice."

I'm proud of my costume. Especially because I've never been a costume girl. At Ranfield, a lot of other kids get really into it at Halloween, but I'd always felt like it was a waste of time.

Isabel begged me, though, and as part of my have-more-fun goal, I tried it, and guess what. It's fun. I squint at Trick. "Are you dressed up?" He's wearing jeans and a white T-shirt under a black down jacket.

He holds up a red baseball cap and tucks it into his back jean pocket. "I'm the Boss." I must look puzzled when he turns around, because he adds, "Bruce Springsteen," and sings a few lines from "Born in the U.S.A."

"Oh, right."

Later, on the chairlift, I need help figuring out Logan's outfit: tan ski pants, a white linen blazer over a pale pink T-shirt, and black Ray-Bans. "Duh, Miami Vice," he tells me.

Oh, right. My pop culture history has always been a weak spot. If I wasn't going to be tested on it, I didn't let it rent space in my brain. Even though the afternoon sun is bright, the wind has picked up. "You must be freezing!"

"Nah, I got Chillys on." He lifts his pink T-shirt to reveal long underwear called Chilly Peppers, which so many of the racers wear. Below us, people zip by in head-to-toe neon spandex, parachute pants, ripped sweatshirts, and fingerless gloves over their regular gloves.

I peer over the lift bar. "Look at everyone!"

Logan studies the people skiing and boarding below our dangling skis. "Wait until you see Isabel."

You can't miss her. She waits for us at the top of Big Blue, clad in what looks like everything Cyndi Lauper ever owned. She has fastened a candy-apple red-blond hairpiece to her ski helmet and wears bright blue and orange Cyndi Lauper makeup. Her crazy layers of skirts and dresses are finished off with a black chain wrapped around her torso. "Time to be totally radical," she calls, skiing off down the catwalk toward Shirley Lake.

• • •

"They didn't have any Diet Coke," Isabel says, pushing a Sprite into my hands and settling onto the couch next to me with a huge plate of self-made "nachos." Her plate bulges with tortilla chips, bean dip, baby carrots, salsa, and what looks like trail mix. "Want some?" she mumbles, her mouth full. "It's a tasty treat."

"Thanks," I say, helping myself to a loaded chip. Chewing what is clearly an M&M with my bean dip, I take in the dozens of people milling around, sitting on the floor, leaning against the kitchen island, most in various states of eighties wear, disheveled from their day on the slopes.

When the slopes closed, Eighties Day migrated to Joy Chang's house. Her hair pulled into a wild, side-swept ponytail, Joy stands on the raised tile hearth of the roaring fireplace, acting as master of ceremonies in a lip-synch contest. Or, as she announces it now to the room, her voice in all caps: "OUR EIGHTIES LIP-SYNCH EXTRAVAGANZA!" When people keep ignoring her, she finally shouts, "Everyone, shut up!"

That does the trick.

Much of the furniture in the living room has been pushed back against walls to make room for a stage. One at a time, different people jump up to lip-synch to eighties hits. I almost pee my pants at Bodie's enthusiastic Cher impression, complete with a long curly black wig and purple eye shadow.

"Well, we can't turn back time," Joy comments at the end of his act. "Or I'd ask for the last three minutes of my life back." Bodie feigns a hurt look. "Just kidding, Bodie. You're a gorgeous diva." There's a lull in the festivities as Bodie hurries out of the room. I turn, searching the room, wondering where Logan went. No sign of him.

Someone dims the lights. "Okay, we have one last lip synch to share with you tonight," Joy announces mysteriously, silhouetted against the flickering orange of the fire. "Sometimes you've got to fight for the right, so put your hands together for the Frost Boys! And Amanda," she adds, grinning.

Logan, Bodie, and snowboardcross Amanda burst into the room dressed as the Beastie Boys. People whistle and scream. Wearing a black leather jacket and backward trucker hat, Logan struts around the room, chains swinging from his neck. He goofily hops around the stage one hundred percent committed to his role.

I can't take my eyes off him.

Isabel, watching me, shakes her head.

"What?" I whisper, my face heating.

"Nothing." She nibbles a bean-dip-soaked baby carrot, her eyes slipping back to the show, where Logan ends by dropping his fake mic and strutting from the room.

After, someone hooks up their iPod to Joy's speakers and people spill into the empty space to dance. Isabel wipes her hands on her jeans, waving to Logan as he comes back into the room, dressed in jeans and a Dakine sweatshirt. "Good stuff, Never."

He takes a quick bow. "Why, thank you."

I brush some hair out of my face. "You were hysterical. I didn't know you had it in you."

He smiles, but his dark eyes send a current through me. "Well, you should get to know me better."

•   •   •

I emerge sleepily from my room the next day to find Trick reading a ski magazine. "Morning," he says.

I pour some cereal. "Morning." I slide into the seat across from him.

"You were in late last night." He doesn't look up from his magazine.

My chest tightens. Is he mad? I should have called. "Yeah, sorry."

"No prob." He stands and starts to clear his bowl. Tucking the cereal box under his arm, he moves toward the kitchen sink.

"Wait—that's it?"

He turns at the edge in my voice. "What?"

"Well, this would be the part where a normal dad says, *Where were you? Why didn't you call?* This is the part where you're supposed to say something like that." I slap my hand on the top of the table, making my spoon rattle against the cereal bowl. We both look at the bowl, at my hand. I am not a table slapper and it feels childish. "And then I would say, *Well, actually, I went to a party, but I should have called!*"

He sets his bowl in the sink. "Sounds like you've got this conversation covered." I glare at him and he clears his throat. "I'm sorry, but when have I ever been a normal dad to you? That ship, I think, sailed a long time ago." He makes a move for the door, pulling his parka from the back of the chair he'd been sitting in.

"Trick!" Another hand slap.

Turning, his eyes wide, he asks, "What? What do you want me to say?"

"Something resembling what a real dad should say!"

Trick fiddles with the zipper on his jacket, his eyes darting around as if he's seeking escape routes. "You have Will for that stuff. He's better at it anyway."

"Yeah, he is." I blink back the ghosts of tears starting to circle behind my eyes, my whole body shaking. "But that doesn't matter. People aren't batteries. You don't swap one out for another. You're my father. That's biology. But I'm giving you a chance to be a dad and you keep ruining it."

He swallows, avoiding my eyes, and doesn't say anything. As usual.

Someone knocks at the door and Trick hurries to open it. A tall man with close-cropped salt-and-pepper hair and a gunmetal down jacket that I know for a fact sells for $375 at Neverland takes a step into the room. Something about him, not just his height, fills the whole space, and the cottage quickly feels the size of a breadbox.

"Trick?" His voice is polished, crisp. He slips his hands into the pockets of his designer jeans, and his gaze sweeps the room like a search lamp. "Sorry, didn't mean to disturb. Just wanted to let you know we're here. Decided to come for Ski Week after all." The Stones. The family who owns the massive house and this cottage.

"Right, is everything okay with the house? I turned the water on, got the stoves all going." Trick looks uncomfortably from Mr. Stone to me. "Chuck, this is my daughter, Mara. She's staying with me for a few weeks. Mara, this is Chuck Stone."

Mr. Stone has a hard-angled face that must dominate in boardrooms, the kind that so many of the fathers of kids at Ranfield have. When he smiles, his gray eyes shine with a practiced light. "Mara, a pleasure."

"Nice to meet you," I say through a dry mouth. None of this feels pleasurable. In fact, something unpleasant definitely simmers beneath his words.

"Well, I'll let you two get back to your morning," he says to Trick. "Perhaps we can talk later? I'd like to discuss the Airstream currently parked in my driveway. When you have a minute." He flashes another polite smile in my direction.

"Um, yeah, sure." Trick shakes Mr. Stone's hand awkwardly and closes the door behind him.

"Did he know I was staying with you?" I ask, after I hear the crunch of Mr. Stone's boots on the snow fade away. "Or that Oli was staying here?"

Trick sighs. "Nope."

•   •   •

Later that morning, Oli pulls his Airstream out of the Stones' driveway. Leaning out the driver's-side window of his truck, he asks if I want to come with him and get some runs in on the mountain. I grab my gear.

On the hill, I keep falling. I can't concentrate. People jostle and push at the lift lines and cut people off on the hill more than usual. Their energy, combined with my earlier fight with Trick, makes me sloppy and frustrated. Oli shoots me a concerned look as we ride silently up the Big Blue, but I ignore it, studying the contrast of sky against snow.

Funny how our moods can determine the shape humanity takes around us. Today, I almost hate everyone. After a near miss with a snowboarder at the base of Gold Coast, I sit in a clump, near tears, until Oli skis over to me. "You okay down there?"

"I hate people."

He tries to hide a grin. "Anyone in particular or just all people?"

"All of them. Not you," I hurry to add. He laughs in his easy way, and the sound of it lifts part of the heaviness from my chest. A smile twitches the corners of my mouth. "And not that guy," I say, nodding to a man gliding happily behind his three-year-old son, who wears a ski leash and an Edgie Wedgie to hold his skis in place. "But definitely that guy." I point at the thirtysomething guy in a splashy ski outfit who pushed in front of us in the lift line earlier.

Oli follows my gaze. "Well, that guy's a tool." He offers his hand to help me up. "Want to call it a day?"

I grab his hand and let him lift me up. The mountain has cleared a little and I feel suddenly brave. "Actually, can we ski Mountain Run?"

•　　•　　•

Mountain Run is the highway of Squaw Valley. It connects the upper mountain to the lower, spitting out just behind where the funi takes off. It's an especially long run, but I make it all the way to the bottom without taking a break. Oli skis near me the whole time. Even when I can't see him, I can feel his presence close by, making sure I'm safe.

We ski as far as we can before we have to take off our skis. Loading them on our shoulders, we clomp by people lounging at the outside bar with plastic cups of beer or hot chocolates, red cheeked from a day on the mountain. "You want something? Coffee or something?" Oli asks as we walk into the main stretch of the Village.

"I'm sorry the Stones made you leave."

He sets his skis in a rack near Elevation. "Their house, their rules."

I'm angry at the Stones for their dumb rules, angry at Trick for not making it work out, for not trying harder, for not caring where I was last night. For a lot of things. "It's not fair."

He turns back to me, his hands in the pockets of his parka, his eyes like the slice of Tahoe visible from Big Blue. "I don't waste my time with what's fair and what's not. Not when someone just crushed Mountain Run. With no falls! Come on, that's at least worth something warm to drink. Do you kids still drink regular hot chocolate or does it have to be something mixed with fifteen different types of fancy syrup and have a name I can't pronounce?"

I prop my skis next to his, pulling off my helmet and running my fingers through my messy hair. Following him into Elevation, I marvel at how he just rolls with what happens, doesn't try to fight what he can't control. "I'd love a regular old hot chocolate."

• • •

Logan meets me at the funi at nine on Wednesday. "Ready?" We hit Gold Coast first and then take the Big Blue for some runs on Shirley Lake. My skis feel strong beneath me and I find myself picking up speed, my body warm even though the day is cold and leaden. On the lift, we do the Venn diagram thing with the movies, books, and music we like, trying to find the places where they overlap. I'm surprised by all the shared space. We both like spy movies and reading books set in foreign countries. We both loved Harry Potter as kids. "You should come over this weekend and we can have a Harry Potter movie marathon," he says. "I'll make you pizza."

"You'll *make* it?"

"I make great pizza. What do you like on it?"

"Mushrooms and olives."

"I make my own dough and sauce. That's the secret." He raises the safety bar as we approach the end of the lift. "But if you've got other stuff going on, no big deal." I can tell he's trying to keep his voice light.

"I have absolutely nothing else going on," I say, and even mean it a little. We exit the lift, gliding to the right toward Shirley Lake. I follow Logan down the shoot, my body smooth even as I push my muscles, feeling them heat and burn. Logan is a beautiful skier, his lanky body like liquid. He makes wide smiles with his skis, encouraging me to track him, and as we play follow the leader, I study his comfortable form as he moves down the mountain. Oli's right — it's also very much how he moves through life.

We hit the lift line at Shirley. I pull my goggles away from my face, letting the patches of fog that built up on the last run fade from the lens. "How'd that feel?" Logan leans into me just barely, his arm firm against mine. "You're doing great out there."

My whole body warms, but it's not from the compliment; it's from how close he is, the weight of his body leaning into me. "Thanks." I peer up at him, taking in his slightly chapped lips, the color the exercise and cold make in his cheeks, the laid-back focus of his eyes through his goggles as they study the line of people in front of us. In line, he always takes the outside because he knows I don't like being on that side of the lift. It's a small thing, but it feels huge all of a sudden.

He catches me scrutinizing him. "What?"

I'm sure my face is already flushed from cold and skiing, so I don't have to worry about his noticing how it heats for all sorts of other reasons. "I'm looking forward to that pizza."

His face melts into a smile. "Excellent — how about Friday?"

"Friday," I echo. The air is supposed to be thinner at elevation, but in this moment it solidifies around us, swirls with the weight of the way Logan is looking at me.

A voice cuts in. "Looking good, San Diego!"

Beck Davis, auditioning for Guy with the World's Worst Timing. I struggle to remember what I found so interesting or charming about him those first few weeks. He and a couple of the Frost Boys hover just outside the Shirley lift line. I stare straight ahead, sliding up in line, the air around us thinning.

Beck scoots forward on his skis, mirroring our progress in line. "Awww, come on. Are you still mad about the stupid car ride? I wasn't going that fast." Other skiers notice, their gaze darting between Beck and me. I don't respond.

Logan's body turns rigid beside me. "What car ride?"

"We're hitting Granite Chief," Beck calls out. "Come with us."

"We're good, thanks," I say, still looking straight ahead. Logan says nothing, his face blank, no trace of the smile left.

"You can ski Granite Chief," Beck insists, even if we're almost at the front of the Shirley line. "Come on, where's that overachiever I know and love? Push yourself."

Logan and I hop onto the lift and it carries us away. After pulling the bar down, Logan says stiffly, "He's right, though. You could ski Granite. At least some parts."

"Isn't it a black? I haven't skied a black yet. I know I should try it, but I don't even feel comfortable on blue runs yet." Even though I crossed that one off the list. "You can go ski it if you want. Don't let me stop you." My voice comes out jagged, still edged with left-over annoyance from Beck's ill-timed arrival.

"Hey." Logan puts his hand on my leg. "I'm not saying you *should* ski Granite Chief. I'm just saying you could. But there's always next season."

His kindness sands away some of the edges. "I know. It's not you. It's Beck. I'm just so sick of him." I tell Logan about the car ride the Friday he and Isabel were in Mammoth.

"You can't let him get to you. This is what he does."

Watching the skiers zip down Shirley's bowl below us, I say, "You know, for someone who claims to be so chill and philosophical, Beck sure needs his friends to agree with him all the time."

Logan laughs and leans back into the lift chair, his skis swinging. "Beck doesn't have friends. Beck has disciples."

TWENTY-SEVEN

I smile when Logan's number comes through my phone. Pizza date tonight. "They better not be out of olives."

"Come to the store." Logan's voice sounds frightened.

I sit up on the couch, my chem textbook falling to the floor, my body buzzing with the worry in his voice. "What's going on?"

"Oli's missing. He went backcountry skiing and there was an avalanche and —" He breaks off to talk with someone, their voices muffled as if he's put his phone against his chest, then says, "Just come over."

My throat grows tight. "I'm at Trick's —"

"Beck and Isabel will pick you up." He hangs up.

Ten minutes later, Beck's Jeep pulls into the driveway and I jump in the back before he pulls to a full stop. Isabel fills me in. Oli and a couple of his friends went out on their Tele skis in an out-of-bounds area in Alpine Meadows this morning and there was an avalanche. Beck makes the right turn onto Squaw Valley Road, adding, "They're experts and they have the gear. They'll be okay."

Isabel stares out the window, and I can see the fear in her profile. I can't quite hear her, but I think she says, "Maybe."

We run through the Village, pushing through the door at

Neverland. It's busy in the way that waiting for news creates busy-ness, people milling around, making calls, talking in hushed voices — the whole room crackling with uncertainty. Isabel makes a beeline for her mom. April leans against the counter, a cell phone pressed to her ear. She nods and nods but says nothing. She disap-pears into the back before Isabel can reach her.

I'm left standing with Beck. "How does April know Oli?" I ask, mostly just to toss some words into the awkward silence.

Beck's worried eyes settle on me. "I keep forgetting how new you are to all of this, how much you don't know." He isn't being mean. He just says it, simply. As fact. But I realize it's what drew me to him in the first place. Sometimes, we need people who don't know our histories, who haven't already built up their view of us, because we hope they will see us in a new way. We need them to. And he did.

He nods toward where Isabel waits for her mom. "When Isabel's dad left, when she was six, they both had a hard time. I don't really remember it. We were just kids." Beck clears his throat. "But Oli took care of them." He swallows, his eyes on the group of men standing by the far wall, all dressed in jeans and Patagonia jackets. "I should go see what they know." He walks away.

Outside, the afternoon darkens. Feeling helpless, I cross to Isabel. "Can I do anything?" I ask. "Do you need anything? I can go get us tea?"

"Thanks, no — Logan went to get some."

I notice she's holding a card. I can't quite see what it is as she absently runs her thumb over it.

"What is that?"

She reddens slightly, slipping it into her pocket. "Nothing — you'll think it's dumb."

"I'm surprisingly open-minded."

She pulls it out and hands it to me. "It's my mom's."

I study it. The card is ink blue with a hooded robed figure holding a lantern and a staff. He stands on top of a snowy mountain looking down. "What is it?"

She peers at it. "I don't know that much about it. It's a tarot card. The Hermit. That's Mom's nickname for Oli." Isabel thinks for a minute. "Mom says the Hermit is one who lives in solitude by choice, and in his solitude is at peace. He's comfortable with who he is in the world and doesn't seek outside approval." She shows me the card again. "See here, he's looking down because he doesn't need to look around and see who's watching him, who's noticing. He lights his own way." She clears her throat. "Anyway, Mom wanted me to bring it to her so she could, you know, hold on to it." Her voice catches and I feel its waver in my gut.

"That's nice," I say quietly. Any way someone wants to hold on to her hope in a moment like this one makes sense to me.

Soon, April comes out from the shop and Isabel looks at her expectantly, but April simply crosses to her, her long arms encircling her daughter.

They don't know anything yet.

Across the store, I see Trick slip out the front door and disappear. Following him, I find him several stores away around the corner sitting on a bench, his breath powdery in the cold dark. The falling night in Squaw tastes like metal, and I shiver as I take a seat next to him. "Trick?"

He stares straight ahead, wiping quickly at some tears edging his eyes. "I keep telling myself he's fine. But it's been a long time. And it's getting dark."

"They'll find him."

He lets out a shaky breath. "You know, when your mom left, I lived with Oli for about four months. He was like that for people. If someone left or got hurt, he'd fill in for a bit until things started to right themselves. He did that for me, for April. He even took Beck in once when he was about fourteen when Jason threw him out." Trick stares at something far away — a memory — or maybe nothing at all. Finally, he mumbles, "I just want them to find him." His head dips, his hair shaggy, curling over his ears. He doesn't even have a hat on. Something about this detail — about how exposed he seems out here in the cold — thickens an ache in my chest. Why haven't they found him yet?

I chew at one of my fingernails, watching him. "Listen, it's freezing out here. Can I get you a beanie or some gloves or something?"

He shakes his head. "You know the thing about Oli? He never judges you for whatever baggage you show up with. He says people get dealt crazy hands and then spend most of their lives just trying to put the cards in order. He thinks our one job as humans is to not keep adding messed-up cards to the pile."

"That sounds like something he'd say." I think of Oli following me down the mountain with that same spirit, always a steady presence in case I fell, and the thought of him lost out there sends tears spilling down my cheeks. I wipe quickly at them. "When we were skiing once, he told me we shouldn't worry what other people say or think about us because most of the time they aren't thinking about us at all. Most people are just trying to find their car keys."

A smile glimmers on Trick's face. "That's classic Oli."

After a few minutes, he takes another shaky breath. "I need to tell you something, Mara."

It's as if all the cold from the air around us concentrates in my body and I'm afraid to even breathe. Still, somehow, I manage to say, "Okay."

"About my accident." He turns to me on the bench, his green eyes searching my face. "It was . . . the thing is . . . you were with me."

My body goes liquid. "What do you mean?"

"You were with me, skiing. I had you on my shoulders. I was goofing around — I'd do that sometimes because it would get you laughing . . . this belly laugh that just lit up the world. Anyway, I had you on my shoulders and I caught an edge. You went flying and I tried to . . . I tried to catch you, and that's when I jacked up my leg. And then there you were, just this little crumple in the snow, not moving." His voice shakes with the memory. I can't feel my face anymore or the tears helping to freeze it. "Your mom tried not to blame me and I tried not to blame myself, but, well, you were so tiny in that hospital bed, with all those wires and those beeping machines." He drops his eyes, his face pale.

I don't remember any of this. "But I was fine."

His face pained, he whispers, "You almost weren't . . . fine. You almost weren't. You were lucky. As bad as it first seemed, you just had bruises and a sprained knee. But when your mom saw you in that hospital bed, she had every right to leave."

I shake my head, running my hands absently over my knees. It's weird to not remember. "Oli said anyone can fall."

"I should *never* have had you on my shoulders. I was cocky and careless. I was careless with *you*." His voice breaks and he slides away on the bench, angles his back away from me, his shoulders shaking.

Feeling paralyzed, I study his back. Around me, lights come on

255

in some of the windows of the Village, yellow and soft, and there is a band playing in a restaurant somewhere near the main corridor. Two guys walk by us, en route to the main drag, their banter full of the day they just had on the mountain, their faces bronzed. They glance at Trick, their laughter dying down as they quicken their pace through the empty corridor past where we sit, until their voices fade completely.

Quietly, Trick says, "She decided it would be better if I just wasn't in your life."

"She did?"

"She was right."

I slide closer to him on the bench. "No, she wasn't. She was angry."

He doesn't respond because the air fills with footsteps slapping on the icy walk and a flurry of color emerges from around the corner. Isabel and Logan appear, panting. "They found him. They found him. He's okay. Broken arm. They're taking him to the hospital in Truckee."

His eyes pained, Trick looks at me. "Go," I tell him, my limbs flooding with relief.

He races back toward Neverland.

·   ·   ·

I sit by the fire Saturday afternoon at Elevation, sipping a latte and reading *Catcher in the Rye*, when I see Logan pull open the door of the café. "Hey!" He crosses to me. "I was looking for you. Did you get my text?"

"I did."

"I owe you a pizza."

"Last night was a little nuts." I went with April and Isabel to the hospital to see Oli, who didn't look at all like he'd been caught in an avalanche except for his left arm in a cast. "She'll get me someday," he said of the mountain. "But not today."

Logan takes in my ski clothes. "Did you already ski today?"

"Just a few runs this morning." I'd woken feeling both wound up by and exhausted from the drama of last night, so I'd let the mountain work out the knots.

He's also wearing his casual ski stuff. "You want to grab a few more before the slopes close?"

My eyes stray to my laptop. "I have to write a *Catcher in the Rye* essay. I can't put it off any longer."

"How much more do you have?"

"Haven't started."

"We can write it on the mountain." He bends over and starts packing up my stuff.

Laughing, I rescue my laptop before he can shut it down. "How exactly are we supposed to do that?"

He plucks the book from my hands, studying its plain white cover before stuffing it in my bag. "I've read it. What are you writing about?"

"I have to write about why Holden is an unreliable narrator."

"Who isn't an unreliable narrator? There, essay done." He stashes my stuff behind the counter and makes for the door.

"Wait, what do you mean?" I ask curiously, following him out of Elevation. "Logan!" But he's heading toward the funi.

•   •   •

A half hour later, we head up Big Blue, our skis dangling below us as we float through the bright, cold air. "Explain again how this is writing my essay?"

We're the only two people on the lift and Logan leans lazily in the corner, using his poles to knock snow from his skis. "You're not going to let this go, are you?" He looks up, the blue sky reflecting in the mirror of his goggles.

I shake my head. "I want to know what you meant about everyone being an unreliable narrator."

He leans forward on the bar, which still makes me nervous, and asks, "You want to ski Shirley or do a warm-up down Mountain?"

"Logan!"

He drops his head into his folded arms. "You're unbelievable, you know that? Such a good student."

He's lucky I don't hit him with one of my poles. "Yes, I am. And I think maybe you said you'd help me just to get me out here and you don't really have an idea one way or another about my essay."

He shoots me an impressed look. "Oh, right, play to my competitive side."

"Stalling . . ."

He sits back again, watching a skier zip by beneath us. "No, wait — I do have an idea about this. Holden's unreliable because he's telling us a story, but it's *his* version, and we don't really know if what he says is true." He raises the bar as the lift approaches the top of Big Blue. "So here's what I think: Isn't that *everyone*? Everyone only has one version, right? One way of looking at the world. Mostly, we tend to see what we want to see in it, so aren't we all, essentially, unreliable? Bam! Essay written." He pushes off the lift, and slightly stunned, I almost forget to follow him off.

I ski up to him. "Um, what was that?"

"Oh, I'm full of surprises," he says. "You'll see," he adds before skiing down the catwalk toward Shirley Lake.

After a few runs on Shirley, we hit the Gold Coast building for some fries. At this hour, the deck is almost empty. The day is unusually warm and it makes me sleepy. After we eat, we kick back on a bench seat, dropping our helmets on nearby chairs, and take in the warm light, our eyes closed.

After a moment, I feel him watching me.

My eyes flutter open just in time to see how close his face is to mine and his kiss catches me off guard. He tastes like salt and the sweetness of the Coke he just drank. Without thinking, I lean in, the kiss unwinding me, its sweetness much more than just the soda.

Before I know it, I'm crying.

He pulls back. "Oh, wait — you're crying?"

"I'm sorry," I mumble, trying to pull it together.

He looks embarrassed. "Okay, crying. That's an all-time low. I had a girl laugh once. But, yeah, never crying."

I shake my head. "It's not what you think. That was exactly right — it was amazing and exactly right."

He pulls back from me on the bench, reaching for his helmet. "Yeah, I can tell, what with all the sobbing." He hurries to put his helmet on.

"Why did you have to be like this," I blurt, wiping at my cheeks. "I came up here to take a break and get my head on straight and then you . . . you happened."

He snaps the buckle closed on his chinstrap. "Sorry?"

Words start spilling out. "You had to be so . . . you. So wonderful and sweet. I came to Tahoe to sort things out, to Live in the Now, but I can't do it! I keep worrying about what's next, what it all means for the future. I'm the worst Now Liver to ever . . . live. F-minus for Mara!"

He tries to hide a smile behind his glove.

"Right, laugh at me. I'm a mess. I make all these lists that I end up tripping over and waste time on stupid rules when, clearly, this whole time, I should have been, I don't know . . . I should have been kissing *you*."

As I try to stand, he grabs my arm, lightly. "I agree."

I shake my head. "I'm leaving next week! We have a week to hang out. That's not enough!"

His eyes flick to the side. "Actually, I'm skiing a race in Utah this weekend, so I'm not back until late Monday night."

My heart sinks. "Ugh, I have the worst timing. Two months I should have spent with you and they're just wasted, completely wasted."

His arms move around me. "Not wasted." He unhooks his helmet, tossing it on a nearby chair, takes my face in his hands, and says, "Kiss me now, and this time, try not to cry all over me. We'll talk about that other stuff later."

I'm barely able to move, but I whisper, "Okay."

His kiss sends a shock wave through me I've never felt before. He tightens his arms around my back, moving one hand into my hair at the nape of my neck. When he pulls away, his brown eyes meet mine for a moment before he hugs me to his chest. As I rest against him, he leans his chin on the top of my head. I hear Squaw around me — the slice of skiers and boarders moving through the snow, the wind, the creak and whirl of the lifts. It's like the music they play for babies to get them to sleep.

"You okay?" he finally asks.

"For now."

TWENTY-EIGHT

I pull my safety goggles off and make one last notation in my lab notebook. "Done," I say to Isabel, who has been hanging out on a stool nearby for the last five minutes waiting for me to finish. "Or at least as done as it's going to be."

"Well, it's hard to do chemistry through the googly eyes you and Logan were shooting at each other the whole time." She laughs, pulling her backpack on. We wave good-bye to Malika and head out the door. She nudges me. "He told me, by the way."

"About my crying. Yeah, that was awesome."

She grins. "He thought so."

A man passes us in the hall, a lanky history teacher named Micah, and he gives me a familiar wave. "When are you just going to enroll?" he teases as he walks past us.

"Tomorrow," I joke back, which is what I've been saying each time he asks.

This time, though, Isabel, stopping to tie her shoes, says, "You should."

"What?"

"Enroll."

I roll my eyes. "Right."

Standing, she adjusts the straps of her backpack. "Why not? You like it here, we like you, Logan *really* likes you." She grins at my flush. "You should just stay. This shouldn't be your last week."

I follow her into the student lounge. "I can't just stay."

Isabel flops down on the couch next to Amanda, who is French-braiding her own hair. "What's up?" she asks, wrapping an elastic band around the end of a braid. The other half of her hair hangs waiting, and she starts gathering it in her fingers.

Isabel fills her in. "I think she should stay and go to school here for the rest of the year."

Amanda nods as enthusiastically as she can without wrecking her hair. "Oh, totally."

Bodie wanders in, carrying his guitar. "What?"

"Mara should stay and go to school with us," Amanda tells him.

He looks confused. "How would that be different from now?"

"She was just here for a break," Isabel reminds him. At his blank look, she adds, "You're coming to her going-away party at Logan's this Friday night. She's going back to San Diego, remember?"

"Lucky," he says, strumming his guitar. "San Diego has sweet surfing."

"I don't surf," I explain, even though this is not the point at all. "It doesn't matter anyway. My mom would never let me stay."

As I say it, though, I shiver with the start of an idea. Would she let me stay?

•   •   •

I wake up off and on all night, my mind spinning with lists. Staying lists. Leaving lists. I can't seem to stop the cycle. The fire

262

crackles — awake! Asleep again. The cottage creaks — awake! With each jolt, I lie in bed, staring into the dark, thinking, *Can I stay? Or do I leave on Saturday as planned?*

I think about all the goals I made to live in the now while I was in Tahoe — meditate, sleep in, kiss a boy, stay off social media, slap on lavender oil.

Check, check, check, check, check.

Have I completely missed the point?

Wednesday morning, I open my backup binder and look at the original Now List.

6. Simplify & downsize!!

Done.

I crossed it off that first night in Tahoe because of living with Trick, because I brought only four pairs of socks and three sweat-shirts. But I never truly *simplified my life.* If anything, I made things more complicated. In trying to maintain all of my Ranfield work and goals and plans, *plus* adding my two different versions of the Now List, I just made everything harder.

Maybe I can fix that.

Dressed in jeans and my parka, I grab the first tram up to High Camp. Stretching out around me, the snowcapped mountains give me courage and my idea churns through my mind. A couple from Wisconsin distracts the cable car attendant through our glide up the mountain, so he doesn't try to talk to me. I bask in the soli-tude, the ride its own brand of meditation. Check.

When we dock at the top, I make my way off the car, head inside, and find a spot in the restaurant by the window. Almost dizzy from the sweeping views (more likely it's the email I'm about to write), I sit down to make a third version of my Now List, the one I dreamed about last night. The one that jolted me awake for the final time in the thin light of dawn.

Only it's not really a list.

It's an explanation to Mom. Turns out, I've been going about this whole Now thing all wrong. I thought Now was a single place in time, an isolated moment when people do crazy-brave stunts like skydiving or learning to ski or kissing a random boy without worrying about the consequences.

But Now isn't any of those things.

I open my laptop and begin an email to my mom.

Subject: The Now List III

Guess what. I figured out what Living in the Now means to me. Now isn't isolated moments on a checklist. It's not meditating or drinking a kale smoothie. Now is the time when you look hard at everything, weigh it, and then take the next step. Now is everything that happened before, leading to everything that might someday be possible. Which makes Now this crazy-powerful thing, right? It's the ultimate hybrid. And it's different for everyone because it's my specific past balanced with my own potential. To live in the now, I have to respect everything from before while at the exact same time opening my heart to everything I might change so I can create the future I want. Now is the ultimate tightrope walker, the sweet spot in tennis, the snowplow (pizza slice, French fries, pizza slice).

Now is the choice right before Next.

I want to stay in Tahoe, Mom. I feel balanced here. I'm pretty sure it's my sweet spot. The great thing is that the reason I know this is because of everything that came before, because Ranfield (all the competition and busyness and stress) built me and wrecked me and then put me here. For a reason. So I want to stay. This is what my Now taught me.

Thank you for letting me come here and figure this out. Please say yes.

Love,

Mara

P.S. I included a link to Crest Charter's schedule and college acceptance list (UCLA, U of Oregon, Pomona, Dartmouth! to name a few) and a list of classes. Note: Advanced Naps and How to Party Like It's 1999 aren't on there!!

I read it over a few times, making small changes, taking breaks to let my eyes rest on peaks out the wide windows of the restaurant. I should probably call her, but I want her to be able to read this all the way through before she starts arguing with me, before she starts giving me reasons why I'm wrong.

I press SEND.

•　　•　　•

The next morning, I'm curled up in bed reading a book Isabel gave me about a teenage ghost detective (a book on no suggested reading list anywhere). I'm trying to ignore the fact that Mom hasn't responded to my email yet. Or to the six texts I sent since the email. Mom never waits this long to respond to anything, so my mind spins possible reasons:

> She dropped her phone in the ocean.
> She has driven off a cliff.
> She is being held hostage.

I shared all of these options with Logan at dinner last night. He suggested that maybe she just hasn't decided yet, but I kept checking my phone anyway until he finally took it away so we could have an actual conversation.

Now I notice Trick hovering in the doorway. He wears neon-blue ski pants and a black parka. "I'm taking you skiing."

I sit up, my heart catching. "Really?"

"Get dressed."

I motion at his pants. "What are you *wearing*?"

"What — these?" He models the ski pants, turning around so I can fully appreciate the hot-pink accents on the back pockets. "These are rockin'."

"I think the word you're looking for is *relic*."

"Don't question the pants." Laughing, he heads back into the other room, calling out, "Get dressed. We'll miss all the good snow."

I can't stop smiling as I hurry to yank on my ski gear.

A half hour later, we're heading up the funi. Like Oli, Trick doesn't talk much when he's skiing. We take a few runs down Big Blue, head over to Gold Coast for a run, and hit a couple of different shoots on Shirley. Trick's leg makes him slow, which is fine with me because I tend to prefer the wide turns and breaks, but his form comes through. He has a steady ease on the mountain that I'm not sure I'll ever have. At one point, we ski near a small terrain park where boarders and skiers do flips and jumps and other tricks on the half-pipe. Trick slows to a stop a dozen yards away, watching them, his eyes unreadable behind his mirrored goggles.

One boy skis backward on his skis, picking up pace until he's speeding up the side of the half-pipe, twisting his body into a knot, and then landing face-forward. "Wow, that was cool." I glance at Trick.

He pinches his lips together. "Not bad. Come on," he says, pushing off on his poles and continuing down the hill.

After another run, we stop at Gold Coast for some lunch. While I stack our helmets and gloves on a nearby chair, Trick opens the small backpack he's been carrying and pulls out a metal water bottle, salami, crackers, cheese, chocolate-covered almonds, and some baby carrots. "Set this stuff up," he tells me before heading inside to get us some hot chocolates.

As we eat, we watch the skiers and boarders sail past us. The sun warms my shoulders, and a slight breeze moves the hair from my face. I almost stop thinking about Mom not getting back to me yet. Finally, my phone buzzes just as we're packing up.

The food lumps in my stomach. She writes:

Has Trick talked to you yet?

Wait, what is he going to say to me? That I can stay? That Mom and Will said yes? Before I can help myself, I start speed-listing images of my life in Tahoe:

walking the hallways at Crest
skiing with Logan and Isabel
bonfires
more eighties dress-up days
Logan making me pizza while I sit by his fireplace

Stop it. She hasn't said yes yet.

Fireplace, fireplace, fireplace.

I text back: not yet.

No response.

"Let's go." I hop up, gathering up the remains of our lunch.

We pause at the top of Big Blue. Trick motions to a spot farther down the catwalk. "You want to do a different shoot on Shirley this time?"

"Trick? Can I ask you something?"

He literally braces himself, putting weight on his poles, as if he knows what I'm about to ask. "Sure."

My mouth dries out, but I manage, "I'd like to stay in Tahoe, live here, and go to school here." I'm not sure I've ever lived more in the now than *right now.* This moment.

"Yeah, I talked to your mom last night." He swallows and fishes his water bottle out of his pack. Maybe dry mouth is a genetic condition. "It's why I took you out today. So we could talk." We have been doing no talking whatsoever.

"Oh?" I can't bring myself to say anything else. People whoosh past us, some stopping to take in the view and others just transitioning right into the run on their boards or skis.

"I don't think it's a good idea," Trick says, tucking the water bottle away.

The world tumbles around me — all the wind and sky and pine and snow and slice of blue Lake Tahoe spinning away. "No, it's a great idea, see — I could live here. And finish high school here. With you."

Sighing, he shakes his head. "Listen, I know it seems like a good idea right now. It seems easy and beautiful and fun."

I nod. "Right, yes — all those things."

"Those are my genes," he says sheepishly. "Path of least resistance. All those years ago when your mom said you would be better off without me in your life, I just accepted that. It was easier that way. No struggle. But I was wrong about that, Mara. Absence, avoidance — they're sometimes necessary but shouldn't become a lifestyle choice."

I shake my head. "But that's not what I'm doing. I'm choosing what's better for me. The slower pace, the mountains. I love it here. I *belong* here."

"Maybe you do. But Tahoe's not going anywhere. And you have some unfinished business at that fancy school of yours. I was a coward all those years ago and I have to live with that. I have to find peace with that and it's not easy, trust me. But you — you have a chance to make it right. Now. To walk in there and show those kids it didn't beat you, that it didn't break you."

Quietly, staring down at the snow on my skis, I say, "But it did."

He puts a gloved hand on my arm. "No, it didn't. It *changed* you. And the most important things in our lives change us in some way. When we let them. Go back to Ranfield, make peace with what happened there. Like I said, Tahoe isn't going anywhere. You can always come back. You know it's here when you need it."

My lip quivers dangerously. "Great, just great, you choose *now* to start acting like a dad. Just my luck."

"You're very lucky. I think you know that."

I can't believe this. From Trick McHale of all people. "What about how stressful San Diego is? You told Isabel I needed to have some fun."

He sighs. "Fun's great. It's essential. But I don't think you'll be happy without both. The fun and the hard stuff. Not in the long run. Am I right?"

Whatever. I adjust my pole straps. "You know what? I don't really feel like skiing with you anymore." Without waiting for his response, I take off down the mountain.

•   •   •

I call Mom from a quiet bench tucked away in one of the side alleys of the Village. She picks up instantly. "Oh, sweetie. Trick told you, didn't he?"

"Yes." Tears. The embarrassing kind with the ragged breathing and the snot.

"I'm sorry, Mara."

"I . . . I . . . have to come home," I manage, wiping my nose with the sleeve of my jacket.

"I know. He told me. But it's really for the best, honey." She keeps her voice kind, but I detect a smudge of victory underneath. "I know you don't want to hear it, but I agree with Trick on this one. It's best to come home on Saturday like we planned. I've let Ranfield know you'll be back on Monday."

I watch the people move past with their skis, with their snowboards, with their white-lidded cups of coffee. "I just thought I found the right place, you know? I'm ready to be here now." *Now.* That word keeps changing shape on me.

"Life doesn't always work out the way we want at every turn. You have to grow up."

All the people who tell you to grow up always seem to have the luxury of having already done it, so maybe they should stop being so pushy. "Mom, you say that like growing up's a light switch. On. Off. And it's not."

She pauses. "That's not what I meant."

"I have to go." I click off my phone, my hand shaking. I pull my legs into my chest and look up. Minutes ago, the sky had been blue, but now the Squaw Valley sun is more a sheen on the sheet-metal clouds than a single source of light.

It starts to snow. Single, quick flecks. Tiny bits of cut crystal. As if to say, *I am quicksilver and cold and always changing, and I will surprise and surprise and surprise you.*

TWENTY-NINE

Friday evening, I sit with my bags on the couch beside me, watching the flames dwindle through the glass of the woodstove. Today, I packed my life into three neat duffel bags. Only three. And I threw out all of my Now Lists and binders.

My phone says 7:14. I'm supposed to be at my going-away party right now at Logan's house, but I can't seem to get off this couch. In twelve hours, Trick will take me to the Reno airport, load me on a plane, and send me back to San Diego.

Someone knocks at the door, and Logan pokes his head inside. His hair curls out from under a beanie the color of hot chocolate. "Thought you might need a ride."

A few minutes later, Logan pulls his car into the plowed driveway of his house. He looks sideways at me, cutting the headlights so the tiny red chili pepper lights glowing over the front door stand out in the dark. He sees me notice them. "I couldn't find the box with the Christmas lights. Just the box marked BBQ. But I thought they'd look nice. Festive."

"I'm a chili pepper fan," I joke, but my voice catches.

"Listen," he says, leaning toward me, his arm resting on the center console, where he keeps a stainless steel coffee mug and a

272

pair of battered white sunglasses. "I know this isn't how you wanted it to work out. I know you wanted to stay. Believe me, I did, too. But let's not get too sad, okay? I made you your pizza. Olives and mushrooms. Isabel brought Skittles. Bodie has his guitar and he does a few passable Nirvana covers. Let's not think of this as some huge good-bye. You're not moving to a remote outpost in the Gobi Desert. It's not like we'll lose all contact."

Like an idiot, I start to cry. "I know."

He takes my hand, his touch that strange combination of electricity and comfort. "Because the thing is — this isn't an ending." He clears his throat, and even in the dark, a red flush crawls across his cheeks. "I was hoping to think of this more as the start of something. We can keep getting to know each other. I can call you. You can call me."

"I'm not sure I can handle the whole long-distance thing."

"Then let's not call it that, okay? Let's figure it out as we go. Without lists and rules." He clears his throat again, looking nervous. "I like you, Mara. A lot. And at some point in our future, I'd like to kiss you without it starting with tears." He wipes at some of the ones currently taking up residence on my face.

"It's good to have goals," I sniff.

"Come on." He opens the door and scrambles out.

Inside, Isabel is yelling at Bodie. He stands on a swivel chair, wearing a T-shirt that reads SAVE IT FOR FACEBOOK, and clutches one end of a half-drooping sign in his hand. Isabel holds the other end. "You have to attach it to something, genius — this won't reach!" She spots Logan and me. "Oh, hey, sorry — we would have the sign up, but Frank Lloyd Wright over there thinks he can get a better angle."

Bodie frowns, the sign dipping again. "*The Phantom of the Opera* guy? What does he have to do with anything?"

Amanda giggles on the couch, paging through a snowboarding magazine and eating straight from a bag of barbecue potato chips. "That's Andrew Lloyd Webber. Frank Lloyd Wright was an architect."

Logan crosses to the kitchen. "Did you at least put the pizza in?"

They all look at one another. "Oops." Bodie shrugs. "Sorry, bro." He tapes the sign quickly to the kitchen island. In wobbly Sharpie letters, the sign reads SEE YA, MARA!

"Bodie made the sign," Isabel says apologetically, pushing bowls of chips and salsa in my direction.

"Yeah, I did." He nods, proudly studying his work.

"It's a great sign, Bodie." I grab a chip from the bowl and jam it into my mouth, a chip shield to hold back any tears threatening to resurface.

My body grows heavier as I watch them. Logan puts the pizza into the oven. Isabel moves the poster back to where she must have wanted it in the first place. Bodie takes a running leap, hurtling over the back of the couch and landing next to Amanda, and crunches her bag of chips. "Nice," she says, her curtain of hair hiding the obvious eye roll I hear in her voice. Bodie unearths the bag and tips the remaining crush of chips into his mouth.

They will go on like this here. I will leave tomorrow and they will make pizza and race one another down mountains and see the alpenglow wash the evening mountains with rose-colored light. And I will be gone.

The front door opens.

Beck.

Logan pauses at the counter where he was about to roll out another pizza, and his eyes dart to Isabel, who shakes her head as if to say, *I didn't tell him.* Beck slips off his beanie and stuffs it into the pocket of his green parka. This is his secret, I realize, watching him — he makes disinterest and messiness so appealing.

"Didn't want to miss the grand good-bye," he says in that way of his. Some people can say the simplest things and still make them sound like they're predicting misfortune. "You doing okay, heading back into that police state you call a school? Back to being a drone."

"Stop it, Beck," Isabel says from behind the counter, unwrapping a package of mozzarella.

Beck's eyes glint with a dark amusement. "I was just asking."

"Well, just stop asking." Isabel violently grates the cheese.

The room grows warm with the smell of pizza. The fire crackles and casts a flickering light into the room. They just want to say good-bye to me — pizza, some board games, Bodie's guitar — nothing major.

But Beck has to bring in an ice storm.

"Why is this what you do?" I ask him as he moves past me toward the counter to grab a handful of chips.

He pops a chip in his mouth. "What do you mean?"

"Did you *not* notice that when you walked in the door, the temperature dropped about forty degrees?"

"If you say so." He turns his back to me, picking through the open can of olives.

The other thing about leaving? It makes you brave. "But since you asked, I'd like to answer your question, even if it was just you being predictably rhetorical and obnoxious." This last bit gets a snort of laughter from Amanda and Isabel. "The answer is no, I'm not excited about heading back into that police state I call a school. But I'm not a drone. You've got that wrong. Just because I get good grades and work hard and —"

"Jump through hoops like a trained monkey," Beck interrupts, barely turning to me.

Logan leans into the counter, wiping his hands on a towel. "Hey —"

I stop him. "No, it's okay. I got this." And surprisingly, it's not anger I feel. Quite the opposite. I start laughing. "Yes, Beck. That's what I am. A trained monkey. Because I want to do well in school and go to college and find a job I actually like. Yep, I'm a huge conformist idiot."

He turns to give me an odd look. "Your words, not mine."

"You know what, Beck? At least I care. You think you're so anti-system but you're not. Because we all choose a system, whether we like it or not. Yours seems to be of the *Dad's a jerk so I'm a victim and the whole world sucks* variety. Congratulations. But you're not as deep as you think you are. It's not deep to trash things all the time. It's not deep to make other people feel small because they want something different from you. That's not deep. It's sad.

"You know what I've realized here in Tahoe? That I would *love* to have this life. I just can't right now. Maybe someday. But I'm not going to sulk back to San Diego. I'm going to go back and work hard because that's how I want to show up in the world. I can't fix everything that's wrong, like hurricanes and homeless people and war, but I can work hard and be a decent person. That's a choice. So are the excuses we make. You're not the only one in this room who has a dad who let you down. It's not fair, I get it. But hiding behind your pseudophilosophies and being such a jerk all the time? That's on you."

The air in the room has thickened into an uncomfortable hush. Beck looks like he might respond. It would be his right to say something like *Really, all this from the girl hiding out in Neverland?* But he doesn't. He just lowers his eyes, moves across the room, and leaves.

Isabel goes to the door, staring out into the dark. Bodie and Amanda check their phones so they don't have to make eye contact with me.

But Logan does, and the way he looks at me feels like warm towels from the dryer. I unclench my hands, feeling the little moon-shaped nail cuts left on my palms throb. My whole body shakes like I've just run a race. "I guess that was kind of harsh."

Logan holds a piece of pizza on a paper plate. "You just said what we were all thinking. Much more articulately, though." He holds out the plate. "Mushrooms and olives?"

"Thanks." I take a bite. It's delicious, and as I eat, some of the adrenaline begins to drain away.

Logan watches me eat. "It's good, right? I make a pretty awesome pizza. Not as awesome as your speeches, but close."

My phone buzzes on the counter and Logan frowns at it. "It's Beck," he says, handing it to me. Wiping my fingers on the cuffs of my sweatshirt, I check it. It says simply, have a safe trip, san diego.

Isabel comes and peers over my shoulder at it, shaking her head.

"He must know how sick we get of him being such a downer all the time, right?" Amanda asks.

I wonder if Beck knows, if any of us truly knows. Do we deep-down know who we are in the world? How we affect other people?

We must have an inkling, right? Based on the way other people move to surround or avoid us? Maybe some of us don't care. Or maybe we can only know if we choose to be honest with ourselves and stop pointing fingers in opposite directions. The world is a mirror that reflects us, but having the courage to look must be one of the hardest things we do as humans. Because it's not always pretty what's staring back. Sometimes it's a scared, exhausted mess who would rather hide in the mountains than deal with the aftermath of her own perfectionism.

Still, we have to look if we want things to change, right?

· · ·

Logan pulls into Trick's driveway a little after eleven and cuts the engine. He looks sideways at me, his hand still resting on the keys in the ignition. "What time's your flight tomorrow? You all packed?"

"All packed. We're leaving at seven."

He hands me a package wrapped in grocery-bag brown paper and tied with what looks like the lace of a snowboard boot. "Um, I got you this."

"Nice wrapping job." I try to be light, but his gift sends an ache coursing through me. I open it, and inside rests a black Frost Boys sweatshirt and a CD titled *Songs to Bring You Home*. "I love it." I pull a pack of dark-chocolate coconut cookies from my bag. "For the record, your gift's better than mine."

He holds my gaze. "Not a competition."

I study his shadowy face, the curve of his jaw. "You are the sweetest guy, you know that?"

He looks away, running his hands over the top of the steering wheel. "I know, I know, I think I need to be more of a jerk. The jerks get all the girls."

"Not all of them." I put my hands on either side of his sweet Logan face and pull him in to kiss me. "Look, no crying."

He wraps his arms around me and I melt into the warmth of his kiss, at the way it takes a delicious eraser to my world. Because right now, there's nothing else. No wash of winter stars, no plane leaving tomorrow, no mountains to race down or futures to plan. Of everything in Tahoe, I will miss Logan the most. He's the fire in the woodstove you take totally for granted but, when it goes out, leaves everything cold.

THE NOW LIST II

1. ~~Get Trick to talk more!!~~
2. ~~Let my phone run out of power~~
3. ~~Focus, Mara!~~
4. ~~Be brave (thanks, Will)~~ ✳ ✳
5. ~~Ski blue runs with confidence.~~ Black runs? (Next season?)
6. ~~Stop and smell the alpenglow~~
7. ~~HAVE MORE FUN~~
8. ~~Be more spontaneous!~~
9. No boys!

THIRTY

As we drive out of Squaw Valley, the rising sun turns the stretch of sky amethyst. We're silent until Trick pulls into the passenger unloading zone at the Reno airport. "Here we are." He gets out and lifts my bags from behind the truck seats.

We stare at each other.

"You got everything?" he finally asks.

"I think so." I clear my throat, swinging my carry-on over my shoulder.

"Mara?"

"Yeah?"

Without saying anything more, without meeting my eyes, he pulls me into a hug that smells like wood smoke and snow. Figures with Trick, my first hug from him would be when I'm leaving and absent of words. But it's okay. We have started something here, something we can cultivate. Somehow in so much silence, we've managed to grow a few roots.

Inside, I check in at the counter with the tired-looking Southwest desk clerk as he hefts my bags onto the conveyor belt. I move through security, thinking about the carnelian stone and Frost Boys sweatshirt tucked safely into the carry-on bag I place in the beige airport tub. Once through, I find a café and hand a woman five dollars for a latte in a white paper cup with a black plastic lid. The guy behind me shuffles, annoyed, mumbling comments about how long the line is, how long it's taking. When he finally gets to the counter, the barista says, "Thanks for your patience," and for some reason it makes me think of Natalie and Elevation, and I walk away smiling.

On the plane, I study the other people coming up the aisle, looking for a nook for their own bags. It strikes me that each of these people has a single life, with dreams and defeats and joy and sorrow, and each has to go through the daily steps to get where they want to go.

Oli said most people are just looking for their car keys. Which means they aren't looking at me at all. It's up to me to put what I want to be in the world and deal with the consequences. How people respond is out of my control. That video hurt — the comments, the whispering, the thousands upon thousands of views — and I'm still ashamed of what happened. But I can't change it. It partly happened because I spent so much time trying to be perfect, I forgot to be, well, just Mara. Not Tahoe Mara. Or Miss Perfect Mara. Just Mara.

Now I have a choice. I can either let the world turn me sour and hateful and afraid. Or I can be the Mara I want to be and face it with as much grace and humor as possible. Wherever I land, I'm the common denominator in my own life. It's not about geography. I can work hard for something out there in the future, but I need to take breaks to appreciate the things I already have. For those of us lucky enough to be born into my type of life, it's often about our point of view, to believe we're already winning just by getting out of bed.

•   •   •

When I land, Mom meets me outside, her Lexus idling. I have my stuff mounded onto one of those pushcarts and she looks relieved, as if she's thinking, *At least I've raised a daughter who knows how to pile her things on a pushcart and make her way home.* As we leave the airport, Mom turns the Lexus onto Harbor Drive. The view both familiar and strange, I stare out the car window. On the right, sailboats dot the glittering water of the bay. I see the single cruise liner, the *Star of India*, docked, and the USS *Midway* museum aircraft carrier with the Coronado Bridge beyond. On the left, we pass the pink art deco administration building and then there is the high-rise cityscape of San Diego. Palm trees and bleached stucco and vast blue water.

Home.

Mom is talking but I've missed most of the beginning of what she is saying, and now she's handing me a folder. "What's this?"

"It's the packet from AYS. You don't even have to reapply. You're in." She looks so happy for me. I stare down at the yellow folder. AYS stands for America's Young Scientists, a six-week summer program I took last year after a grueling application process. "Very elite," my counselor said. "It'll look great on your college applications."

"Actually, Mom. I don't think I'm going to do AYS this summer." I set the packet at my feet.

She bites her lip, frowning, but waves it off as she changes lanes. "You don't have to decide that now. Oh! — and I made you an appointment with a woman named Ashley Callahan. She specializes in college advising with students who have unique circumstances like yours. You can talk with her about it."

I turn back to the window, hiding a smile. It strikes me as funny that someone has a job specializing in kids like me, ones with *unique circumstances.* Aren't circumstances, by definition, unique? I would love to see her list of clients. A bunch of privileged kids whose parents think not being able to get into a first-tier school qualifies as a crisis. I can just picture our first meeting. *Hi, Mara. Your life won't be as perfect and award-winning as you initially thought*, she'll say, adjusting her six-hundred-dollar glasses, *but we'll find you something else. That will be two hundred dollars per hour, please.* I tip the air-conditioning toward me; it's probably fifty degrees outside but it feels hot. *Something else.* I smile into the flow of air. *Something else* will be just fine.

Mom looks sideways at me. "Are you hungry? Do you want to stop for a salad somewhere?" I shake my head, staring out at the passing traffic, my senses recalibrating to San Diego zipping by outside. "It feels good to have you home," she tries again.

"Thanks, Mom." Before I left, I heard Trick on the phone with her, letting her know he'd told me about the accident. Staring out at the passing cars, I wonder if she'll ever talk to me about it, or if, like so many things with people, it will be left unsaid. Maybe the knowing is enough.

I take a deep breath. San Diego is a beautiful place. Busy and fast and full of the vibrant things that make up cities everywhere.

But right now, it's not my favorite beautiful place.

It's not San Diego's fault. This is Josie's place — she seems made to be here, made of sand and salt water and sea air. Not me, though. Turns out, I belong tucked into a mountain range somewhere. Some people feed off the busy, but I have the opposite reaction. I need the stillness, the smallness, to remind me to settle, to breathe. But the gift of Tahoe is that I know this now. I know that no matter what happens here, I will always have a place I can return to when I need it. My geographic insurance policy.

My body feels light, like snowfall, and studying Mom's profile, her blond hair newly trimmed and highlighted, her linen suit stylish, her French pedicure perfect in her sandals, I realize this is her place. Where she feels the most like herself. Maybe San Diego saved her when she was at her lowest point the way Tahoe saved me when I was at mine. I fill with a silly kind of childhood love for her — all her Google calendars and spreadsheets and checklists.

Because sometimes love looks like a spreadsheet.

"Actually, I would love some Mexican food." I smile sideways at her. "Tahoe just didn't have the Mexican food I'm used to."

A stripe of late afternoon sun brightens her face as she moves back into the slow lane. "Absolutely. I know the best place," she says, turning on her blinker and taking the next exit.

•   •   •

A lit-up sailboat moves across the dark waters of the ocean. Josie points it out before pulling a Ranfield Ravens sweatshirt over her head. We sit on the cool sand of the beach at La Jolla Shores, where we came to eat sandwiches and watch the water grow black. A breeze blows the salty ocean air through my hair. The windows of the houses to the south begin to twinkle in the dark, the pier is drenched in shadow, and the crumbly waves move against the shore. A shaggy-haired man in a faded sweatshirt and jeans walks barefoot down the beach, and it strikes me that people come here to disappear, too. Tahoe has ski bums. We have beach bums. Maybe everywhere has its own version of people who duck under the radar.

"You can feel free to add to that." I motion at the present I've just given Josie. "It's a work in progress."

Josie uses her phone as a light to read it. "This is cool, Mara — thanks." She studies the Be a Better Friend to Josie List I made. I'd even decorated it with some sparkly ocean stickers and slipped it into a clear plastic sleeve.

> Go with you to parties even when I don't want to.
> Talk about boys when you want to talk about boys.
> Talk about everything else, too.
> Spend Friday nights *not* studying.
> Watch boring ocean documentaries.
> Tell you how I'm feeling (most of the time).

She tucks it into her bag along with her phone, and the sand turns shadowy around her again. "First day back tomorrow," she says. "It'll be great — you'll see." She returns to watching the boat's slow progress. "Don't be nervous."

I run sand through my fingers. I *am* nervous. There is no way I won't be nervous. It's my nature in the same way I can't help but have blue eyes or the freckles that pop up when I get too much sun.

Tomorrow, I will walk into calculus with the tall windows and the desks set in rows and my stomach will twist into a thousand knots and I'll feel like I might faint.

But I will survive it.

I will go through the steps: walk through that door, sit down, take notes, write down the assignment, listen to the lecture. And then it will be over. And I'll have done something that two months ago I was pretty sure I'd never be able to do again.

"You're nervous, I can tell." Josie tugs the end of her glossy ponytail, her dark eyes concerned.

"I can't *not* be nervous, Jo. Mostly because I don't know how to feel anything other than how I already do. But I'll be okay." I wiggle my toes in the sand. "One of the hardest parts is that I still don't know who posted the video. I'll walk into class not knowing and that person will just be sitting there. I'll see all those faces and think, *Was it you? Was it you? Or you?*"

"I know." Josie follows my gaze across the waves, the light of the moon wriggling across them. "But you're forgetting the most important part."

"Which is what?"

She threads her fingers through mine. "You know who it *wasn't*."

·   ·   ·

And so I do it. I walk into calculus, my chest in a clench, my palms slick with sweat. Students sit at their desks or on top of them, chatting with each other. A couple of kids seem to be hurriedly finishing last night's assignment. Mr. Henly writes out tonight's homework, his black dry-erase squeaking across the stretch of whiteboard. This morning, before school, I brought him a paper shredder from Costco with a shiny red bow. He'd looked up from where he sat grading papers at his desk and said, "Good girl."

Eyes swivel in my direction and, for a moment, nothing — and then some murmurs, some whispers, and the hair on my neck stands on end. I'm about to ask Mr. Henly where I should sit, navigating the silence like a dark alley, when Jaydon Barris, a senior boy who spends most of his time trying to get everyone to come see his improv group perform at a random café somewhere, pops up from a desk. "Mr. Henly, I can't find my phone! I need the pass — it has *all* of my new sketches on it." He darts down the aisle, nearly knocking me over. "Oh, hey, Mara — wait, did you have mono or something?"

"What?" I barely manage. "No."

"Oh." Jayden grabs the oversize protractor, which Mr. Henly uses as a pass, from its hook by the door and bolts from the room. *Not just car keys, Oli*, I think — *sometimes also phones.*

Mr. Henly catches my eye. He wears one of the plaid shirts he always wears, tucked into a pair of navy blue trousers. "Mara, same seat," he offers, with a wave of his hand toward the row where I'd ripped up all the tests, where everything had gone blurry, where someone had filmed it and posted it for hundreds of thousands to see. He motions again, giving me a faint math-teachery smile.

I sit down, opening my binder to a blank piece of paper. The board reads *Differentiation Formulas* in Mr. Henly's crisp, boxy handwriting. Just as the bell rings, Chris Locke slides into the seat next to me. "Hey," he says, flipping open his green binder. "Welcome back."

THIRTY-ONE

In the last week of May, we sit on our patio, the dregs of Saturday dinner in front of us. The twins play paddleball on the lawn, or their version of it, which is mostly trying to bean each other in the head with the rubber ball. Mom gets up to refill my iced tea. Will holds up his iPad from across the table. "Look, Mara. Dog shaming." He shows me a picture of a cream-colored French bulldog, his muzzle stained green, with a sign hanging around his neck reading I ATE ALL THE JELL-O. "Look how many views he got." Over a million.

"I know how that dog feels," I quip, pleased that I can actually joke about the YouTube video now. I return to the novel I'm reading. It's not for school. It has mermaids and aliens in it. Mom saw it at Costco and bought it for me, which is her way of trying to ease her own foot off the gas pedal.

Will laughs, scrolling through more pictures. "Lots of shameful dogs in this world." He shows me another one. Amused, I study my stepdad, my heart swelling as I remember the Shells of Wisdom he had waiting when I got home from Tahoe.

MISSED YOU

Mom slips back into her chair with a glass of white wine. "What finals do you have on Tuesday?" She tries to sound offhand, like she's just remembered I have finals next week and hasn't secretly been planning a study schedule for me in her head.

She's gotten better, but she's still Mom.

"French and English." She starts to say something, but Will flashes her a warning look. "I'm studying with Josie tomorrow at her house," I tell her. Closing my book, I add, "But just so there are no surprises, I'm getting a B in calculus and probably one in AP US history. Maybe an A-minus."

Her mouth, whether she likes it or not, makes a thin line. "Okay, well, I'm sure that will be fine." Fine is a sour taste in Mom's mouth. Like I said, she's trying.

My cell rings. Looking down, I see the caller ID: Trick.

He's called off and on since I've been back from Tahoe. Predictably, the conversations are mostly short. He tells me about the store and stuff I already know about Isabel and Logan since I talk to both of them more than I do to him. Isabel continues to inch closer to qualifying for the US Ski Team. Not yet, though. Not this season. In April, I sent a congratulations card for a great season. I might be more impressed that she keeps trying than if she had actually made the team. Trick never talks about Beck and I don't ask. And Logan. Well, my Things That Make Logan Amazing List just keeps getting longer.

Now I hold up the phone. Mom doesn't like us to answer phone calls during dinner, and technically, even though I'm reading, we're still all sitting here. "Do you mind if I take this?" I ask, and she motions for me to answer it.

"Hi, Trick."

"Oh, hey — didn't know if you'd answer. Any big Saturday night plans?"

I look around the yard. "Yeah, huge."

"I won't keep you," he says hurriedly.

"I'm sitting in the yard. Not really breaking any party records tonight."

"Oh, okay. Anyway, I was talking to Matt Never today and he's looking for someone to work at the Tahoe City shop this summer part-time, and, well, I thought of you."

I sit up. Mom and Will exchange a look. I repeat his offer. "I'm putting you on speaker with Mom and Will."

Mom leans toward the phone. "Hi, Trick. That's a really nice offer, but Mara's busy this summer. She has a six-week science program she's enrolled in." I shake my head at her. "No," I mouth, but she waves me off, which lights a flame of annoyance in me.

Silence on the other end, until, finally, "Okay, right. You already have plans. I didn't think about that. When I was a kid, summer was just, you know, summer."

"It's not like that anymore," Mom says, gripping her wine glass.

It might be like that, though, for some kids.

He clears his throat. "Okay, well, I just wanted to throw it out there. Think on it."

"Thanks, anyway," Mom calls out, standing, collecting plates, glasses, forks.

I hang up and help her carry some dishes into the kitchen. "Mom, I'm not doing AYS this summer. I told you that."

She yanks open the dishwasher. "We hadn't really made a final decision about that."

"Yes, I did."

She puts the lasagna pan in the sink to soak. "Tahoe's not an option."

"Why not?" Tahoe for the summer. I'm itching to text Logan and Isabel.

She scrapes lasagna off a plate into the garbage disposal with a little more force than necessary. Liam's plate. He always picks out all the mushrooms. "Because you have commitments here. You need to start your college applications."

"I can start my college applications in Tahoe. Squaw Valley has Wi-Fi." What she really means is *I need to be with you while you start your college applications*.

"You can't just hang out at Neverland all summer." The way she says it sounds like I might be considering starting my own meth lab.

I move the rest of the lasagna into a Tupperware. "Why?" I really want this to be my summer.

She stacks our plates and glasses and silverware into the dishwasher in her ordered way. "You know, Mara, there's a reason Wendy *leaves* Neverland. She realizes she has to live her real life."

I'm surprised she hasn't brought that up before. Taking a moment to choose my words, I try to explain an idea that's been stirring in my mind for the last few weeks. "You know what? I think Neverland has nothing to do with geography. I think maybe it's a state of mind, an attitude, and not a place at all. Anyone, anywhere, can choose to check out, to not grow up, to be selfish or live only in dreams or shirk responsibility. Anyone can choose that. No matter where they live." To appease her, I even add, "I think I might write my college essay about it."

She blinks, seeming momentarily impressed that I've put some thought into my essay already. Drying her hands on a striped kitchen towel, she starts the dishwasher. "I know you're going to think I'm being condescending, but I need to say something to you. I think

292

you will regret not taking the opportunities you have right now if you throw them away to go hang out by a lake. You can only do AYS for one more summer. And it will look great for college."

I listen to the whoosh of the dishwasher for a moment. "AYS isn't my only opportunity. I think going to Tahoe is its own kind of opportunity, Mom. To know Trick better, to live in the mountains, a place where I feel like I belong." She shakes her head, turning away from me to scrub the lasagna pan under hot water. "Besides," I add, "isn't growing up about making choices and then dealing with whatever happens because of them? I'd be doing that. Clearly with a great deal of warning from you." Her shoulders sag, but in their release I can feel her yielding. The possibility of Tahoe hits me.

Will appears in the doorway, clearing his throat. "Hey, just checking on you two." He smiles gently at me and I am awash with gratitude for my stepfather. For his steadiness and sense of humor. "So, Tahoe could be cool. I've always wanted to rent a house there for a week. Maybe mid-July?"

Her eyes downcast, she gives the lasagna pan a final rinse. "Okay." She hands me the pan. "Dry this."

Smiling, I dry the pan, letting the towel do an extra victory lap for me.

• • •

Tahoe City looks different in June. The lake sparkles in the warm sun, but the far mountains are still topped with snow. People boat, paddleboard, and kayak on the blue water. Trick pulls the truck into an empty spot in front of Neverland's Tahoe City store.

"I didn't tell him you're coming." He grins, leaning on the steering wheel. "Just like you asked."

293

I try to catch a quick glimpse of my reflection in the truck's side mirror. I chopped my hair to my chin last week, hoping for a cute, boxy look, but I'm afraid it might be more fussy news anchor than I'd hoped for. "It looks great on you," Trick assures me. I open the door and step onto the sidewalk, swinging the door shut behind me. Before Trick can pull away, I rest a hand on the open window.

He sees me and turns the music down. "What's up?"

I lean in. "Thanks for having me here this summer."

He lifts his trucker hat and runs a hand through his hair before pulling it back on. He drums his thumbs on the steering wheel, which I'm learning means he's thinking about something. "Mara, I know as far as dads go, well, I've been pretty much junk." He stares straight ahead, his thumbs still drumming. "But all those years . . . I was always your dad, even if it looked like, well, like I wasn't. I just figured being out of your life was the best thing I could do for you, but it turns out —" He shakes his head, looking pained. "I guess I'd just like to not keep screwing up with you if I can manage it." His voice breaks off, and he takes his hat off and on again.

"Trick?"

"Yeah?"

"I know. All we can do is go from now with the cards we've got, right?" I hand him a slip of paper, a grocery list I'd written on the plane. "Speaking of now, here's a food list. Can you pick this stuff up before tonight? I know what your kitchen looks like when I'm not here and I don't want to starve." Looking relieved, he takes it, and I wave as he drives off.

Turning, I look at Neverland, and this time the whirls in my stomach are definitely more butterflies than knots. A sheet of sun gleams on the storefront, but as I get closer to the shop, I fall into the shadow of the overhang and can see Logan through the window. He stands in the center of the store, wearing Bermuda shorts, a T-shirt, and flip-flops. He's holding a kayak paddle, demonstrating the swing you use to a silver-haired woman in board shorts and water shoes. He sees me through the window and freezes, his face shifting from surprise into a smile. He has clearly stopped mid-sentence, because the woman's eyes move to me away from the demonstration. Handing the woman the paddle, Logan motions for me to come inside.

I open the door and step into Neverland. "Hi."

"Excuse me for a minute." He smiles at the woman. Slipping his hands into his pockets, he takes a few steps toward me. "You took the job?"

"I took the job."

He motions to the blue binder I have tucked under my arm. "What's that you got there?" The kayak woman still stands next to him, holding her paddle, her eyes locked on us, interested. When she sees me notice her, she pretends to examine a dress on a hanger nearby, but her eyes keep slipping back to us.

I show him the binder. "Oh, this? It's my Summer in Tahoe List. I actually made it for you."

He raises his eyebrows. "Great. Another list. Too bad we're nowhere near a ski lift right now."

"Don't you want to check it out?" I offer it to him.

He walks down the store aisle and takes it, flipping it open to reveal the single sheet of paper inside. On it, I've printed one word:

Logan

"Nice list," he says, flipping it shut, his eyes sending shivers through me.

I hold his gaze. "And, you know, I'd also like to learn to paddleboard."

A smile plays at his mouth. "I think we can manage that."

I grin back. "And also kayaking and hiking the Pacific Crest Trail and —" I add until he smothers me in a bear hug, probably to shut me up.

It works.

AN AUTHOR'S GRATITUDE LIST

1. *The Possibility of Now* would not exist without the hard work of two amazing women: my editor, Jody Corbett, and my agent, Melissa Sarver White, who (insert favorite climbing-a-mountain metaphor of your choice here) patiently guided me through *multiple* drafts of this novel. A special thank-you also needs to go out to the wonderful people at Scholastic, who work in countless miraculous ways, but especially Yaffa Jaskoll, Beka Wallin, Sheila Marie Everett, Roz Hilden, Alexis Lunsford, Elizabeth Whiting, and Anna Swenson. And shout-out of gratitude to Molly Jaffa at Folio Literary for her tireless efforts on all things international.

2. Every writer needs her people, and I'm lucky to have a whole local bookstore full of them — thank you to the staff at The Book Seller in Grass Valley, California. I'm also particularly grateful to Gary Wright and Mark Wiederanders for their writer minds and hearts and support along the way. Michael Bodie and Loretta Ramos give the best pep talks, and I'm so grateful. Once again, thank you to Tanya Egan Gibson, who has read more of my novel openings than she probably cares to be reminded of — thanks for always being my go-to girl. And to my writing group: Kirsten Casey, Annie Keeling, and Jaime Williams — well, ladies, I simply don't know what I'd do without you.

3. Thank you to Tahoe, a very real and special place. I tried to remain true to the world there, but I did take some liberties with certain details and facts (especially in relation to restaurant and

store names and the ski racing/ski practice/ski week schedules). Many people helped me make this world as authentic as I could — any mistakes are mine, not theirs, or just my stretching the lovely taffy that is fiction to fit the health of this story.

4. Like Mara, I'm new to skiing and want to thank the people who have been so patient with this novice: Lillian Llacer and Gary Reedy took me out that first day (after much coaxing from my daughter!), and, in the days since, the Dixons, the Thiems, and the Hatchers have been so patient with wobbly, slow me. I want to also thank Sean Costley of Squaw Valley Ski Patrol for his mountain experience. Finally, thanks to Amanda Courtney and Cody Lamarche for the ski conditioning you put me through so I could actually survive a day of skiing. It was, as you knew it would be, totally worth it.

5. Maybe all writers are like this, but I seem to spend a lot of time processing my work and couldn't do it without my friends and family, who always lend an ear (and a shoulder and a heart!) when needed. There are too many to mention, but I want to especially thank Dawn Anthney; Erin Dixon; Crystal Groome; Sands Hall; Krista Witt; and my parents, Linda and Bill Culbertson, for their unwavering support (or at least being really skilled at nodding along and seeming interested!). Thank you, too, to my San Diego sensory detail reconnaissance team, Brandon and Erika Culbertson, who didn't bat an eye when I texted questions like, "What do you smell at La Jolla Shores at night in early March?"

6. A special mention must go to Emily Gallup, who generously shared her skills as a therapist and spent hours with me discussing the struggles we're both seeing in many of the teens we work with

regarding anxiety, stress, and current cultural expectations. Thanks, Em.

7. Over the years, I've had incredible students in my high school classes. They have shared their dreams and fears, and a huge part of this book is for all of them, but a special thank-you goes to Autumn, Bobby, Davia, Bethany, and Aliyah, who gave me some much-needed insight during the writing of this book.

8. Finally, the biggest thank-you to Peter and Anabella, who are always and forever the most important parts of any list I make.

ABOUT THE AUTHOR

Kim Culbertson is the author of *Catch a Falling Star*; *Instructions for a Broken Heart*, a Northern California Book Award winner; and *Songs for a Teenage Nomad*. When she's not writing young adult novels, she teaches high school creative writing. Kim lives with her husband and their daughter in Northern California. For more about Kim, visit www.kimculbertson.com.